NEVER ALONE WITH REX MALONE

It is 2054 and Britain's society is shattered. Two nuclear attacks have left most of London obliterated and the rest of the country blasted and desolate.

But one national shrine is preserved and venerated – the mausoleum of Britain's demi-god, the Prime Minister, Rex Malone. And one survivor, caged in an underground prison, keeps her secrets of his rise to power.

Natalie Klein was imprisoned for life for a sordid murder committed before she knew Malone. The dark consequences of her deed had made life a nightmare until he befriended her, and in gratitude Natalie devotes her horrifying bent for crime and violence to Malone's cause, though without his knowledge, to ensure his election as Prime Minister.

To some, Malone might seem an odd candidate – an Eastern European peasant who made a million in post-war Britain, then concentrated his energies on newspapers and politics. To Natalie, he is a shining hero the world must acknowledge. Her private campaign becomes a strange succession of murder, blackmail, sadism and terror.

Never Alone with Rex Malone is a provocative satire of twentieth-century vices.

NEVER ALONE WITH REX MALONE

Eleanor Beckman

COLUMBUS BOOKS
LONDON

First published in Great Britain 1986
by Merlin Books Ltd., Braunton, Devon

This edition published by
Columbus Books Ltd.,
19-23 Ludgate Hill,
London, EC4M 7PD.

British Library Cataloguing in Publication Data
Beckman, Eleanor
Never alone with Rex malone.
I. Title
823'.914[F] PR6052.E29/

ISBN 0–86287–313–4

Typeset by Falcon Graphic Art Ltd
Wallington, Surrey

· PART ONE ·

The Limbo of Miss Natalie Klein

The year was 2054. Highgate Cemetery was one of the few parts of London left intact after the hydrogen bombs of April 1997 and December 2053.

The first of these two attacks was not ordered by the Soviet Government. Boris Apresky, the captain of one of their submarines, somewhere in the Atlantic, had borne a private grievance against Great Britain. Londoners often pronounced his name with the stress on its first syllable and he had read mockery in their mispronunciations.

Outwardly, Boris Apresky was a calm, balanced man. He hid his obsession with his name so successfully from his peers that he was appointed Soviet Ambassador to London. His paranoia festered within him. It drove him to drink and sharpened his homicidal tendencies.

As a professional computer operator, it had been easy for him to violate the programming of the master computer on his submarine, the *Michail Lermontov*. He used the next number to be logged and entered a false, complexly coded message to the effect that the Soviet Union was at war with Great Britain.

The forgery reduced two-thirds of London to rubble.

The second Russian bombing attack on London in December 2053 was officially authorized by the Soviet Government. What little was left of the city was cordoned off from those few Londoners who had survived.

Since the hydrogen bomb of 1997, an extension had been built on to Highgate Cemetery. It was built to accommodate the Malonist Vault in which Prime Minister, Rex Malone, and his wife, Hortense and their children had been laid to rest after they had been wiped out.

Malone had been Prime Minister of Great Britain for over twelve years. He had been democratically elected twice and was liked by the electorate because of his prepossessing appearance and rough diamond charm, as well as his contribution to abolishing inflation, unemployment, poverty and national debts without being corrupt or undemocratic in his methods.

A detailed analysis of his policies and the manner in which he activated them is not needed. The comments of the European press, from Left to Right, were sufficient in agreeing that Great Britain under Malonist rule was as close to a Utopia as any cynical philosopher would have deemed possible.

His popularity may have been enhanced by the fact that the Western world lived under the increasing threat of a holocaust and the nation needed someone strong but human to worship. It was because of his promotion from national hero to god overnight that the monument accommodating him and his family was erected. The Malonist Vault had a long black rectangular base approached by a flight of black steps. It was entered by a doorway beneath the words HOUSE OF MALONE in gold letters. The doorway led first to an outer chamber and then an inner chamber. This was divided by a marble block higher than the rest of the construction. It was here that Rex Malone and his wife were laid to rest.

The block was divided by a space, enabling one part to be

occupied by Malone and the other by Hortense. At the top of the block, two giant hands, a man's and a woman's, were clasped in defiance of the blackening sky at which they pointed in an embrace for the rest of eternity.

Their children had been laid to rest in the lower part of the vault. On the father's side lay the sons. On Hortense's side, the daughters. A replica of each child was sculpted in bronze and their hands were crossed like medieval saints.

Outside the vault was a pedestal on which a biblical quotation was painted in gold letters:

'They were lovely and pleasant in their lives
and in death they were not divided.'

In smaller letters underneath, the results of Malone's leadership were summarized in the words of Longfellow which could have applied to the inhabitants of Great Britain under Malonist rule:

'Alike were they free from fear that reigns with the tyrant,
And envy the vice of republics . . .
Their dwellings were open as day and the hearts of their owners.
There the richest were poor and the poorest lived in abundance.'

* * *

Jeremy Klator was the Keeper Elect of the Malonist Vault. It was his responsibility to supervise its maintenance and cleaning both inside and out. A team of cleaners, known as vaultmen, worked under him. A man referred to as First Vaultmate Vernon was responsible for the cleaning of the giant-sized effigy of Malone in battle clothing occupying the inner chamber of the vault. Klator and the vaultmen wore white overalls, white gloves and beekeepers' headshields.

Their bodies were encased in radiation-resistant polythene.

Klator's family had all died of radiation except his five-year-old son, who had cancer. The doctors said there was a chance this might be cured. They manned an emergency underground clinic called Harley Zone One, twenty feet below the site where Harley Street had once existed. The hope that his son might be cured gave Klator an incentive to live. This, combined with the honour of being Keeper Elect of the Malonist Vault, cheered his otherwise dreary existence. He looked sadly at the dour black sky and swung his arms to protect himself against the gusts of wind lashing at him through his polythene covers. He approached the vault to inspect its cleanliness.

He found the vaultmen lined up in a row in front of Malone's effigy. As he entered the inner chamber, they saluted him.

'Is the work done?' asked Klator.

First Vaultman Vernon came forward and lowered his head.

'Yes, sir, the work is done,' he said.

'Good. You may go to your shelters now.'

'And you, sir?' asked Vernon.

'I? I shall stay here awhile.'

'Yes, of course, sir, I understand.' Vernon turned to leave and put on his headshield.

'Vernon!' called Klator.

'Sir?'

'I'd like you to have this.'

He placed a coin worth a hundred pounds in Vernon's hand. Inflation had altered substantially since 1997 when the Malones had been killed by the lunatic whims of Boris Apresky. On the gold coin was a carving of Malone's face in profile, intricate enough to show his acute, penetrating stare. Vernon looked at it in astonishment.

'One hundred pounds, sir! That's ever so generous. I'll be

able to buy a half-pint can of beer on the black market for that.'

Klator turned away and went back into the inner chamber. He removed his headshield and knelt before the effigy of Malone and spoke out loud:

'Malone. Master, don't let my son die. Make the doctors cure his cancer. Be merciful as you were in life.'

A pile of soggy leaves was blown through the doorway of the vault and into the inner chamber which it had taken the vaultmen three hours to clean. Klator rushed outside in despair, deliberately failing to put his headshield back on.

'Filthy Russian bastards!' He shook his clenched fist at the sky. 'You've destroyed everything that's dear to us. Can't you have some respect for what we hold sacred?'

Autumn had come early to the wasteland that was London. Klator staggered through the brutal storm towards the nearest tow-cart terminal that had once been the London Underground. The tracks could still be used but there were no trains. The tow-carts were pulled by heavy chains, manually operated by closely supervised convicts who had sold secrets to the Russians. Their foreheads were branded with the mark of the Hammer and Sickle. Part of their punishment was to have direct contact with the survivors using the terminals. Embittered travellers would spit into the faces of these men as they wound the handles of the Victorian-looking machines occupying the platforms.

As Klator was about to go down to the tow-cart terminal, another gust of wind whistled past him and nearly knocked him over. He looked at his watch and noted bitterly that the month was June, which had been a warm and sunny month in his childhood.

'Where to, Mrs Mopp?' asked a cheeky convict operating the makeshift lift leading to the tunnels.

'Harley Zone One, you cock-sucking commie,' rasped Klator. 'It will amuse you to know my son's got cancer.'

'What's that?' asked the convict, who had the brain of a cretin, which was why the Russians had used him.

'A disease,' said Klator. The convict let out an involuntary, idiot's titter and Klator broke his jaw without knowing he had lost his temper until he saw the convict's dentures on the plank supporting the lift. He felt much better.

* * *

There was a big underground prison on one of the isles off the coast of Scotland, known once as the Hebrides, now Northern Strip Eight. The prisoners were treated kindly and organ music was played continuously over loudspeakers to placate them.

A slow, but rousing tune called 'Once To Every Man and Nation' now a national hymn, was being played even more slowly than usual that day in June. The tune was an old favourite of Jeremy Klator's. When he walked through the part of Highgate Cemetery that had not been cordonned off, he would sing the words to give himself strength and invite other people to join him.

These people would congregate daily to visit the vault. The ones who had died of cancer and plague were the lucky ones. It was the screaming, the crying and the dying who needed the comfort of Jeremy Klator to bring them out of themselves through the hypnotic tonic of the song.

While the tune was playing in the prison, two warders were standing in the corridor talking. The eldest, Ethel, had worked in the prison for fifteen years. Her colleague, Beverley, had just joined the personnel. Both had Edinburgh accents. Ethel said:

'Our oldest prisoner's a hundred and one, just turned. She's a lifer. First degree murder. She's an extraordinary old woman who hugs the bust of some obscure Frenchman all day and never lets go of the thing.'

'Is it the bust of a man called General de Gaulle?'

'No. I think the man's name was Napoleon Bonaparte. He was probably some Left-wing Christian social worker.' was probably some Left-wing Christian social worker.'

'What's the old woman's name?'

'Her name is Natalie Klein. She was a close friend of the Malones before they were killed by the bomb in 1997.'

'The Malones?' exclaimed the younger woman. 'You mean she *knew* them?'

'That she did. He and his wife were very kind to her and she loved them. He used to come and visit her before my time.'

'What would a fine man like that want to associate with a common murderer for, Ethel?'

'She committed the murder long before she met him. He knew nothing about it until the Law came for her. She worked for him. I'm not sure exactly what she did but whatever it was, it wasn't what he told her to do. It was what she thought ought to be done in his interests. Although he won on a landslide in his first election and she helped him win, it wasn't the way he wanted her to help him.

'She committed other crimes, all with intent to help him, but he had such a sense of decency and fair play that he was bitterly disappointed when he found her out. Even so, he still remained her friend. The nation knows that his steadfast loyalty, even to the fallen, was one of his most outstanding virtues.'

'What did the old woman do when she worked for Malone?' asked the younger warder.

'I don't know. I was ill at the time it all came out and I didn't see any newspapers. All I know is that he was angry and upset and he told her so, but she still believes she did right and she is proud of it.'

'You say she committed a murder before she met Malone,' said the younger woman. 'Whom did she murder?'

'You don't know much, do you? I suppose it was before your time. She killed another woman in cold blood, called Dolores Murphy, and pushed the body down a mineshaft.'

'Why?'

'Because – or so the papers said – Dolores Murphy was blackmailing her. The old woman was only twenty-four at the time.'

'What was Dolores Murphy holding over her?'

'The papers said she had threatened to tell the old woman's common law husband that she had been having an affair with Seamus Murphy, Dolores's brother who was killed in a car crash after receiving an abusive letter from the old woman. They had had some quarrel.'

'Is it true she had been having an affair with Dolores Murphy's brother?'

'Most definitely. But that's not all. The case involved something much more sinister than that. The papers said Dolores was blackmailing the old woman about the love affair but that's not true. Dolores had some personal information about the old woman that was incriminating enough to cause her ruin.'

'Whatever had she found out about the old woman?'

'I'd like to tell you but I can't. The old woman knows she hasn't long to live so she told me the truth. She said I could sell it to the *News of the World*.'

'What's that?' asked the younger woman.

'You're the most ignorant person I've ever met in my life! It's a newspaper read by filthy old men in black rubber mackintoshes.'

'Why would they wear those? They're not radiation resistant!'

'Your ignorance and stupidity gets on my nerves sometimes but I don't mean to be unkind. I know you've barely been out of a shelter all your life. Anyway, the old woman told me I could sell the story after she dies and not before. I'd been talking about my domestic problems one day. She's a good listener. One day she asked me why I was crying when I went into her cell. I broke down in front of her and told her how bored my husband had been getting with me recently and how he threatened to leave me unless he could be kept amused with a hologram viewing room installed in our shelter.

'The old woman took pity on me. She told me that she too had loved when she was young. I went to the *News of the World* offices in Fleet Strip One. They're not a paper that can be relied on but they're my only hope. They promised me two million pounds which is just enough to get a hologram room installed. I'm not spilling my story before I give it to the newspaper and I can't do that before the old woman dies. It wouldn't be fair on her.'

'Is it a very sordid story?' asked the younger woman conspiratorially.

'Yes. It's what you might call pretty tacky. Can you imagine a newspaper like that being interested in it if it wasn't?'

There was bitterness in the older warder's voice which confused the young woman. She was afraid of being snubbed again so she decided not to ask any more questions about current affairs, of which she knew nothing.

'May I go and look through the door of the old woman's cell?' she asked timidly and was relieved to be able to ask a question without exposing her ignorance, which shamed and embarrassed her.

'Go and make friends with her,' said the older warder. 'You'll find her a bit strange but there's nothing to be afraid of. She's extraordinarily serene despite her solitary confinement. Perhaps it's because we're not allowed to hold a mirror to her face. They say she was a beauty when she was young. Her serenity isn't only due to that. It's because she's convinced she's more important than she is. She keeps talking about how she found glory in her youth and how much she loved the Malones. She says she's not in prison at all and that her soul is free because Malone saved it. She seems happy but it's common knowledge here that she's pretty batty.'

The younger warder looked through the door. Natalie Klein was moving backwards and forwards on a rocking chair in time to the tune of 'Once To Every Man and Nation'. She was holding a porcelain bust of Napoleon Bonaparte in her black-gloved hands. Her face was veiled. Her long hair, which had once been as black as a raven's wing, was arranged in a plait, just as she had worn it in childhood. She held the bust like a baby and spoke to it as if it could hear her. Her voice was deep and harsh but strangely resonant and musical in its intonation. Her accent was like the hair of a woman who wasn't sure which colour to dye it. While being distinctly Welsh, it would lapse unexpectedly into a cadence that was almost Churchillian and at other times it would sound curiously Germanic. She was articulate but her only verbal flaw was her occasional use of clichés, in particular the histrionic repetition of the phrase 'the days of old'.

'I was called a coward in the days of old,' she said, 'and the brand of cowardice is a cancer of the soul.' Beneath her veil, she looked sadly and penetratingly into the eyes of the bust.

'I sought you, and this is my St Helena. I found glory by helping to bring about the attainment of power by one far more glorious than I and one far wiser than I. But I killed once, long before I found glory, when a funny law existed and the taking of another person's life was called "murder". A hundred and one summers have passed me by, if you can call a season that ends in June, summer. A hundred and one summers have passed me by and I have only to wait for the Reaper to call for his pound of flesh. But I am not afraid because he shall know how I found glory in the days of old.'

The young warder left the prisoner to her monologue.

'Did you know the warder before you came, the warder who met Malone when he came to visit?'

'Muriel Lowther was her name. I met her once.'

'Did she say anything about Malone?'

'She said he was a lovely man.'

'Tell me about old Miss Klein. What was she like when she was young?'

'Long before she met Malone she ran a funeral business with her lover when she was in her twenties.'

'What other things happened to her – except that thing you're not supposed to speak about?'

'I'll tell you as much as I can over the brown-pill break.'

They found a table in the canteen and stirred caffeinated capsules into cups of hot water.

'They've started putting Laropepinine* into the browns. That's why there's always such a rush to the canteen.'

The two women sat down. The older one took a swig of the hot liquid and smiled contentedly.

'So you want to hear about the old woman, do you?' she asked, wiping her mouth on the sleeve of her overall.

* * *

Camberwell, London
The Late Twentieth Century

At the age of twenty-four, Natalie Klein was graced with a fashion model's looks. She was five foot seven inches tall and weighed eight and a half stone. As a child she had worn her jet black hair in a plait that reached her waist, but she had cut most of it off by the time she was twenty. Her hair was thick and lustrous. It was cut in layers and curled naturally, falling

* LAROPEPININE: A powerful, popular, non-addictive drug comprised of opiates and a neutralizing mineral and chemical compound. The drug caused euphoria, but because of the compound, left no hangover in its wake.

below her shoulders. Her complexion was healthy and her skin tanned, giving her an Indian appearance. Her nose was quite small in proportion to the rest of her face and was mildly aquiline. Her profile had often been compared with Donatello's *David.* Her hair was swept back from her face and secured by two combs, showing a pair of elfin ears. The only unprepossessing feature of her face was a pair of pale, slate-grey eyes that although quite prominent, were cold and suspicious unless focused on someone dear to their owner. Her voice was on the deeper side of average and unvarying in pitch. Her accent, unless checked, was Welsh. It was not an accent which could be mimicked easily and yet Natalie Klein had a gift for mimicking others.

Her speech was also strangely uncontemporary. She tended to use the kind of language used by colonels in the 1930s. Often, her use of English was pompous, old-fashioned and flowery, but it would be interspersed without warning with the coarse language of the gutter if she wished to shock or humiliate.

She was sympathetic and pleasant towards friends who confided their innermost secrets to her but never told anyone anything about herself. Sometimes she would make mockery of the sensitivities of others without knowing where the barrier lay between friendly joking and unkindness. Occasionally, she would ask unsolicited personal questions to tease, but would not tolerate anyone doing the same to her. She related to men more easily than to women but was unintentionally thoughtless of their feelings and sometimes hurt them without knowing she had done so.

An example of her brutal and yet merciful behaviour can be seen in an isolated incident.

She was on her way from London to her father's house in the country. Her father was on his way to the same house but had started his journey ten minutes later than she. She came across a hideous and gruesome road accident. A man's legs had been crushed by a hit-and-run driver. She got out and went up to the man who was conscious but in too much pain to scream. She put her hand near his mouth to see if he was breathing. He was.

'He's not dead,' she said. Her voice was devoid of compassion or emotion. A crowd surrounded the man. An ambulance arrived just as Natalie had risen to her feet and in its wake came a van commandeered by an ex-Army Police Inspector. He gulped when he saw the man's crushed legs and held a handkerchief to his mouth. Natalie was outwardly unmoved by the man's suffering. She went up to the Police Inspector and slapped him on the back.

'Hey, you there,' she said within the wounded man's hearing, 'get that thing off the road. My father's due to come along any minute and if he sees it he'll faint.'

This was the sort of behaviour, both savagely cruel yet kindly and loyal that typified much of her character.

Klein and Elliott was a small but prosperous firm of Funeral Directors and Monumental Masons near the bottom of Denmark Hill in Camberwell. It was run by Natalie Klein in partnership with her lover, Charles Elliott. Natalie was the daughter of Selwyn Klein, a prosperous, well-known figure in the world of journalism. He was editor of the widely read *Derbyshire Echo* as well as numerous prestigious London publications.

The Klein family were Welsh and until Selwyn Klein had settled in England, his forefathers had seldom ventured from Welsh soil. The Kleins, though Welsh, were of marked Spanish descent.

Proof of their Spanish ancestry was traced through the registers to the descendants of the refugees who landed at the time of the Spanish Armada. Initially, the Spanish settlers were clannish and married spouses of their own nationality. It was only in later generations that they intermarried with the Welsh, which enabled Welshmen of

Selwyn Klein's generation to be categorized as being partly Spanish.

Selwyn Klein was a quiet, kindly, serious, hardworking and good-humoured man who was liked by all who met him. His original name was Rhys-Clynndyddwynn but he was so bored with having to spell it out that he changed it by deed poll to Klein.

Natalie Klein's brother, Ethelred Klein, was a famous writer. He was good looking as well as brilliant and knew it. If so much as a week passed by without his name appearing in print, he would become depressed and bad-tempered.

'What's the matter, Ethelred, dear?' his family would ask him at breakfast, as he rattled the pages of one newspaper after another like a dishcloth.

'My name's not in print, godammit!' he would snarl and sometimes throw a jar of marmalade at the luckless person who had questioned him.

When Ethelred was in a happy mood he liked to stand on the balcony of a hotel his family used for summer holidays and stare at naked women on the beach through binoculars.

'Ethelred, you went to America common and you came back vulgar,' his father said on one of these occasions, but Ethelred was a prosperous as well as talented writer and such words had little, if any, effect on his vanity.

Natalie Klein was self-conscious about coming from such a literary family and at the age of twenty-one was determined to make a fortune for herself in her own right. After a long and intimate friendship with Charles Elliott, a Cornishman and former gravedigger who had impressed her by his kindness, honesty and good looks, she persuaded him to go into partnership with her, and her father reluctantly put some capital into the business. He agreed that no recession could stop anyone dying. She charged fifty pounds less than rival firms in her field and demanded payment in cash. She had not declared any income tax for three years. By the time she was twenty-four, she had amassed a sizeable fortune in her own right. Instead of being ashamed of her dishonesty, she was proud of it.

'I've had to call several times. Are you deaf?' Charles Elliott, whom she called 'Charlie', was calling to her in her study upstairs.

Natalie Klein was sitting in a darkened room decorated with *mementi mori*. She had her feet on the desk, a pocket calculator in one hand and a brown paper bag of radishes from which she was eating in the other.

'What do you want? I'm doing the accounts.'

'Our Branch in Dulwich Village needs a car at two o'clock this afternoon. We've got two spares. I've got to manage a job in Croydon where the boys are working on the Talbot widow.'

'She's not very good news, that woman. Is she pretty bad?'

'She's the screaming, breast-beating type, Latin temperament, one of those. You never warned me about her. I've put Valium in her tea.'

'That's about the only advice of mine you've ever taken. I'll get the car and take it now.'

'You don't have to go so early. You can leave at one.'

'I'm going now because I'm going to the cinema. You know I go to the cinema in the afternoons.'

'You always leave all the work to me, don't you?' he said.

'You are right. I leave it to you because I own the place and if I wish to go to the cinema in the afternoons I shall do so.'

'But you don't do *anything*. You won't even talk to the customers any more.'

'I've become squeamish about facing the bereaved so I stick to admin. Besides, I haven't got the right manner. I get nervous and I'm too abrupt.'

Elliot mimicked the voice of Humphrey Bogart. 'You can say that again,' and added, 'I still don't see why I must do everything. We're one pallbearer short. Mr Sprout's got flu.'

'Flu? You never told me about this. Has he been on the premises with it?'

'Don't get worked up. He hasn't been in here and you won't catch it. Don't you ever think about anything besides your health?'

'No.'

'To think I could have built a boat and put to sea by now instead of living with a hysterical hypochondriac.'

'How dare you! I am not a hypochondriac!'

'Let's say no more; but a little help once in a while wouldn't go amiss.'

'I count the dough, don't I? I fiddle the books.'

'That's it. You do all the things you enjoy doing and you leave the duties to me.'

'That is as it should be. Which car is it I'm to take?'

'The third on the left in the garage.'

She turned the ignition on and revved up the engine. She ground the gears as she exited from the garage on to the driveway and churned up the gravel. The vehicle screeched to a halt.

'Easy, now, easy, this is not a racing car,' said Elliott.

She leaned out of the window, looking over her shoulder slowly and deliberately as if to suggest the business she was running was no more than an absurd joke.

'Why, you astonish me,' she said, mimicking a Southern Belle, 'until now I could have sworn it couldn't be anything but!'

'You can be quite comical when you want to be.'

'Aren't you going to open the gate? I can't bomb this thing over to Dulwich if you don't open it.'

He leaned through the driver's window, his face angry and stern.

'One doesn't *bomb* hearses anywhere, Natalie, one drives them with fucking reverence!'

'Don't swear, dear, it's common.'

*   *   *

There was an unexpected hold-up in traffic going from Camberwell to her destination just beyond Dulwich Village. About four vehicles had stopped in front of a zebra crossing. A man she didn't see was walking on the pavement near the crossing, waving a half-empty bottle of whisky in the air, shouting. He was about six foot tall, mustachioed and wearing tinted glasses. He had on a navy blue coat over a tight-fitting blue denim suit. He had already tried to get into the passenger seats of two cars and was about to get into a third car.

Natalie could not see what was going on. All she could hear was a lot of shouting. She got out briefly and then got back in. She took out a paperback book of Edgar Allan Poe's poems. The book fell open at *Ulalume*. This was her favourite and she liked to read it half to herself and half out loud when agitated or impatient. Suddenly, she was startled by a stranger reading over her shoulder.

'A bit dour,' the stranger said, and removed his tinted glasses. His eyes were brown, melancholic and bloodshot. He waved his half-empty bottle of whisky as he spoke. He had a strong Southern Irish accent.

'Who are you and what the dickens do you think you are doing in here?'

'Can you take me to the nearest pub?' replied the man and Natalie feared he would get violent if she didn't behave reasonably.

'If there is one on my route I will drop you there. Your methods of getting people to do what you want are very unorthodox.'

'It's the only way to get what I want.'

'In your case I have no doubt it is.'

The first of many silences ensued. She looked at him closely and his tight-fitting jeans pleased her. She smiled at him. He drank more whisky from the bottle and passed it to her.

'Want some?'

'I'm behind the wheel, you cretin.'

'I've had all I want. More than I need.'

'That is evident,' she replied coldly and threw the bottle out of the window. The man laughed inappropriately and went on laughing for ten minutes. It was not the laughter of a happy man.

'Why are you so sad?'

'I'm very happy!' the man shouted aggressively and banged his fist on the dashboard. 'I've nothing to be sad about.'

'You are lying, but your sadness is not unattractive.'

'Christ, you're pompous!'

'People who drive vehicles like this have to be pompous, otherwise they go bust.' The man turned round and looked over his right shoulder.

'Is this a hearse?' he asked, taken by surprise.

'No, it's a plane. A damned silly question gets a damned silly answer.'

There was another silence. The man looked at Natalie and Natalie looked at him.

'Natalie Klein's my name. What's yours?'

'Seamus Murphy.'

'Irish? I can tell by the accent. It's rather pretty.'

Murphy banged his fist on the dashboard a second time. 'And what of it?' he shouted.

'Nothing of it. I was only saying you have a charming accent.'

'It's an accent that has kept me out of work for five years. After two, I stopped trying. I was sacked for poor time-keeping. I couldn't wake up in the mornings. Whatever shop I went to, no one would sell me an alarm clock because of what you call my pretty accent.'

Natalie began to giggle uncontrollably and turned her head

away. Murphy felt slighted by her reaction. The whisky had sharpened the grudge he bore. He raised his voice in anger.

'Beneath what you see, I do have some pride left. Now I have sunk so low, I can't sink any lower. Hence, in having nothing, I fear nothing. In that way you are weak and I am strong. Will you give me some money?'

She had never met anyone like this before in her life. She gave him a ten pound note.

'Thank you. All my family are dead but I still do have a sister.'

'That comes under the category of unsolicited information. What's your sister's name?'

'Dolores.'

After another uncomfortable pause, Natalie asked, 'Have you any hobbies?'

'Reading, drinking and poker.'

'In the first two, we are on mutual ground at least.' Then suddenly, she asked: 'Do you like Edgar Allan Poe?'

Her tone when she asked this question suggested a sort of recklessness in exposing a side of herself that her more cautious instincts would have told her to hide. Her speech had become stilted as if she were talking about something personal to her, a sacred thing, seldom shared with anyone else.

'You're not as frightened of me as you were earlier, are you?' he asked. His power of observing the frailties of others was reptilian and she read mockery in his voice.

'I am frightened of nothing and no one. I asked if you liked the poems.'

'They are absurd, pointless.'

'You are mad. How can you say such a thing?'

'All books that have ever been written are about life and life is pointless, so the act of writing about it is as meaningless as being born. Everything is meaningless. I spend my life doing the things that ordinary people enjoy: drinking, walking and reading. What is that, just escapism.'

'You're a dismal blighter, aren't you, Seamus?'

Murphy did not say anything but sat in silence with his head in his hands. She did not know whether to pity him or find his melancholia erotic. She also feared him and she knew he could sense her fear.

'You're a nice person underneath all this crap,' he said, and smiled – his was a very charming smile.

After another silence she extended her left hand and seduced him. She was surprised to see how quickly he was roused and was very nervous.

'Change down!' she said in the voice of a sergeant-major addressing a lance-corporal late for parade.

'What?'

'Change the gears, man! How many pairs of hands do you think I've got?'

'You're a peculiar woman.'

'I'm moving into a side street. The indicator is on the left of the wheel. Push it to the right.'

She moved over to the passenger seat and kissed him on the mouth, violently but with no emotion.

'We will have to go in the back. There are blinds in the back. Get out of the car,' she said.

He got out mechanically, his mind befuddled by drink, bewilderment, mental depression, desire and general confusion. He stared at the ground.

There was a standard joke in the Klein family about a General who had befriended a great-aunt of Natalie's and whose method of getting others to do things was to bark staccato orders with disarming repetition in a voice that increased in volume like a machine-gun. He liked Worcester sauce with everything he ate, whether savoury or sweet and if the Worcester sauce was not on the table he would say to his butler: 'The Worcester the Worcester the Worcester the Worcester the Worcester . . .'

'What are you laughing at, Natalie?' asked Murphy.
'Clothes off clothes off clothes off clothes off.'
'You've a very peremptory manner.'
'I'm a peremptory person. I am accustomed to say "do this" and it is done.'
He took off his coat and threw it on the ground. She produced a bottle of water.
'You laundered?' she asked curtly.
'What do you mean – am I laundered?'
'Have you got any venereal disease, you slow-witted fool?'
'No,' he said flatly. He was too depressed to get aggressive and strangely fascinated by her manner.
'Wash yourself first, please,' she said and because he felt so gloomy he did so without argument. 'All right. You can get in now. The hatch is open.'
The bier rollers dug into him but he was too flattened to complain and too roused to care about the discomfort.
She knelt astride him and took his face in her hands and ran her fingers through his hair. It was her first gesture of affection or tenderness towards him. He smiled and she returned the smile. She said:

'Come up through the lair of the Lion
With love in her luminous eyes.'

'Fine words, those. Are they yours?'
'Aye, to be sure they are, b'fockin' Gorrah!'
He took her by the scruff of the neck and turned her over.
'Go on, I like it rough,' she said.
'Then to be sure you'll be getting what you came for! I'll teach you not to mimic my accent.'

* * *

It took Natalie ten minutes to satisfy herself with Murphy. When he got out he looked more downcast than when he got in. He stood by the road, looking as if he might be mounting the steps of a scaffold. When she stepped outside she looked pleasantly baffled. She was overwhelmed by his technique and stunned but happy. He had done exactly what she wanted the way she wanted it done. She took the bottle of water and washed her hands while he watched in puzzled distraction.

'To be sure I admire your cleanliness,' he said in a flat voice.

'Get back in, Seamus, there's something I wish to say.'

He didn't answer. He got in and stared vacantly into space.

'Unemployed for five years, you say?'

'Aye.'

'You what?'

'I meant "yes" for Christ's sake. Perhaps you don't understand our humble paddy's parlance.'

'Not again, please, Murphy dear, it's awfully sordid to talk about Ireland straight after sexual intercourse.'

Murphy said nothing. She began to feel very ill at ease and raised her voice to a clipped military bark:

'Well, you've proved yourself to be a damned good man about the hearse. You may consider yourself employed. I shall want your services on Mondays, Wednesdays and Fridays. Each time you will be paid fifty pounds in cash. Here's fifty pounds for the work you did today. I will have to see you at your residence so what is your telephone number?'

'I'm not on the phone.'

'Where do you live?'

'The top floor of a squatters' block – 139 Albany Road.'

'Good. A rough area but conveniently situated, nevertheless. I will come to see you at 2.15 on Wednesday and thereafter on a regular basis on Mondays, Wednesdays and Fridays as stated.'

'Why not Tuesdays and Thursdays?'

'Those are the days I go to the cinema.'

'And you say you'll pay me in cash?'

'In cash. You will be earning a hundred and fifty pounds a week as well as your dole money, so you'll be rich in no time.'

'I don't understand why you are making this arrangement with me.'

'Must I be reduced to spelling it out?'

'Aye.'

'Can't you say "yes"? "Aye" sounds damned silly.'

'Yes. I'd like you to tell me the reason.'

'Because I need what you've got to offer.'

'I've nothing to offer you except a nihilistic view of the meaninglessness of things and the misery and uselessness of life.'

'The state of your mind does not concern me. I'm not interested in what you think or how you think. I am referring to the work you did for me this afternoon. I told you I wanted it rough and you gave me what I asked for. That is satisfactory.'

'You sound like some fockin' old colonel. Do you mean you want me to be your whore?'

'Dead people have travelled in the back of this vehicle, Seamus. In pomp. In style. In reverence. So please don't use language like that in here.'

He looked over his shoulder as he had before and waved his arms in a bemused, Gallic gesture.

'I don't understand you at all. You're a raving lunatic.'

'You are probably right, but fortunately I know it. I'm going to have to bung you out, now, because I've got to deliver this car in a spirit of dignity. Buck up. Out you get!'

'You will come on Wednesday at 2.15, won't you?'

'What I say I'm going to do, I do.'

As he got out, Murphy noticed the gold-lettered engraving saying *Klein and Elliott.*

'That's the same firm that buried my mother and father. Charles Elliott is an old friend of mine.'

'Is that so?' She tried to conceal her surprise. 'I haven't time to hang about talking. Slam the door, will you?'

* * *

On Wednesday at 2.15, Natalie Klein went to the top flat at 139 Albany Road. The banisters felt loose as she mounted the stairs. Alcoholics, meths drinkers and junkies sat on landings and on the stairs, huddled in groups. The walls were covered in graffiti. There was an overpowering smell of human waste.

Murphy's room was quite clean and tidy. Antique-looking books had accumulated in neat piles on the floor. She was puzzled to see that some of their titles were in German. Murphy was in bed, reading a book about the philosophy of Nietzsche which was also in German.

'Do you really read German, or is this just affectation?' she asked.

'I may be Irish but that doesn't make me uneducated. Yes, I speak fluent German,' he said defensively.

'Well, I'm not Irish and I don't speak German. The only German I know is "*Chamberlain ist ein Arschloch*"*, which Hitler used to say from time to time.'

Murphy laughed, a strange, tortured laugh but a laugh nevertheless.

'You're the only person I know who keeps promises,' he said.

'Then you must keep peculiar company.'

'Are you going to get in with me?'

'No. I'll be using the floor.'

'The floor?'

'You heard me, and here's fifty pounds. Keep it rough but don't knock me about.'

'You don't have much respect for men, do you?'

* By courtesy of Mr Martin Hale (*The Fourth Reich*). This author does not take kindly to plagiarism.

'Apart from the man with whom I live and the men that are in my family, no.'

'I'm going to the bathroom for a few minutes.'

'Buck up, then. I'm going to see a film in Leicester Square which starts at 4.15.'

'What are you going to see?'

'*The Texas Chainsaw Massacre.*'

'I've never heard of it. Is W. C. Fields in it?'

'No, he isn't. Do buck up and do whatever you've got to do!'

After he had satisfied her he went back to bed. She saw a pile of long-playing records lying by a gramophone and looked through them to see what sort of tastes he had. There was nothing there that wasn't classical. This impressed her but she did not say so.

'May I use your bathroom, please?' she asked.

Murphy suddenly got hysterical. 'I don't want anyone going in there!' The vehemence in his voice startled her.

'Why?'

'It's not very nice in there. I don't want you to see it, so don't ask any more questions about it.'

'Very well then, I must be off.'

'I think I love you,' he said in a frail voice as she was about to leave.

'Why?'

'Because I feel safe that you will treat me like a tramp and not ask anything of me that I'm not prepared to give. I'm no more than a worthless parasite.'

She looked at her watch. It was 3.20. She had plenty of time to get to Leicester Square.

'Come, come, my man, you underestimate yourself.'

'I can only take. I have never given anything to anyone in my life. That is why I hope you will never love me in return.'

'You're a good roll in the hay but nothing would induce me to love you.'

'Do you dislike me?'

'I neither like you nor dislike you. You do what I want the way I want it done, so I'm not indifferent to you.'

'You put on this cold act to hide your fear of strangers,' he said with sudden hostility. The remark jolted her a little but she did not take it seriously enough to brood over it.

'I've got to get on now, Seamus. I'll come back the day after tomorrow.'

She was just in time to see *The Texas Chainsaw Massacre.* Its grisly contents cheered her far more than the events of that afternoon.

* * *

For three weeks the arrangement had worked out well. Natalie had been satisfied with Murphy and had now become virtually dependent on his services. When he did not answer the door one day, she was shocked, not because she feared he was out, but because of her reaction to his absence and her knowledge of her addiction to what he provided. The heavy, two-inch door was unlatched. She threw her weight against it. Murphy was asleep with his book on Nietzsche's philosophy open in his hand.

'I'm not surprised it sent you to sleep!' she remarked, her mouth an inch away from his ear. He turned over but still did not wake up. She saw a loose brick in the wall above his head. Behind it, wrapped in polythene, was something she thought was washing powder. She was irritated that this man should be asleep when she had called and remembered his request that she should not go into the bathroom.

'Wake up, you idle bugger, or I'll go in your bathroom!'

The bathroom consisted of a dusty bath, basin and water closet. There was a toothbrush in a glass, some toothpaste, soap and a bottle of mouthwash on the shelf above the basin. Lying across the drain was a small syringe, half full of blood.

Some of the white powder had been spilled on the floorboards. She told herself it was Vim. She tasted it. The taste was unfamiliar but she knew what it was and how thriftily it had been saved with the regular income of its slave. She crushed the glass in the palm of her hand. The glass cutting her hand made her unaware of her tears.

Murphy had started sneezing and sweating. He staggered into the bathroom in a semi-stupor, unaware of the time and knowing only that he needed another injection.

'What's the matter?' he asked in a weak voice that was deceptively gentle in its frailty. 'You can tell me. I won't tell anyone.'

She composed herself and said in a steady, unfaltering voice: 'I won't be coming back any more because I found out that you take this stuff and I do not want to watch you dying.'

* * *

He held his stomach to lessen the cramps. He tried to stand up straight as he saw her go into the bedroom and remove his savings from a tin on the floor. They totalled three hundred pounds. She began her hurried descent downstairs.

Instead of going to his supply hidden in the wall, he ran after her in an instinctive fit of rage. The need for the drug and the knowledge that he had been duped gave him the strength to chase her.

'Hey, stop, will you! I need that!' He saw the door slam behind him with its lock still on and realized he would not be able to get back in. His fury had reached a climax and as he lumbered down the stairs, he fell and sprained his ankle, not noticing the pain.

She had reached the ground floor. Her path was blocked by the same group of dossers who were swaying backwards and forwards, singing a tuneless old song:

'I don't want to join the Army. I don't want to go to war.
I'd rather hang around Piccadilly Underground
living on the earnings of an wh . . .'

'Watch it, Tom,' said the one dosser who wasn't singing, 'it's 'er that goes up there.'

'. . . *'igh born lady!*' sang the dosser addressed as Tom, in a voice more contrived and theatrical than the voice he had used earlier. He and the others divided like the Red Sea to make a path for her.

* * *

Traffic conditions had caused her to take longer than usual to get back home. She turned the notice on the door to 'Closed'. She felt ill and disgusted and was about to go to bed when she heard two hushed male voices.

'I know it's not the first time I've asked but I've got to have some money,' said a voice with a familiar Irish accent.

'You've had five hundred pounds already from me in the past month. It's true it comes from my personal funds and it's nothing to do with her, but my personal funds are exhausted because of you.'

'Then use the firm's funds! I've got to have the stuff.'

'You should never have got onto it. She watches the accounts like a hawk. The answer's "no". She'll find out and I know better than to cross a woman's path. It's no good kneeling, licking my hands. Go to hospital. Anything. I said "no" and that's the end of it.'

The door to the office banged open unexpectedly, knocking over a vase of plastic flowers on a table behind it.

'Why didn't you tell me you had given five hundred pounds to that man and why is he licking your hands?' asked Natalie.

'I . . . well, he and I have an agreement.'

'To do what?'

'I've never really been educated and he's known me for

over ten years. He helps me with my English.'

'Your *English*? What are you talking about? You *are* English.'

'He has often taught me things about Shakespeare,' he began defensively.

'I find that an odd motive for him to be licking your hands. Are there any homosexual elements in his relations towards you?'

'If that's your implication, I'll leave here tonight. This man is a junky. He is also a very old friend. I've tried to persuade him to go to hospital to withdraw but he can't, and so I've been giving him my own money. His name's Seamus Murphy.'

'I know. I've met him before.'

'Oh? Where was that?'

'He was hitchhiking and I gave him a lift. I also gave him money. I gave him a hundred and fifty pounds on three occasions, making a total of four hundred and fifty pounds. That's why I'm concerned that you have given him an additional five hundred pounds. We've given him a total of nine hundred and fifty pounds between us, and if he'd spent all that on heroin he'd be dead by now. He has more to say to you than to me, so perhaps you'd be good enough to ask him where it all went. I won't tolerate this sloppy, irresponsible behaviour.'

She had to shout all this because Murphy was lying on the floor, screaming. Neither Natalie nor Elliott showed outward emotion at the horrible spectacle of suffering and degradation, but each kept their private and totally different griefs to themselves.

Johnny Rucelli, a six-foot, husky-voiced, forty-year-old New Yorker of Italian descent, was banging frantically on the door. He was surprised to find it closed at 3.30 on a Wednesday afternoon. His loud, Bronxy voice attracted more attention than Murphy's screams.

Natalie said: 'Don't waste any time. Take him down to the cellar. The chains I used in my S.M. days to pay back gambling debts are still there. Shackle him. Keep him on whisky and valium until the cramps wear off. It's cruel but there's no choice and there's a man banging at the door.'

'But that's sadistic! We can't! We . . .'

'Shut up! Take Murphy down and I'll softsoap the man outside.'

'I won't have any part in torturing him. We ought to get an ambulance.'

'An ambulance! An ambulance! I can't have an ambulance coming to a place like this. I'd be the laughing stock of the neighbourhood. It would mean getting the police out as well. I'm not having some junky who wants to die anyway, interfering with my profession. Take him down and do as you're told!'

'No, I won't!'

'What? I can't hear with all this screaming.'

'I'm not taking him down to the cellar. It's not heated and there are rats down there.'

'So what? That's the last thing a junky would notice. Do you think a junky's conscious of room temperatures or surroundings?'

Johnny Rucelli could hear a lot of noise coming from within and tried again, this time more persistently. He hammered at the door and rang the bell.

Natalie opened the door and greeted him with a benign, understanding smile.

'Say, are you guys closed all the year round?' said Rucelli. 'Don't people die no more in Great Britain?' The Italian lilt in his voice, combined with his expensively tailored clothing, gave her the impression that either he or his family might have had Mafia connections in the past and that money was no longer any object to him. She made a mental note to charge him more.

'I am sorry you were kept waiting like that. Would you very kindly wait and I will check the telephone is manned.'

Elliott had been persuaded that she had been right about Murphy. 'I'll put him below,' he said. 'You deal with the client and don't be too abrupt with him. Remember he's not your lover.'

'Won't you come in, sir,' she said. 'I apologize most sincerely for the confusion over the sign. It must have been deeply distressing for you.'

'Yeah, it was. You seem a pretty laid back, spaced-out bunch of guys. Maybe people don't die so much no more, huh?'

'Would you come in and sit down and we can discuss what you would like us to do for you.'

'I guess I chose to come to London to bury Sammy because I'm pretty wound up right now about da American way of death. There's only one thing more obscene than that and that's da American way of life. I know the British know how to throw a downmarket, low-key, low-profile type of fooneral. Back home in the States, you can't back out in no style no goddam more without a fleet of flash caddies, fat flash morticians and a fat flash casket carried like it was some goddam bag of groceries. Sammy had heart trouble and knew he had to go and just before he died in that hospital he said: "Blossom dear, I either gotta have me a British fooneral or else I don't get buried at all." '

'Your name is Mr Blossom?'

'Nah. That's just what Sammy called me. Johnny Rucelli's my name and Sammy and me was making it just fine.'

'I am sure we shall be able to do exactly what you want the way you want it done.'

'Yeah. I chose you because a fella from this part of town I met at some races you call the Durby, said you guys didn't charge as much as da other goddam flasher parlours.'

'Your friend was indeed right. We try to exploit sorrow as

little as we can. Our consciences force us to charge one hundred pounds less than other firms like ours, regardless of the modest lifestyle we lead which, as believing and practising Quakers, we believe it right to follow.'

'Say – what's a Quaker?'

'A Quaker is a member of a religious sect that advocates clean living, modesty, chastity and godliness.'

'Sounds whacko, but Sammy wanted a simple job, so I guess I came to da right tomfool joint.'

'You have indeed, sir. We believe in religious values and not in profits, but we do insist on our clients paying in cash. It is not that we doubt your honesty. It's just our rule.'

'I guess that's fine by me. I've got a hell of a lot of dough with me right now. Just make da job simple and dignified, huh?'

She gave him a charming smile. 'Your wish is always our command. We will charge you seven hundred and fifty pounds, inclusive of VAT, for the simple burial you ask for. Other mercenary firms such as *Crumblebottom and Bongwit* down the road would charge no less than one thousand pounds, because to them profits come before people.'

(*Klein and Elliott's* standard overall price for a simple burial was four hundred and fifty pounds inclusive of VAT.)

'Sounds like a good deal,' said Rucelli and handed her a bundle of fifty pound notes from a maroon crocodile hide wallet. He had given her a thousand pounds without his knowledge. He had at least five thousand pounds left.

'With respect, I must ask you to let me count it first, just to make sure you haven't overpaid me. I didn't see you counting it and I wouldn't want you to be dealt with dishonourably.'

She counted the notes. 'You haven't overpaid me, sir. You've only give me seven hundred pounds, so I must entreat you to give me another fifty if you would be so good.'

Rucelli handed her another fifty pound note without question.

'Forgive me for intruding on the more painful side, but your Sammy, would you mind telling me how tall he was?'

'Four foot three inches.'

'A child – your son? How very tragic for you, sir.'

'Nah. A dwarf. Him and me was hittin' it off real cool. I met him in a gay joint patronized by freaks in L.A., and I guess it was love at first sight. Pa'd already made his roll in prohibition and passed his dough to me, so I gave Sammy a home.'

'I am truly very sorry, sir. Have you any particular preferences – any special floral formations, any personal touches?'

'May I see your casket catalogue?'

She nearly laughed but controlled herself as she replied, 'Certainly, sir. Here are our patterns. This section at the back is used for the loved ones shorter in stature.'

The catalogue varied from the very conventional to the ridiculous. Rucelli chose a model with a *Vuiton* cover.

'I will see to it that you have that model, sir. Would you kindly excuse me for one minute.'

'Yeah. I got all day.' Rucelli sat with his arms folded, chewing gum.

Natalie went to the cellar and called Elliott to shut Murphy up. The withdrawal symptoms were at their worst and he clawed at Elliott when he came to give him a glass of whisky mixed with Valium.

'Undo the chains!'

'No. She's captain of this ship and I must do what the captain says.'

'Captain of this ship! Captain of this ship!' Between spasms of choking he repeated these words for about fifteen minutes until he reached an orgasm of pain and rage.

Rucelli had witnessed many revolting murders even as a child, during his father's Mafia days, and was unruffled by what he overheard.

'Say, lady, do you mind my asking – what the hell's all that shouting?'

'Shouting?'

'Yeah, I can hear two fellas screaming and shouting like they was bustin' each other to pieces. What's da big idea, huh?'

'Oh, that. You must excuse me. I'm most embarrassed and I can't apologize enough. My nephew's mother won't allow him to watch the television at home so he comes over here to pester me in the afternoons. He's watching a video downstairs. I've told him to keep it down but he turns it up loud because he's very deaf.'

'What sort of movies does your nephew like watching, for God's sake? Snuff movies?'

'And what sort of shit is the captain of your ship?' screamed Murphy more loudly than before.

'This afternoon my nephew's watching *Mutiny on the Bounty*. Please accept my apologies. Some tea?'

'Nah. Don't wanna abide by no British customs except da burials.'

'I hope everything will be to your satisfaction. Just one moment, please, that horrible boy has turned it up again.'

'Take a look at him. We'll have to get him to hospital,' said Elliott when Natalie reappeared.

'No. Knock him on the head with something. I've got a batty American upstairs complaining. I've just taken one thousand and fifty off him.'

'In other words you've swindled him.'

'Of course. I was raised on the work ethic. I wouldn't have any self-respect if I wasn't a good capitalist. The American wants us to do a four-foot three-inch dwarf in a *Vuiton*.'

'A *Vuiton*?'

'Yes.'

'We've only got one and I kept it as a relic. But it's four foot long so how are we going to manage?'

'Cut its feet off, you cretin! Use your head. But stop that noise or the man will ask for his money back and take his custom elsewhere.'

'I'm so sorry about that, sir,' she said, coming back to the office. 'I can assure you it won't happen next time we meet. Which hospital did your poor friend die in?'

'Da goddam London Clinic, surrounded by a bunch of good-for-nothing Ay-rabs.'

'How shocking! Is he in the mortuary there?'

'Sure thing.'

'Then I will have him collected and all you have to do now is leave everything else to us.'

'You promise there won't be no goddam noise? Hell, I want this thing done with some reverence, man!'

'I can assure you that the boy will never be coming here again. He is most selfish but there again it must be sad to be a little boy and be deaf.'

Rucelli was softened by the remark. He smiled for the first time and shook her warmly by the hand.

'Thanks a lot, lady. Sorry I got hostle.'

'Indeed, you were not hostile. It gives me pleasure to take the sting out of death for you and to relieve what we know to be an unendurable sorrow. Here's my card and if there's anything else you want to discuss, you may call me at any time of the day or night.'

* * *

It took Murphy's body three days to get accustomed to the absence of heroin. The physical craving was replaced by severe depression. Natalie would not go near him, so he confided his misery to Elliott.

'As there's nothing I can do to make someone happy, I'd like at least to be able to make someone unhappy. Every time I hurt someone, I delight in hurting myself much more. By hurting myself, I am hurting the memory of the parents who brought me into this world. When others have interests and motives for living, I despise them. The only fulfilment I get is from finding someone's weakness and destroying that person.'

'What you need is a doctor. I can't help you.'

Later, Murphy asked to be shown round the house.

'So, this is your bedroom, is it?' he asked.

'That's right.'

'Are you not well? You've got an awful lot of medicines here.'

'None of them is mine. The bottles of pills are all hers.'

'Is she ill?'

'No, there's nothing wrong with her. She has a morbid, pathological fear of illness, germs, anything like that. I know how silly it must seem to you. I've had to live with it. She actually believes that if she doesn't take enormous quantities of pills every day, she will die. Hence, she lives in permanent fear. She won't even go into a chemist because she's so frightened of germs. She's got a friendly local chemist, a Chinaman who delivers crates of pills here once a week. He comes because she tips him generously.'

The sly expression on Murphy's face baffled Elliott. When their eyes met, Murphy turned away.

'I thought she wasn't afraid of anything,' he said.

'That's what I thought,' replied Elliott, 'but illness is the only thing she has an irrational and unnatural fear of.'

'Why?'

'I don't know. I wish I did. Let's not talk about it any more. It depresses me. We'll go out. I don't know where she's gone but I'll buy you a drink anyway.'

Murphy agreed and within a month returned to his old room in Albany Road. His heroin supply was still intact. He felt a sense of complacency that he was no longer dependent on it, combined with relief that it was still there.

Natalie wanted to forget him, but a recklessness within prompted by her memory of his primitive technique as a lover, drove her to his lodgings one afternoon when she had walked out after ten minutes of a film that bored her. Her feeling of lust had overcome her vindictiveness towards him for having used her.

'Hullo, Seamus, may I come in?'

'I thought you would never come back.'

'You thought wrongly, didn't you?'

'I want to ask a big favour of you.'

'What do you want?'

'See this piece of paper here? It's a ticket for some medicine from John Bell and Croyden's.'

'It would be easier if I used my local chemist. John Bell and Croyden's is a very long way away.'

'They are the only chemists that have the original prescription. They are holding it until it is picked up. Won't you do this just for me?'

'What's the medicine called? We keep a lot of medicines in our cupboard. John Bell and Croyden's is most inconvenient.'

'It's medicine to help the psychological effects of heroin withdrawal. I know you won't have that in your cupboard. Please do this for me.'

She softened on seeing his charming smile, not knowing the extent to which he hated her for having him put in the cellar.

'All right, Seamus, I'll get it for you. I'm very pleased you've stopped having the injections, and it's nice to see you are better.'

Wigmore Street was more crowded than usual that day. All sorts of exhibits from weighing machines to weight-losing machines stared at Natalie from the windows of John Bell and Croyden's.

She remembered the scene from the film *Taras Bulba* when the hero rode over the ravine to prove he was not a coward. To her, the door leading to the chemist was the ravine, for such was the pitiful depth to which her hypochondria had sunk. She tried to bribe passers-by to enter the building on her behalf, explaining that she'd had a row with the management, but was dismissed as a crank by everyone she approached.

She did not know that Murphy had followed her on the Underground. Nor did she know he had watched every move she had made to avoid entering the chemist. But she did go in, strengthened only by the imaginary sound of the galloping horse's hoofs in her ears. She went straight to a counter selling disinfectant and poured Dettol on her hands which she covered her nose and mouth with. Murphy watched her from another part of the shop as she approached the precriptions counter.

An anaemic-looking man with a harrowingly loud cough was sitting on one of the chairs used by the collectors of medicines. A woman sitting next to him wiped the sweat from his forehead and loosened his tie. The man was leaning with his head on the back of the chair, holding a white handkerchief in front of his mouth. When Natalie looked in his direction again it was covered with blood.

'It's ever so lucky they can cure tuberculosis these days, isn't it, our Alfred?' said the woman in a heavy Lancashire brogue.

Natalie poured more Dettol over her hands and covered her face. She went pale and trembled all over with fear, a fear so violent that if she had been faced with the choice of dying at that moment, she would have taken it.

Murphy suddenly approached her.

'You lied to me when you said you were afraid of nothing, didn't you?' His shouts reverberated round the chemist's. 'I even believed you. But you're scared of illness. Look at you, you gutless, cowardly bitch, you're scared to death.'

'I am not!'

'Why are your hands shaking?'

'You came in here to torture me when I've never wronged you and you took unfair advantage of me.'

'I came to prove I could see through you. You only work with the dead because the dead can't turn round and tell you you are a coward and a hypochondriac and worth nothing.'

'I am not a coward!'

'Prove it, then. Go near that man with the handkerchief. Go and ask him if he wants a glass of water.'

'No! I'm getting out of here.'

'Not so fast, daughter! You had me taken to your cellar where you had me chained up, didn't you?'

The heads of many occupants of a poorly attended queue, not unlike queues waiting for food in Russia, turned unanimously towards the stormy couple.

'Let me go!' She bit him hard on the hand. He let out a sharp scream.

'Excuse me, sir and madam, is this noise really necessary?' asked a white-coated man claiming to be the Assistant Manager of John Bell and Croyden's. He was obviously more concerned about the noise than by the length of the unattended queue.

'I thought I told you to ask that man with the cough if he wanted a glass of water,' said Murphy, after the Assistant Manager had gone.

She tried to shake off his grip as they fought at a distance of ten yards from the man with the cough.

'Hey, mister, you over there, do you want a glass of water?'

'Go right up to him and say it nicely. Let me take you by the arm.'

'No! No! Help! Rape!'

'I'm sorry, sir and madam, but I must insist that you both leave at once. There are some very sick people here and this kind of disturbance is totally inappropriate,' said the Assistant Manager.

'Don't blame me,' replied Murphy, 'I didn't want to come

here in the first place. It was her. She was afraid to come alone because she's a hypochondriac as well as a coward, do you hear?'

'Lower your voice, sir, for mercy's sake!'

Natalie hailed a taxi. The taxi driver was a Negro with gold-plated teeth and a flashy smile.

'Denmark Hill, Camberwell, please.' She wound down the window as the taxi moved away and called to Murphy. 'You'll pay for this the hardest way you've ever paid for anything before. No one hurts or insults me without being punished.'

The Negro was pleasant and sympathetic.

'Hey, I don't mean to butt in on you,' he said, 'but people insult me every day of the week and if I cried every time someone insulted me, the streets of this city would be flooded and everybody would be swimming to work, not walking.'

'You are most kind. All I can say is that if anyone wanted to insult someone as nice as you, I think it's damnably offensive of them.'

* * *

Elliott was typing invoices with one finger when Natalie stormed into the shop.

'Hand over the machine and two sheets of paper. This is an emergency.'

He was good-natured and did as he was asked.

'Thank you. Let me by. I've got to take the typewriter upstairs.'

He slapped his left hand with his right and muttered, 'Keep out of her way, Charlie boy, when she's like this.'

It took Natalie two hours to destroy Murphy's soul as if driving a stave through a vampire's heart. Her letter to him was two hundred and fifty words long. Its tone was below the belt, vitriolic, vicious and deadly, but redeemingly articulate, scholarly and academic. The education and gift for language shown in its prose turned what might have been a string of fishwife's abuse to a missile of death without actually committing murder.

When either Natalie or someone dear to her had been shabbily treated or slighted, she would pursue the guilty party with obsessive and inveterate hatred. Her punishment was one stage more severe than the act that had provoked it.

'An eye for a tooth and a limb for an eye' was her motto and no form of persuasion, however logical or reasonable, could intercept her missiles or prevent her from launching an additional fleet of missiles in their wake, regardless of the subsequent psychological state of the target. Only when the target grovelled at her feet like a backstreet masochist, would she relent and bring her vicious vendetta to a standstill.

The words 'I will write them a letter' were not infrequently on her lips. Her letters to 'offenders' were legion and their tone, varying from moderate criticism to cruelty, was dependent on the severity of the irritation caused to her.

When she wanted to injure someone, she preferred ink to the spoken word. She had the power to turn ink to cyanide and the pen or typewriter ribbon to the bomb from which it had emanated.

When she had finished she had torn shreds of skin from the index fingers of both hands. After she sealed the letter she felt as if a weight had been lifted from her.

'What have you done to your fingers?' asked Elliott.

'Bind them.'

'What's the matter?'

'I said: bind them.'

The telephone rang after she had posted the letter.

'I called to say how sorry I am I hurt you,' said Seamus in his soft Irish voice. 'I did not want to hurt you. I wanted to hurt myself because I'm an odious man with no respect for people with something to live for.'

She opened her mouth on instructions from her heart to explain the contents of her letter and to tell him not to open it, but her tongue rebelled like a striking miner. She replaced the receiver.

For two days, her guilt over the crushing wording of her letter to Murphy conflicted with recurrent fury about his behaviour in the chemist's. She appreciated his decency to apologize. Part of her wanted to forgive him but the greater part felt that no apology, however genuine, could undo the unmotivated humiliation she had had to suffer in a public place. She took steps to forgive but every time she tried to take the initiative, her compassion was drowned by a surge of hate.

Elliott sensed her anxiety. He suggested taking her to the Vagas Cabaret off Jermyn Street. It was a club that specialized in singing the songs of Tom Lehrer. She had found it cheerful and amusing and had enjoyed herself when he had taken her there before. She agreed to go with him that night.

The club was crowded. A woman with a shrill, clear voice was on the stage singing a black-humoured song to a traditional polka tune. The song *Rikkitty Tikkitty Tin* was about a woman who killed each member of her family one by one. The occupants of the tables clapped in time to the song:

'Her mother, she could never stand, sing rikkitty tikkitty tin,
Her mother, she could never stand and so a cyanide soup she planned.
Her mother died with the spoon in her hand
And her face in a hideous grin, a grin, and her face in a hideous grin.'

'Have you got a light?' asked an old lady. Elliott was bored and disliked the song but Natalie was animated and elated. She got up and lit the old lady's cigarette.

'Excuse me, madam,' said the waiter carrying a small silver tray with a telemessage on it.

'I ordered another gin and tonic. Is it coming?'

'Is your name Miss Klein?' he asked.

'It is.'

'This arrived five minutes ago. Someone working in your house delivered it here.'

'How strange. Will you please bring me a double gin and tonic while you're about it.'

'Very good, madam.'

'She cut her baby brother in two, sing rikkitty tikkitty tin.
She cut her baby brother in two and served him up as an Irish stew –
And served him up as an Irish stew and invited the neighbours in, 'bours in,
And invited the neighbours in.'

'What's the matter? You're not laughing any more,' remarked Elliott. He had not noticed the delivery of the telemessage, nor had he seen her open it.

She leaned against the table. The paper fell to the floor. She lost consciousness and, as he bent over to see if she was breathing, he found it beside her. The communication was verbose and uncommonly long for a telemessage. It read:

> 'I LAMENT THE DEATH OF MY POOR BROTHER, SEAMUS MURPHY, WHO WAS KILLED DRIVING INTO A TREE. HE DIED WITH A POISONOUS LETTER IN HIS HAND. PLEASE GOD HIS VICIOUS MURDER SHALL NOT GO UNAVENGED. AND AS HIS SISTER I SHALL PURSUE HIS MURDERESS UNTIL SHE DIES.
>
> SIGNED DOLORES MURPHY, EVER-LOVING SISTER OF A MOST EXCEPTIONAL, AND BELOVED BROTHER.'

The manager of the club came to the table.

'Do you need a doctor, sir?'

'No,' replied Elliott, 'I'll take her home. She's had a shock.'

That night he kept her sedated on a higher dose of her own sedatives. His kindness gave her strength. To avoid surrendering to apathy, she forced herself to work again the next morning. She was busy in her office, calmed by some blue capsules which she referred to as her 'comforting blue boys' and Elliott banged about in his workshop.

'You're prettier than I thought you were, daughter,' commented a strange, menacing, low-pitched voice. The sepulchral huskiness of its tone made Natalie shudder. It showed a soft Southern Irish accent, stronger than Murphy's.

The visitor was a cadaverous woman who looked twenty years older than her forty years. She was dressed from head to foot in black and her head and shoulders were covered with a black lace shawl. Natalie was struck by the fact that she only had one front tooth. This, combined with a pair of piercing small eyes, blazing from hollow sockets in an emaciated face, made her look very sinister indeed.

Natalie bent over and took a swig of whisky from a bottle on the floor. She wiped her mouth with the back of her hand and sat up to face her attacker.

'What can I do for you, madam?'

The visitor tapped the floor with her walking stick three times. 'My name is Dolores Murphy. My brother's body is in the mortuary at King's College Hospital. I wish your firm to dispose of his remains in strict Roman Catholic tradition.'

'My name is Natalie Klein. I received your telemessage. You have me at a loss for words since I have none to offer. Anger is a natural emotion to feel when a person is bereaved, and even if death is precipitated by natural causes, it is equally normal to feel the need to blame someone for it . . .'

Dolores tapped her walking stick on the floor again.

'You talk far too much, more than becomes you, daughter.'

'You are right. Perhaps I do, but I can and must assure you that in absolutely *no* circumstances did I kill your brother, nor did I contemplate so doing.'

Dolores rose to her feet and leaned over the desk. She was taller than Natalie and therefore more frightening. She gripped her by the arm and did not allow her eyes to wander from Natalie's face. She continued: 'I have earned my living as a clairvoyant and fortune-teller. I work in fairgrounds. I earn little but enough to survive. A curse has been put on you. You will never know lasting happiness as long as you live. The day will come in a year's time when you will think you have found it, but it will not last. I've already seen to that.

'You will meet an honest man and you will become a close friend of his and his wife's. He is a very famous man, a man of self-acquired wealth, a man who knows no evil, a man who has suffered much and who dedicates his life to relieving suffering in others. The man will not know you when he meets you. He will treat you like his daughter because he will not know what you are, but one day he too will find out.'

'What am I?'

'Even you do not have that knowledge, yet, but you will know before the day is out. The man of whom I speak and whom you will not meet before a year has passed, is a man who will never fully understand what you are because vice is alien to him, but when what must be known is known by all, the man of whom I speak will have made you proud to be his friend, so you will be sorry when in the end even he will have to be told.'

'Told what?'

'What you are. And once you have come to know him you will live in fear that he will ever have access to such knowledge.'

'Who the dickens are you talking about, madam?'

'You have not met him or his wife yet. You will, and when you do, you will not remember the time I first passed you by or what I said either.'

Natalie was very superstitious. She hid her shaking hands behind the desk so that her fear would not be detected.

'How do you know all this?'

The cadaverous face peered into her own.

'The acts you commit will be acts of evil, some only of folly. That is part of my curse on you, and you will not know the folly of your acts until after you have committed them. You have crossed my path and you shall live in hell on earth. Do not think I predict fortunes with hands. I predict them with faces and your soul is damned.'

'Excuse me. This calls for Mr Elliott's attention.'

'Mr Elliott is known to me. He cannot save you.'

'Good morning, Miss Murphy,' said Elliott, entering the room. 'I understand how painful it is to have lost a brother. I'm willing to take care of Seamus's burial free of charge, but I will not have you frightening and intimidating Miss Klein.'

'Will you pick my brother's body up, yourself? He was your friend, was he not?'

Elliott loosened his collar. He was unnerved by this woman's manner but not as severely as was Natalie.

'Of course I will. I'll do so straight away. You stay here with Miss Klein.'

For two hours that seemed like several days, Natalie remained in the office alone with Dolores Murphy. A maid came into the room when she heard the bell ring.

'You called, madam?'

'Yes, I did. Would you please bring some tea.'

The servant made a gesture imitating the opening of a bottle and the emptying of its contents. Natalie nodded at her and raised one hand above her head, keeping the other at waist-level, as if stretching an accordion. This was a signal that she did not simply want the tea drugged. She wanted it loaded enough to stupefy. She was immune to the effects of tranquillizers unless taken in heavy doses, but her guest was not.

'Will you pour it out, please? And I'd like you to stay in the room.'

'Very good, madam.'

She hid her shaking hands under the table. She drank three

cups of the foul-tasting brown liquid. She was still fully alert ten minutes later but her palpitations were less violent. Dolores drank only half a cup and became drowsy within a few minutes. The powerful narcotic was working on Natalie, if only very mildly. Her face clouded over with a serene, beatific smile. The two women stared at each other while the maid looked at them both in bewilderment, wondering who was going to pass out first. Neither did. The surface hate and fear had vanished from their faces but the loathing they felt for each other was still alive.

'Your brother is in our Chapel of Rest, Miss Murphy,' said Elliot politely. He had just returned after a heated, bureaucratic argument with Reynolds, the half-witted mortuary attendant at the King's College Hospital. Although Reynolds exaggerated his act of being irritatingly slow and thick, Elliott forced himself to keep his temper with him. He would not allow Natalie to have any communication with him because she had once slapped him across the face in front of his colleagues when he had spelt the name on a label incorrectly.

'How is he got out?' Dolores asked Elliott.

'You asked that he be shrouded. The mortuary regulations state their bodies are not allowed to be moved unless they are fully clothed. Because of our concern for you and our deep sympathy with your suffering, which we feel is personal to us, I was able to persuade them to grant your request. Had they not known me, this would not have been possible to arrange.'

'I see.'

'Thank you is the word I think you are groping for,' said Natalie.

'Please forgive Miss Klein. I agree her manners are nothing short of disgusting but she is not herself today,' said Elliott.

'She's herself every inch of the way, young man. You're in bad hands and shall come to a bad end if she stays with you.'

'Your remark is totally out of order!'

'If you say so, I'll leave it at that for now. What about my brother's physical state? Are the injuries bad to look at?'

'The injuries which caused his death are internal. The precipitating cause was a blow to the brain but his face is entirely intact. Please don't think that either of us is insensitive to your suffering, because we are not. I will take you through and you shall see him.'

'Thank you, Mr Elliott. It is Natalie Klein who shall suffer.'

'That was quite unnecessary, Miss Murphy.'

Behind the closed door of the Chapel of Rest, Dolores knelt before her brother's body and prayed, holding forward a heavy brass cross which she wore round her neck. Natalie went back to the office where Elliot was waiting.

'That woman's scaring me to death. How does Murphy look?' she asked.

'Still in rigor. His face is statuesque. An artist might say it was beautiful.'

'Indeed? Perhaps it would be respectful for me to go and see him. I ought to. After all, it would seem the right thing to do. What do you think?'

'Go and see him if you think it would be right, but please don't do anything silly or eccentric. That's all I ask.'

'No.'

Dolores came out. Natalie knew how horrifying it must be to lose a brother and tried to be kind to her client. She extended her hand to support Dolores.

'May I go in, Miss Murphy?'

'I will wait for you in the office with Mr Elliott. Whatever prayers you have to say, if you intend to say them at all, will not shake off my curse.'

'That was unnecessary, Miss Murphy,' said Elliott. 'If you continue to be rude to Miss Klein, you will make things worse for yourself. While I grieve the loss of Seamus and recognize that his loss is worse for you than for anyone else, it does not justify bad manners. It may be Miss Klein's profession not to show her feelings but that doesn't mean she hasn't any.'

'She's not the kind that would.'

'If you say anything more about her, arrangements will be made for you to dispose of your brother's remains elsewhere. We ourselves are charging you nothing. Consider yourself warned.'

'I've naught against you. You are right to warn me, taking my finances into account.'

Natalie bolted the door in the Chapel of Rest. It had been used as a bedsit before the building had been converted into an undertaker's shop. The see-through mailbox was still on the door but she had become so used to its being there that she had forgotten about it.

She stared at the lifeless body of Murphy. Her tears were not those of bereavement. They were shed because Murphy's appearance in death had moved and roused her. His was a sacred beauty that had never struck her in life.

She knelt as she had when she first met him and took his face in her hands. She repeated the words she had uttered that day and ran her fingers through his hair.

'Come up through the lair of the Lion
With love in her luminous eyes.'

This was the closest to an utterance of prayer that she knew.

She stayed with Murphy for ten minutes and took care to leave him exactly as she had found him, betraying no evidence that she had done anything untoward. She was out of breath when she left the Chapel of Rest and the colour had returned to her cheeks.

Dolores was kneeling outside the door which opened inwardly. The drug made her lose her balance and she tumbled down the steps like a grotesque black rubber ball. Had the circumstances been less unpleasant, Natalie would have laughed at her ludicrous appearance. Dolores sprang to her feet and grabbed her by the throat.

'I saw it all, daughter. I've got it on record.'

Natalie lost her head and shouted like a maniac, stabbing the air with her finger. She backed away from Dolores, who was advancing towards her.

'I don't know what you're talking about. Let me pass, you mad Irish bitch!'

Dolores took the cross from round her neck and waved it in front of Natalie as if auditioning for the part of Jonathan Harker.

'Is that fucking thing for sale?'

Dolores was not used to being shouted at. She was so shocked by her adversary's foul language and irreverence that she dropped it. Natalie pushed her way past her and rushed into Elliott's workshop.

'Charlie, this is an emergency. We can't have this woman wandering around here loose. She's evil and dangerous. Please promise you won't allow her to be alone with me.'

'Calm down. Try and behave like an adult. Look at it from her point of view. She's just lost a brother. How would you like it if it happened to you? She can't harm you.'

'Yes, she can. I don't think you realize how bad she is. Can't we shove her on to *Crumblebottom and Bongwit*? It would teach the sons of bitches a lesson!'

'Keep your voice down, Natalie.'

'Those bastards are always poaching from us. They think they own the dead. They need a maniac like that woman to keep them in their place!'

'For Christ's sake calm down and stop shouting. You've done enough harm to *Crumblebottom and Bongwit* already. Only the other day, you pasted a notice on one of their windscreens when they were waiting to do a formal job, which read, "Am Drunk. Will Remove Vehicle When Sober." Mr Sprout took half an hour to scrape it off and went without lunch. All right, so the Murphy's sister's a pest. The way to win with her is to get Seamus buried free of charge. Once we've done that she won't pester us again.'

'You'll be sorry if you're wrong.'

He read hate in her eyes and went back to his hammering.

'Women!' he muttered under his breath. 'They're enough to drive any poor bastard to sea.'

Natalie Klein and Charles Elliott did all that was in their power to placate, comfort, console and humour Dolores, whose brother's interment was conducted as requested, according to strict Catholic tradition. Even professional actors would have concealed their repulsion less expertly than they.

* * *

There were times when Natalie despised Elliott for the gentleness, patience and tolerance that she so desperately lacked. His stoicism and failure to show his feelings after Murphy's interment made him appear like a caricature of the English. They were driving away from the graveyard when she turned on him, berating him for being boring, timid and benign.

'All my life I've learnt to get along with people and I come from nothing. You were born with everything but you quarrel with everyone you meet,' he retorted.

'Yes.' She banged her fist on the dashboard. 'Because no one values me for what I am. Only for what my family do. Why else do you think I chose a trade like this? I did it to attract attention to myself by deliberately being peculiar. If I quarrel with everyone, it's because the majority of people I meet are shits.'

'All right! I'm sick of your bad temper and your persistent tantrums. Knock it off!'

Three days after Dolores's request had been granted,

Elliott brought Natalie breakfast in bed. He had learned to accept the domestic role reversal she imposed on him.

'You were right all along about Dolores Murphy,' he said. 'She's quite mad.'

'I am always right.'

'She wants to have her brother's body exhumed now. She's been very offensive and abusive. She says she doesn't want anyone near Seamus's grave.'

'Why?'

'Ask a psychiatrist. Don't ask me. I've sent her packing. She says she'll make our lives impossible, but if she comes back I'm getting the police on to her.'

In her confusion Natalie accidentally knocked a jug of coffee on the floor but ignored it. 'Whatever you do, don't do that! We can't have the police here. It's out of the question. We'll do as she asks. I don't care any more. All I want is to be rid of her.'

'Stop shouting, woman! You've got to understand there's no limit to what Dolores might ask. She's dangerously insane. She's been here upsetting people every day when you've been at the cinema. She's going to bring our trade to a standstill. Seamus never complained about her but maybe he was trying to be loyal. He talked a lot about his sister, but he never said she was a psycho. If we don't get the police and a Court Order, she'll ruin us.'

Natalie suddenly sat upright.

'No!'

'Do see reason.'

She got out of bed and paced up and down the room, wringing her hands. 'I am seeing reason, I'm not attracting any more attention to us. Dolores will simmer down. She'll stop coming back if we ignore her. All right, so she's mad and we'll have to placate her. We'll exhume her brother. We'll do anything.'

'You're attracting enough attention as it is. Why must you

bellow as if I were five miles away? I will not tolerate this perpetual shouting!'

'I can't help it. I'm trying to cut it down.'

'You went to the grave, didn't you. You went several times. Why did you go to the grave?'

'I – I don't know.'

'But you do know you're not allowed in after the gates are locked, don't you?'

'Yes.'

'Dolores saw you there. That's why she wants him exhumed. She thinks you're mad.'

'*She* thinks *I'm* mad?'

'Yes. She's completely whacko herself, but she's under the impression you want to dig him up. That's why she wants him exhumed and burned.'

'Well, exhume him, then! As long as I don't have to hear about it. I don't want to be burdened with other people's mental illnesses. All I ask is that you don't get the police out.'

'You make it sound as if you've got something to hide, even from me.'

She picked up an ashtray and smashed it on the floor in a fit of rage. 'Do see sense, you stupid rustic! Even if an establishment is respectable, no businessman wants the police wandering around it. People see them hanging about. They might think we keep a disorderly house or deal in drugs. Then all our trade will go to *Crumblebottom and Bongwit*.'

Elliott wiped his forehead and showed no emotion. He looked physically and mentally exhausted. 'You may be right, boss. We'll exhume him,' he muttered hoarsely.

And so the remains of Seamus Murphy were removed from the earth and transported to a crematorium. Another religious service was held. Natalie did not attend. Whatever was left of Seamus Murphy drifted, just as he had in life, through a squalid-looking chimney into a grey sky of nothingness.

Dolores took possession of a silver urn containing her

brother's ashes. It was a *Klein and Elliot* urn and a *Klein and Elliott* gift. Dolores made an exaggerated, theatrical issue over her ownership of the urn because it was the only object she had possessed that had both material and sentimental value. She was aware of the financial worth of solid silver. Rather than keep it in her rented rooms, she liked to be seen carrying it everywhere she went, like an amateur athlete who had won his first cup.

She was known throughout Camberwell as 'The Ash Lady'. Jokes would be made about her in public houses; songs would be invented, their vulgar content bawled drunkenly on Saturday nights. In a self-centred way, Natalie thought she was making a greater idiot of her than she was of herself. The idea of her carrying the urn around with her nauseated her and revolted her. Not only did it give Dolores a warped sense of pleasure. She could not bear to see anyone's remains reduced to such an impersonal and inappropriately small size. Because she was in principle opposed to cremation, she was bitterly insensed by the exhumation on humane and moral grounds. The denial of the perverse pleasure of visiting Seamus's grave distorted her vision beyond logical proportion. Gradually, she began to develop a sinister and pathological obsession about Dolores's decision to cremate her brother. The idea of her carrying the silver urn, flaunting what seemed to Natalie to be the ultimate form of perversion, tortured and tormented her.

She and Elliott went out to an early dinner the night after the ceremony to celebrate their last encounter with Dolores. Elliott went straight to bed at 8.30 and fell asleep, aided by tranquillizers and wine. Natalie went downstairs to bolt the front door. Her ordeal had not ended. It had just begun.

Dolores waited outside and tapped on the window.

'You were very stupid to come back,' Natalie began. 'You've gone too far this time. Any interchanges between us will be conducted not by me, but by our solicitors.'

She did not have to look her assailant in the face. Her failure to meet her eyes gave her confidence.

Dolores put her hand through the open window and gripped Natalie by the arm.

'You won't be going near any solicitors when you've seen this, daughter.'

'You'd better come in, but if you cause me any serious trouble, I'll fight you to the death like a man and I'll win.'

'I've something here you want but it isn't free of charge.'

'If it's blackmail you'll go to jail for it.'

Dolores produced a photograph from her pocket, gripping it tightly so that Natalie would not be able to snatch it from her. She held it in front of Natalie who looked at it briefly and made an agonized shuddering noise. After two minutes, she composed herself.

'If you're a Catholic, please have some compassion for your enemies. I thought your philosophy was all about that sort of thing. I'm sure your Priest would tell you to hand it over,' she pleaded.

'You are a pagan. You proved that in the Chapel of Rest so let's leave religion out of it.'

'Just hand it over.'

'I'm going to but it's going to cost you.'

Natalie thought for a while. It was a question of Mate in a few moves as long as she didn't make any mistakes.

'How much?' she asked.

'Ten thousand pounds in cash.'

'I know that's a lot of money to you but it's little as far as I'm concerned. I will agree to meet your criminal demands because it's the only way to ensure you won't come back and disrupt my business. We haven't got more than a hundred pounds here in the office. We keep our safe with much of our accumulated savings in it in the garage. That's where burglars are least likely to look. If I honour your terms, will you promise never to come back?'

'I give my word. Have you ten thousand pounds in your safe?'

'At the moment, we have twelve thousand pounds there but the extra two thousand is for pallbearers' wages and essentials such as hearse maintenance, etc. The keys to the garage are in the top drawer here. You can bend over me to see I won't pull a gun on you, if it will put you at your ease.'

'Even if you do kill me, my immortal soul will hold the four aces,' said Dolores in a voice that chilled Natalie and made her feel faint.

'That's precisely what you said only the other day.'

Dolores leaned on the desk and stared Natalie in the eye. 'I'm glad you weren't too hard to persuade, daughter. I thought you'd blow your cool and call the Law.'

'Don't refer to the police as the Law. It's common.'

Dolores laughed. It was the hollow laugh of a Grade B Hammer ghoul.

'Let's go, Dolores. I've got the keys. I want this over as soon as possible because I'm tired and I want to go to bed.'

The older woman smiled, showing her one front tooth. She may only have smiled because she knew it made her look more frightening.

The part of the garage Natalie took her to was full of empty wine crates. She turned on the light, a single unshaded bulb, and guided Dolores over the crates, coils of rope, work stools and nail boxes that hadn't been tidied away.

'We keep our safe over here. Can you see that dark thing by the window?'

'I see it.'

'Good. I'm afraid it will mean having to clamber over all this to get to it.'

She forced herself to trip on one of the crates, dropping the key into it. She rolled on to the floor and let out a wail of pain.

'Are you hurt?' asked Dolores cautiously.

Natalie rustled up artificial but convincing tears.

'I've sprained my ankle. Can you please help me up?'

Dolores wrenched her to her feet. Then, without thinking, she knelt down to look for the key. Natalie picked up a hammer from the tool bench nearby. She hit Dolores on the head with it thirty-two times, holding the hammer in both hands.

She was reassured that her victim was dead when she saw part of her brain emerging through the brutally battered cranium. She took the photograph from her pocket and burned it. She noted that Dolores did not carry a handbag and turned out her other pockets. She found a five pound note, two one pound notes, some Kleenex tissues and a tattered picture of the Crucifixion torn from a prayer book. She burned that as well.

She rolled Dolores's body onto a stretcher with wheels and tied her arms and legs to it securely. She opened the hatch of one of the hearses. The opened hatch made the task of dragging the body as hard as pulling it up a steep hill. She pulled Dolores in from the inside of the vehicle. Such a load would have been too heavy in ordinary circumstances but the emergency gave her extra physical strength that even a healthy young man might have envied. She pulled down the blinds in the bier compartment and locked the hatch.

She rubbed axle grease on the number plates at the back and front and sprinkled dirt on top of the grease. Elliott had already filled the vehicle with petrol. She picked up the keys and reversed out of the garage, checking first that there was no blood on the floor. She wiped the hammer clean and returned it to its exact position on the workbench.

She swept up the ashes from the two burnt pictures and put them in her mouth. When her neat, tidy mind was satisfied there was no evidence of her action, she closed the garage door and drove out, taking care not to rev the engine.

The time was 9.17. Her vehicle could reach a maximum of

ninety miles an hour but she would not be able to reach Bodmin Moor before 1.00 a.m. because of the heavy rain. She took two blue capsules. Within ten minutes she felt so calm that her calmness alarmed even her. The full moon, and the unlikelihood of anyone wandering on the moors in such torrential rain gave her confidence.

She had heard terrifying stories about lesbianism in crowded women's prisons. She knew she would get life if her crime was discovered. She imagined what it would be like to share a cell for the rest of her life with two hirsute women abusing her beauty. If she was going to be caught, she decided she would kill herself rather than face jail, but at the same time the possibility seemed totally unreal. She was not going to be caught.

Elliott had taken her to Bodmin Moor on many occasions. He had catered for her interest in romantic literature, where heroines got lost on the moors, pursued by an adversary, be it a highwayman, an escaped convict or a hound. He had shown her the mineshafts approached by the narrow roads leading off the main moorland road, and had pointed out the ones which were not filled in. He had taken her there most weekends and she knew Bodmin Moor better than he did.

The narrow, unoccupied road across the moor was blocked by sheep that did not respond to her horn. When she drove on the grass to avoid them, her back wheels got in a rut. If she hadn't been drugged she would have panicked. Instead, she remembered a film of the Battle of Waterloo when Napoleon, played by Rod Steiger, was shown getting stuck in the mud on the battlefield. 'Come on, get me out of this!' he had barked at two aides. The memory made Natalie laugh as she got out to wedge the back wheels with a stone to stop them sliding back into the rut.

She got back to the main road from which she turned into an uneven, narrow side road. She found the shaft that Elliott had shown her. The moon illuminated the road and made her task as easy as it would have been in daylight. The wheels of the little wagon were supple; Elliot had kept them oiled. Her extraordinary reserve of strength made it easier for her to pull the body towards the shaft fifty yards away from the path.

It took her half an hour to get the body to the shaft because the ground was uneven, the mud slippery and the vegetation coarse. The effects of the capsules were beginning to wear off. Her sharper awareness of danger made her work faster and more urgently.

She had read in the papers of corpses being identified by their teeth alone. Dolores had one front tooth but the normal number of molars on each side in both the upper and lower jaw. She prised open her mouth, hoping to see that its sluttish-looking owner had never consulted a dentist.

She shone the torch she carried round her neck in Dolores's mouth. Many of the back teeth had been drilled and filled. The others either had minor cavities or were completely decayed.

She took a hammer from the hollow area under the bier compartment and prised open the dead woman's lips. She decided to knock out what teeth remained and scatter them. As she brought the hammer down, she hit her fingers. The pain was sharp and nauseating. Her nerves was going. She decided she would risk the consequences and leave the teeth.

She dragged the wagon with a succession of clumsy, lurching movements and propelled it down the beckoning, gaping shaft. The thud that followed ten seconds later, reassured her that, although the shaft was not as deep as she thought, it was deep enough to hide her load from detection.

She checked she hadn't left the torch and the hammer behind, and filled in the tracks left by the wagon. She went back to the narrow, uneven road. There was nowhere to turn so she reversed for two miles until she reached the main road.

It was 6.00 a.m. when she arrived in London. She burned her clothes in a dustbin which she and Elliott used as a brazier. She returned the hearse to where she had found it, washed it, cleaned the number plates and checked there was no blood on the bier rack. She filled the tank with the spare petrol cans she and Elliott stored and walked back to the house naked with the keys in her hand. If Elliott had seen her, she would have said she had been walking in her sleep. He knew she was pretty eccentric and he would have believed her.

He was still in a drunken sleep when she went to the bedroom. She got into bed and fell asleep. When she woke two hours later, she had no recollection whatever of what she had done or where she had been. She felt very unwell and had a vague feeling that some time during the night she had had a bad dream. Apart from that, she might just as well have had a lobotomy. Her memory refused to tell her what she had done. Instead, it punished her body in the form of physical symptoms. She was frightened, because she had the outward signs of a physical illness but no idea what had caused it. She was convinced she had typhoid and lay on her back, bellowing for her favourite doctor, Dr Heineman.

Dr Sergei Heineman, Harley Street's most envied and accomplished diagnostician, was the Kleins' family doctor. He had a sentimental attachment to Natalie because she was born during the *Se vuol ballare* aria of *The Marriage of Figaro* at the Royal Opera House. He had been invited there by her parents and had taken more applause from the audience for the delivery than the singer. The tempestuous Latin in the role of Figaro left the stage after the aria in a temper and his understudy took over.

To look at, Dr Heineman was a combination of Clark Gable and Ben Gazzara. His appearance, combined with his guttural Viennese accent, set Natalie's blood on fire. He said there was nothing wrong with her except a stomach upset and nervous exhaustion.

She always felt better after his visits, whether there was

anything wrong with her or not. Within two days, she was back at work.

* * *

A year passed. Natalie continued to see Dolores Murphy. Sometimes she would appear in the street, carrying her brother's ashes. She would repeat the words: 'My immortal soul shall hold the four aces,' until Natalie screamed. But the intervals between her appearances became longer and Natalie felt she was getting better. She started to enjoy her work again. Then, one morning, she took a telephone call when Elliott was out on business. The caller said he had an uncle called Augustus Brown who had died in Riverfield, a town in a merged group of Midland counties forming Barfax East. Burial had been requested in London where the rest of the Brown family lived.

Natalie collected the body from the mortuary in the Riverfield General Hospital. She had a flat tyre on the outskirts of Riverfield on her way back to London. A lorry driver, motivated by amused, morbid curiosity, changed the wheel. He dragged Augustus Brown out by binding a chain to the casket and reversed, attaching the other end of the chain to the lorry. He couldn't think of a way to get it back in when the wheel had been changed. She cursed him for his lack of initiative. He drove off in a temper. She paced up and down, chain-smoking, no longer caring that she had made an idiot of herself. She sat by the side of the road, using Augustus Brown as a chair, and thought about her childhood, trying to recall why it mattered to her so much to be thought brave, and what the original underlying cause was of her not wishing to be thought of as a weakling or a coward.

She had been the youngest of the Klein children and the last to be sent away to school. Idleness and solitude made her mischievous and destructive. By the time she went to boarding school, she was a compulsively vain, attention-seeking exhibitionist, and her outrageous behaviour increased her popularity with the more timid children who encouraged her and made her behaviour worse.

She attracted attention to herself in this way to hide how much her fear of illness tortured and shamed her. She felt she could hide her hypochondria by perpetual acts of mischief for other children to develop an interest in. She befriended a girl called Emma Robinson. The two became inseparable friends, their friendship strengthened by Emma's admiration and worship of her apparent fearlessness.

Another reason for her exhibitionist behaviour at the strict Protestant school was her need to be recognized as a person in her own right. Although she was devoted to her father, she did not like being introduced as Selwyn Klein's daughter, and ninety per cent of her misdemeanours were motivated by a need to stand on a pedestal of her own creation. She believed it was better to be an exhibit in the Chamber of Horrors than not be remembered at all.

* * *

Emma Robinson invited her to stay during the summer holidays. The Robinsons found her well brought up but were both horrified and delighted by the anecdotes she told them about her practical jokes and cheekiness towards the mistresses. A boy called Mark was also staying in the house. Under his laughing, stoic exterior, he was a very sad little boy whose father had just died. His mother was a friend of the Robinsons and was temporarily too overwrought to cope. Mark had a cherubic face and a twinkle in his eye. He forced himself to be cheerful and not to let his father's death upset him openly for fear of being considered 'wet'.

He was happy at the prospect of accompanying Natalie and Emma to the cinema one afternoon. Although the girls were only ten, like himself, they painted their faces to compete for his attention and this flattered him.

Mrs Robinson drove the three children to a cinema showing the film *Taras Bulba.* Mark sat between the two girls, both of whom tried to impress him by making him laugh. Natalie was more interested in the film than her companions were. The hero of the film was Taras Bulba's son who was accused of being a coward. He was challenged by his own brethren to ride over a ravine to prove he was not. The sound of the galloping horse's hooves, sometimes only just making it to the other side, and the sight of the pieces of rock falling into the ravine after it had been ridden over, had a hypnotic effect on Natalie. She turned to Mark before the interval.

'Isn't he brave?'

Mark agreed with her but did not share her zealousness.

'I'd give anything to be thought as brave as that,' Natalie added, ignoring the woman in front who hissed for silence.

'Would you now,' said Mark. 'Wait till the interval. I've got an idea. You'll be able to prove you're just as brave, if not braver.'

A middle-aged ice-cream vendor with horn-rimmed spectacles and thick powder stood in the aisle during the interval, while a queue gathered in front of her. 'I bet you don't dare go up to that woman and say: "There's a good-looking boy in the cinema who'll fuck you for a shilling," ' said Mark.

Emma pleaded with her not to do it but Natalie wanted to make more of an impression on Mark than Emma had made.

'Excuse me, madam,' echoed a voice which lapsed involuntarily into a heavy Welsh accent.

'Wait your turn!' said the ice-cream vendor. Her unfriendly tone made it easier for Natalie to be impertinent.

'I've come to say: "There's a good-looking boy in the cinema who'll fuck you for a shilling." '

'One shilling! One shilling! Tell your friend he's going to have to offer me more than one shilling.'

'I did as you said, Mark, but she says her rate is higher than a shilling.'

'Then go back and tell her she's only good for a shilling.'

'Excuse me, madam, my friend says you're only worth a shilling.'

'Get out of it! Don't be so bloomin' rude!' shouted the ice-cream vendor, loudly enough for Mark to hear, so he knew she had accepted the dare. He was surprised she had done so and wondered how far she was prepared to go without his being implicated.

When the children left the cinema, Mark picked up a brick and handed it to Natalie.

'See that red sports car at the lights?'

'Yes.'

'I bet you don't dare throw this at it.'

Emma tried to persuade her not to do it and Natalie said she thought it was a bad idea. Mark reminded her of her wish not to be thought a coward and the sound of the galloping horse thundered in her ears as it had when she had spoken to the ice-cream vendor. She held the brick in both hands and threw it as violently as she could, making a dent in the Aston Martin's paintwork.

The driver was a twenty-three-year-old engineer, taking his girl-friend out and trying to impress her with his new acquisition. He went straight towards Mark.

'I'll smack you up for this, you little brat!'

The children turned and fled with the driver pursuing them. If he hadn't tripped and fallen, he would have caught them. Natalie confessed her crime under pressure. Her parents were so stunned when they heard what she had done that they both had to have a glass of brandy. Natalie was confined to the library and made to learn *The Charge of the Light Brigade*, which was an easy, even pleasurable task. This was partly because much of it rhymed in threes but mainly because she could identify with the theme of misdirected courage. When she was word-perfect she was asked to stand on a stool in front of her parents. Occasionally, one of her brothers would prompt her through the window by mouthing the words of the poem that all the Klein children had been made to learn at some stage of their disciplinary education.

When Natalie had finished reciting, her mother, who had remained pale and shaken as if she had actually been trampled on by the Light Brigade, said: 'I'm so utterly appalled, Selwyn dear. I think we ought to teach her a proper lesson and make her go round and recite it to the Aston Martin driver as well.'

'I think that would be unjustifiably hard on the man, taking the monotonous tone of her voice into account and considering what he's had to go through already,' Selwyn Klein commented mildly.

* * *

Natalie laughed as she remembered the incident, and paced up and down by the roadside. Her feeling of merriment conflicted with a sense of nostalgia for her happy childhood that had passed her by with little chance of being relived. She decided she would keep the promise she had once made to herself and that one day she would prove she was not a coward.

She had given up trying to flag down drivers to help her and, as she grew more aware of the grotesqueness of her situation, she became depressed. Her escapades of bravado as a child had been futile. A man who had meant a lot to her had died, having publicly called her a coward when he had found out what she feared most.

She was also convinced his sister was still at large. Her subconscious had censored the knowledge that she had killed her. Dolores's appearances continued, if after long intervals. Each time she appeared, Natalie was reminded of her cowardice, in the street, in crowded waiting-rooms, at social gatherings, on all occasions when there would be witnesses, and every visit was more painful and more vicious than the one before it.

Three hours passed. No one showed signs of wishing to help her. She sat on top of Augustus Brown, facing away from the road. She was too humiliated to call for roadside services because she wouldn't have been able to describe her predicament without appealing to the blacker side of the listener's humour, and laughing out of nervousness herself. She got up and paced up and down again, her mood alternating between fury and gloom. She knew no one would come to help her and she no longer cared.

But someone did come. As if she might have been a gull with a broken wing, the person who came mended her where she had been broken, and commanded her to fly as she had never flown before, and when she flew she feared nothing, not even illness any more. Her new guide and teacher trained her not to pursue petty, phoney displays of artificial courage, but to dedicate herself to the attainment of a supreme personal glory that she never knew existed within herself.

· PART TWO ·

Captain Rex Malone

Captain Rex Malone was graced with good looks. He was a self-made, self-taught millionaire publisher, newspaper proprietor, football club owner and charity campaigner. He was over six foot tall, and well built as opposed to fat because his wife kept him, if against his will, on a strict diet. She, too was concerned about his image.

His hair was thick, straight and black and swept back from the face showing a widow's peak. The nose was sharp, prominent and straight and in proportion to the rest of the face. The upward-slanting hazel eyes were shrewd and watchful. The smile showed well kept teeth which, although white and straight, were jagged and unequal in length, giving him rather a rakish look. His smile was often combined with a guttural Cossack's laugh which melted the hearts of many women.

He had a very deep voice. His accent, though English, had a mildly northern lilt because he had learnt his English in Liverpool, but if he became heated or emotional, an occasional East European rasping *R* would betray itself. Even if he was not heated a speech expert would have been struck by his occasional use of outmoded slang and the dropping, though not too often, of malapropisms.

When speaking publicly, he was sometimes inclined to use the kind of language that would have made him seem more English than the English, so much so that there were times when he was misinterpreted as being a caricature of the English.

To give an example, a section can be taken from one of his speeches, delivered with the tub-thumping eloquence that made him popular: 'And it's the little things in life that make this smashing country worth living in – yer friendly, apple-cheeked housewife inviting you in for a cuppa! Yer merry milkman calling to give you yer pinta!'

Many people laughed at his speech mode. The millions that were later to vote for him found it appealing.

Malone was born in Eastern Europe between the wars and was raised in conditions of appalling poverty. In his childhood he was influenced by a Rabbi whose teachings endowed him with a passionate sense of ethics, fair play and honesty. His urgent need to compete with others was first manifested at the age of three, when he had to be pulled out of a river when trying to swim, in imitation of other boys older than he.

He would recall, with some good humour, an occasion when he was jilted at the age of eleven: 'I fell in love with a girl three years my senior. I remember being very unhappy as the lady would not take any notice of me and treated me like a little child.'

He left his native country and enlisted with the Allies at the outbreak of World War Two. He escaped from the Gestapo in France and then left French shores in a small boat from which he was picked up by a British destroyer bound for Liverpool.

It only took him six weeks to learn English. When he returned to France in the Normandy invasion force, he met Hortense Le Mesurier, later to become his wife.

She was impressed by his boldness, honesty and aura of firm resolve. Because she was bored by the superficial middle-class snobbery prevalent in some of the circles she was obliged by her peers to mix in, she found relief in the company of this unconventional, fiery, impatient, sometimes even abrasive and moody Slav who said what he thought and who was aggressively intolerant of folly. She was struck by his swings in temperament from extreme friendliness to moodiness, but she admired and respected his resoluteness and singlemindedness. While being capable of spontaneous cantankerous behaviour towards people of low intelligence who contradicted him, he was entirely devoid of malice, mischief, underhandedness or vindictiveness, even towards those who had wronged him. Indeed, the words 'you silly idiot' were the unkindest words he was ever heard to utter.

He told her that he had come home as a boy to see his family herded into a truck to be taken to the gas chambers. His strength to fight oppressors, combined with his lack of subjective viciousness in describing the experience, moved her. Her affection was protective at first. Later, she found she was in love with him.

He saw in her the qualities he would have liked to see in the mother whom he had never met in adulthood. He loved Hortense for her purity, complete selflessness and devotion, both unfluctuating and unfaltering, a quality not commonly associated with French women.

His first ambition had been to win the MC. Through his fearlessness and powers of leadership on the field, he got what he wanted.

Hortense always associated the Brahms 'Hungarian Dance Number 5' with him because it was being played when he proposed to her in a restaurant. The association was also apt due to its dramatic Slavonic swing from massive energy to moodiness.

After the war he changed his name to Rex Malone and moved into publishing by befriending an influential publishing house owner. He borrowed enough capital from his new associate to set up his own company, secured a vast annual turnover for his company and repaid his associate with interest. He was then able to form a merger between his newly found company and that of his associate. The company merged to become Agamemnon International Publications.

'If there were another hundred firms in this country like mine, there would be no balance of payments problem,' he said in a television interview, and he was right.

His inexhaustible energy and capacity to work an eighteen-hour day enabled him to expand and export to over twenty countries as well as countries behind the Iron Curtain.

He also had an interest in politics. Always concerned with the underdog, he became a Labour MP in a predominantly Tory constituency in the south. He was defeated in a subsequent election. It was a period when the Lunatic Left were becoming over-influential with the Labour Party, so he set up his own Party, the Malonist Party, which was a superior replacement of the Social Democrat Party. His constituency, Barfax East, was formed by a group of Northern Midland counties. He made repeated bids for a popular tabloid newspaper and bought a derelict Fleet Street tabloid which he transformed to the *Malonist Voice*. The newspaper carried a photograph of himself (smiling) on the top right-hand corner of the front page. It sponsored bingo competitions and he was always photographed on the front page, drinking champagne with the winner.

Certain men resented him. If they were middle class or wealthy, their resentment was due to envy of a man who had started with less than they and got further. If they were working class they hated him because he was foreign.

He was described in myriad ways as 'both attractive and repellent', an 'opportunist', a 'rogue', a 'megalomaniac', a 'socialist, albeit an idiosyncratic one', and a 'spring-heeled Bohemian and connoisseur of English courtesies'.

An interviewer asked him why he liked England and the English.

'I suppose it's basically that being foreign born, I'm more patriotic than the natives. I'm very fond of this country, its institutions, people, climate and way of living. I am keen to get this country back where it belongs, to the old idea of Empire but not through the gunboat.'

He bought a series of ailing printing firms in close succession, quadrupling their annual profits and providing jobs for thousands of workers who would otherwise have been redundant.

Jealousy of his success increased. Printers on the *Malonist Voice* staged a vicious and long-drawn-out strike. Malone was tough to the end.

'Do you think I'm on an ego trip?' he asked his assembled print workers.

'Yes!' they screamed unanimously.

'If you want a fight,' he said, 'I'll give you one such as you've never had before because, by Christ, you need it!'

The strikers knew they would get nowhere with this fiery, hot-blooded Cossack. They returned to work.

* * *

It was during his campaign to become Prime Minister that he was touring the outskirts of his Barfax East constituency, travelling in a vehicle called the Malonemobile. Like the campaign vehicles of the other political parties, the Malonemobile looked like a Landrover. It was painted white and yellow, the colours of the Malonist Party, and the slogans of the Party stood out in prominent black letters:

> 'YOU'RE NEVER ALONE WITH REXY MALONE.
> VOTE WHILE YOU CAN. REXY'S YOUR MAN.'

The slogans were designed to be simple, eye-catching and

easy to remember. When he approached crowded streets, Malone would recite the slogans over a loud hailer.

Some children were playing ball in the road. They stopped to stare at the yellow and white vehicle, which was the only one that had not hooted at them.

'Vote while you can. Rexy's yer man.
Vote while you can. Rexy's yer man!'

The children stopped him to get his autograph. Politicians from the other parties envied the Pied Piper appeal he had with children.

When he had finished meeting their demands, he began to dictate what were known as 'condolence letters' to his secretary and personal assistant, Miss Bechtold, who was neat, brisk, bossy and efficient and who had been with him for fourteen years.

'Mrs Emily Davis has just lost her husband who died in an industrial accident. Give her a standard letter from Condolence file 43,' Malone instructed her and handed her the local newspaper with an article about the accident. The article had been encircled.

'File 43 would hardly be appropriate, Mr Malone,' replied Miss Bechtold. 'Correspondence in that file begins: "Mr Malone and his colleagues in the Malonist Party are happy to congratulate you on the birth of a son/daughter." '

'Never mind the number. You know the file I mean.'

'You're referring to File 41 – the one in which letters begin: "In circumstances as tragic as yours, words are futile but . . ." '

'That's the one,' said Malone, throwing an apple core out of the window in front of a foul-mouthed cyclist.

'Very well, Mr Malone, but I've told you before, you shouldn't throw things out of the window.'

'All right, all right, matron.'

'Anyone else to get a 41?'

'A few. Yes.' He gave her a list of names and addresses from the *Barfax Herald* which lay open at the Births, Marriages and Deaths page. When he'd finished reading out the details, he threw the paper out of the window because he was in a mischievous mood and wanted to hear her express disapproval.

Suddenly, he stared out of the window with a surprised look on his face. He slowed down, swerving abruptly to the side of the road.

'What the hell's that, Miss Bechtold?'

'A bizarre spectacle, Mr Malone. Probably a joke. We must get on.'

Malone stared in disbelief at the casket lying beside a hearse abandoned by the side of the road, and a young woman in black pacing up and down in a rage.

'I'm not going on. I'm getting out to see what all this is about.'

'There's no point,' replied Miss Bechtold. 'It would only be one vote gained, not to mention involvement in something very peculiar and best avoided.'

'There are some instances when I deal in principles, not numbers, and this is one. If someone needs help I will help them.'

Malone got out and walked towards Natalie Klein.

'Blimey, madam, you seem to have come to a dead end.'

She recognized him as she had seen him repeatedly on television, where she had been impressed by his looks and had respected him. She felt humiliated to be found by him in such undignified circumstances and spoke in abrupt staccato sentences to hide the humuliation.

'You could say that. I've been having trouble shifting my stiff back onto my wagon.'

Malone regarded his new acquaintance, his head raised, his eyes alert, shrewd, fox-like, curious and questioning. He had seen a massive slice of humanity in his life but had never come across a situation quite as bizarre as this.

'I don't understand how it got out in the first place,' he said in a startled tone.

'The wheel had to be changed. A lorry driver had to drag my cargo out first.'

'Your cargo?'

'That's what it's called in the trade and the lorry driver couldn't put it back.'

'Why?'

'Because of its weight.'

'Why couldn't he have used his common sense?'

'Maybe because he had none.'

'Then why didn't you tell him how to use his common sense?' asked Malone.

'If I'd seen an obvious solution I wouldn't be here now. What do *you* suggest I do?'

'It's simple. You solve the problem in five moves.'

Malone put two fingers of each hand in his mouth and wolf-whistled.

'I do wish you'd stop that whistling, Mr Malone, every time you want to attract my attention. It's frightfully common,' said Miss Bechtold.

Malone looked towards Natalie and smiled. 'It's what they do at football grounds,' he said. She returned the smile. Then he turned to Miss Bechtold. 'Get the iron rod.'

'Get the iron rod, what?'

'Get the iron rod, *please*.'

'That's better, you're becoming house-trained.'

Miss Bechtold took a heavy metal stick for wrenching things open from the back of the Malonemobile and handed it to Malone, who took off his jacket and loosened his tie, shoving a cigar in his mouth and spitting its end into the gutter.

As he worked he spoke to Natalie like a lecturer addressing students.

'First you get it open. Then you roll the thing out. Then you put the casket in the back. Then you swing the bastard over your shoulder.'

He winced as he did so. The pain of dislocation was like a knife with its handle rotating. He walked towards her vehicle with the load on his shoulder while she gaped at him in astonishment. After a silence lasting about three minutes she said:

'Are you really Rex Malone?'

'That's me. I'm Rexy to my electorate and Rex to my family and my friends, so you can choose what you want to call me.'

A child aged nine, wearing a brownie uniform, marched towards him and demanded his autograph. He had not had a chance to lay down his burden but the child was unconcerned.

'Your autograph, please, one to keep and two to sell.'

'Smart thinking. This sounds like an order, not a request. How much will you charge?'

'Fifty pence for one extra. I'll get a pound if you give me two extras – that is apart from the one I keep for myself.'

'A shrewd business sense, and a brownie, I see. I bet your daddy's proud of you.'

The child smiled at him precociously and handed him three books one after another.

'Would you mind holding the book steady so that poor Uncle Rex can write his name for you.'

'Who have you got over your shoulder?'

'I'm surprised you didn't ask before. That's poor old Bill. He works for us. He won't stop working even if he's ordered to. Now he's fainted, We've been told to stand him on the head and in fifteen minutes the blood will get to his brain and he'll be all right again.'

Natalie broke into paroxysms of giggles and turned away. The child accepted the explanation and ran off when she had what she wanted. Malone felt as if he had been sprayed with shrapnel and the pain radiated to his waist.

He threw the earthly remains of Augustus Brown into the casket. The head made a strange hollow sound on impact and Malone swore under his breath.

'I am so grateful to you for what you did. Is there anything I can do in return?' Natalie asked.

'What are your politics?' Malone asked hoarsely, after recovering his breath.

'I am an anarchist.'

'Is there an anarchist candidate in your constituency?'

'No.'

'Who the hell do you vote for, then?'

'For Mrs Thatcher, of course. She's the closest to anarchy you can get!'

Malone gave the guttural Cossack's laugh for which he was famous and showed his jagged white teeth in a smile that delighted her.

'I liked that! Miss Bechtold, did you hear what she said?'

'Yes. I heard it.'

'I want to work for you now,' Natalie said to Malone in a serious voice.

'Why?'

'I think you are very good-looking.'

Malone took a few minutes to answer while nursing the pain in his shoulder.

'You'd better come along with Miss Bechtold and me. Leave your gear by the road. I'll have it collected and delivered if you give me the details. We're going back to headquarters. Then we'll collect my own car and you can stay with me and my wife until all this rubbish is sorted out. What does a pretty girl like you want to do this kind of work for, anyway?'

'I have a feeling for the dead,' she said spontaneously, but noticed he was eyeing her strangely and added: 'there's always money in death. No recession can stop people dying.'

Malone felt suffocated because of the heat. He undid the top button of his shirt and loosened his tie further. The gesture attracted Natalie.

'I liked your second explanation better than the first,' he said. 'What's your name?'

'Natalie Klein.'

'All right, Natalie, Miss Bechtold has some work to do at headquarters so come with me. We'll go to my house. I know my wife will like you and so will my children, some of whom are about the same age as you.'

A lilac-coloured Daimler with mauve-tinted windows and a silver miniature statue of the sworded warrior, Agamemnon, on its front, was parked outside the Malonist Party headquarters. Malone got out of the Malonemobile clutching his shoulder. Miss Bechtold walked briskly away with a pile of papers under her arm. Malone got behind the steering wheel of the Daimler.

'Come on, Natalie, in you get,' he said.

As she was getting in, he started the engine. Then he moved off.

'Got any overnight stuff with you?' he asked abruptly.

'Of course not. None at all. I wasn't to know any of this would happen.'

'Someone in my house will give you what you need,' he said. 'Next time you go out on business, see to it that you are better prepared, in case you run into this kind of trouble again. Yours was not exactly the sort of predicament that an ordinary well-wishing passer-by would wish to get involved with.'

His tone gave her no indication whether he was joking or berating her so she shielded herself with the defensive abruptness that she used as armour.

'These things happen. That's all there is to it.' The staccato voice had deteriorated to a military bark. He felt the tone of anger and his mind was in conflict as to whether to consider her appallingly bad-mannered or to admire her for her boldness. He did not comment but continued to look at the unfolding road through the eyes of a jaded emperor surveying a procession of dignitaries who had interrupted his siesta.

For the next hour neither Natalie nor Malone spoke. His silence was due to exhaustion and low spirits exacerbated by his aching shoulder. Natalie was silent because she was not a small-talk conversationalist and only spoke if she had something specific to say. But because she had been brought up to be courteous in return for help, she forced herself, with extreme reluctance, to open a conversation without asking personal questions.

'Is your gearbox automatic?' she asked.

'I suppose so,' Malone replied in a depressed tone. A silence of ten minutes ensued while Malone tried to ignore the pain in his shoulder. Suddenly Natalie said: 'I've just thought of something you'll find funny. A man was travelling in a car with Churchill late at night. The man said to Churchill: "It's very dark, isn't it?" Churchill said: "It usually is at night." '

'It's possible Churchill may have been right,' said Malone, but had he been feeling less tired and uncomfortable he would have laughed. There was another long silence.

'Do you speak French, Natalie?' asked Malone suddenly.

'Yes, I do. Why do you ask?'

'Because my wife's French. Although she speaks impeccable English, she likes to speak her own language sometimes.'

'I'll speak French to her, then.'

'Do you speak other languages besides French?'

'Russian,' she replied abruptly.

Malone smiled. His mood transformed immediately. Russian was among the languages he had spoken since childhood. He asked her questions in Russian. The answers she gave were even more abrupt and staccato than her remarks in English, and because of their terseness they somehow sounded wittier in Russian.

'Where the hell did you learn to speak Russian like that?' he asked (in English).

'I taught myself.'

'You mean you had no lessons?'

'No. You can teach yourself anything if you want to learn.'

'But your accent – it's Siberian. It's excellent and I'm very impressed by it, but wherever did you pick it up? It sounds so strange.'

'By listening to songs.'

'Have you been to Russia?'

'Yes, once.'

'Who did you go with?'

'No one. I went by myself.'

'What – alone?'

'Yes. Why not? I go to a lot of places alone.'

Malone seemed bewildered. She could tell by the expression on his face that he was impressed by her but she couldn't understand why, and because she feared she would have felt an anticlimax if she asked why, she didn't say anything and stared vacantly ahead of her.

He drove through some automatically opening wrought-iron gates bearing the formidable silver-plated crest of Agamemnon International Publications. The muscular silver-sworded figure was identical to that on the front of the Daimler, although it was at least ten times larger, and the sword shone more brilliantly in the evening sun than the rest of the statue. A watchman occupying a booth near the gates raised his hat to Malone, who was chewing an unlit cigar, communicating to the watchman an aura of power, confidence, fearlessness and strength.

He followed a sinuous drive scattered with ramps and notices that said children were playing. The drive was flanked on one side by a glass-walled building, used for the offices of Agamemnon International Publications, and by evergreens and flower beds on the other.

At the end of the drive stood a grey-walled Bath stone house owned by Agamemnon International which was entered by a covered area supported by pillars. Opposite the covered area on the other side of the drive was a tennis court and round the corner was a bigger covered area supported by more pillars, giving the place a Greek-Roman look. A bronze, larger-than-life statue of Agamemnon holding a sword pointed to a flight of steps leading to a garden framed by more flower beds, with a circular swimming pool, sauna bath and changing room in the centre.

A labrador bounded from the garden to greet Malone, and a maid, wearing a light blue uniform, her dark hair wound in a coil on top of her head, arrived on the scene just in time to prevent it from scratching the paint off the Daimler.

'Good evening, Mr Papa,' said the woman, who was in her fifties, foreign and whose smile communicated a feeling of natural well-being and peace of mind.

'Evening, pal! I've a visitor with me. Miss Klein's the name. Natalie, this is Minda who's put up with us for years on end, God help her. I hope you like our house. You've a permanent invitation to it.'

Natalie was still not entirely at ease with Malone but her attraction to him outweighed her fear. She found it difficult to combine gracious, affectionate behaviour with the open boldness which she sensed he admired.

'You are indeed kind,' she said in a stilted tone, alien to the tenor of her earlier behaviour. Her change in speech took him by surprise.

'I'm not kind!' he said angrily, but with intent to convince her that his invitation was genuine. She closed the door of the Daimler very gently, afraid that her instinct would be to kick it in the way she shut the doors of the cars she drove herself.

'No,' said Malone quietly.

'No?'

Malone continued to chew his unlit cigar. 'You have not closed the door correctly,' he said. 'Try again.'

Malone entered the house first and went to a wash-basin in a water-closet near the front door where he washed his hands very thoroughly. She waited in the same way that Murphy had waited when she had washed her hands the first day they met.

'To be sure I admire your cleanliness,' she said, instinctively mimicking an Irish accent. She did not know she had spoken until he fixed her with an alarmed and curious stare. He said nothing but studied her, with his head raised, his expression fox-like, expecting anything.

The house, like its owner, was clean, neat and tidy. A Persian carpet covered the hall which led to a ceremonial flight of stairs. These divided from left to right at the top, beneath a ten foot by five foot mosaic design on stained glass, the colour of which was predominantly blue.

In the hall was a glass-doored cabinet showing chessmen in different models covering ten shelves.

Beyond the hall was a drawing-room full of light from bay windows overlooking the garden. In one corner of the room were a harp and a grand piano on which stood a silver-framed photograph of Malone, Mrs Malone and their children. The furniture was Empire.

Chess sets, some with wooden pieces, some with bronze pieces and some with marble pieces, lay on every occasional table. Although this room was as tidy as a museum, its very walls radiated life.

The room led to a study area which was darker and more forbidding in its sobriety and had fewer windows. Its walls were lined with books, mainly encyclopaedias. There were two leather-topped writing desks. On one was a bust of Malone, sculpted out of clay and making him look inappropriately older than his years. A jumbo-sized egg-timer dwarfed the bust and the combination of the two had an odd effect on the eye. The other desk had nothing on it except a brightly painted porcelain bust of Napoleon which was no longer used as an ornament and had been pushed aside. Natalie assumed it had been an unwanted gift and wished it was hers.

'Want anything to eat or drink?' asked Malone, who had seated himself by one of the windows near the musical instruments.

'I only want tea and nothing else.' Malone liked Natalie, although he thought she was a bit odd. He spat out his well-chewed, unlit cigar and wolf-whistled, putting both hands in his mouth, and she laughed spontaneously.

'What the hell's so funny?'

'I like the way you whistle.' Minda, the maid, came in and asked Malone what he wanted.

'A full cold chicken, please, pal, a bottle of beer and tea for Miss Klein and nothing else,' he said.

'Missus say not good for you to eat so much in one go.'

'To hell with what Missus said! Get me what I want. I won't be ordered around by a bunch of hens!'

Minda returned with the things she'd been asked to bring, and gave Natalie a cup of unsweetened tea and nothing else. Malone wolfed the whole chicken in the same amount of time it would have taken an ordinary person to eat a sausage. He ate with his fingers, pushing the knife and fork provided to one side. He took a long gulp of beer from the litre-sized bottle and looked contented.

'Tea all right?' he asked.

'No. It's not all right at all. I can't drink it without sugar.'

Malone whistled again and told the maid to bring some lumps of sugar in her fingers. She brought four lumps, all of which Natalie put in the tea which she stirred thoroughly, afraid of leaving any sugar untasted.

'Keep your wits about you, pal,' said Malone. 'Miss Klein's got a very sweet tooth,' and as he said this he took his shoes off and threw them into a corner. He rested his feet on one of the tables, chewing another unlit cigar which he had taken from a silver case.

'You've had a long day, so take off your boots,' he said.

'I don't really think I can do that in here. I don't want to.'

'Is this a convent you think you're in? You're tired. Take them off.'

'No.'

'Are you intending to become a nun or something? You've been standing around for a long time, so when I say take off your boots, I mean take them off.'

She did as she was told and tried to imitate his own action. She threw them to a different part of the room from where Malone had thrown his shoes and one of them accidentally hit the pedestal of a chess table, knocking a marble bishop on its side, bringing a knight over as well.

Malone found this very amusing.

'A bishop and knight in one move!' he said. 'You've really got guts. By God, I've never seen such guts.'

She was reminded instantly of Murphy's cruel references to her cowardice and of his sister's words of venom to the same effect. Even in her sleep the words of the two siblings would haunt her and cause her to wake, shaking.

'You only work with the dead because they can't turn round and say you are a coward and worth nothing.'

Now these words were being contradicted. The unmotivated and uncalled-for kindness, shrouded though it may have appeared by a transparent layer of primitive and brash boorishness, touched her. She rose to her feet to give the impression that she was picking something up from the floor, turned towards the study area and wiped her cheek with the palm of her hand and forced herself to cough.

'Christ, woman!' shrieked Malone, banging his fist on the

table. 'What the hell's the matter? We Malones don't stand for this sort of thing. We Malones are tough!'

'No one has ever said anything like that to me before. You are so very . . . kind . . .'

'I do wish you'd stop telling me that I'm very kind! This is the third bloody time you've said I'm very kind since you've been in this house.'

The angry, frustrated words were more helpful in her circumstances than words of gentleness or compassion. Her urge to cry was obliterated and to be seen crying in the presence of such a man would have been the cruellest indignity of all.

When he'd finished the beer, he excused himself, saying he had telephone calls to make, and asked her to help herself to any drinks she wanted. She poured herself half a glass of whisky and studied the room more carefully. The first picture to make an impression on her was that of a woman who could have been any age between thirty and forty-five, with red hair and dressed in Empire clothing. She had luminous blue eyes that were wide and oval and which occupied much of her face. They were bright as well as honest. She had natural, classical good looks.

Next to each other on another wall were portraits of two girls aged about seventeen. They were twins. The only difference between them was that one had wild, fearless eyes while the eyes of the other girl were brooding, demure and histrionic. Both girls looked more like Malone than their mother.

The dog from the garden barked as a car engine was heard in the distance. Malone entered the room unexpectedly.

'That will be my wife,' he said. 'I see you've been looking at my twins. I bet you can't tell the difference. Even I can't always tell, except when they speak.'

'How old are they now?'

'They will be twenty-three in two months.'

An elegantly dressed woman carrying a carrier bag entered the room. Natalie recognized her from her portrait. Her classical, vivid beauty had not been romantically exaggerated by the painter and she looked more remarkable in reality. She wore a tailored pale grey suit, black and gold ear-rings and black patent shoes.

'You're late again, Ma,' said Malone. 'I'd like you to meet Natalie Klein, who's very kindly said she'll help us with our campaign. Natalie, this is my wife, Hortense.'

The women shook hands. Natalie took an instant liking to Hortense and continued to pump her hand up and down absurdly longer than necessary, as if it were a handle that needed oiling. Malone eased her hand away from his wife's. His facial expression gave no indication whether he was disturbed, amused or irritated.

'You are simply incorrigible, Papa!' Hortense exclaimed in a shrill voice and a strong French accent. 'Taking your shoes off in a drawing-room and throwing them into a corner. Even the children knew better when they were small.'

'Sorry, Ma, I was tired,' said Malone quietly.

'Have you offered Natalie some tea?' Hortense asked, and looked in disgust at the chessmen lying on their side, which she put briskly back in their original places. Malone looked towards Natalie and smiled.

Hortense muttered the word 'barbarian' under her breath and kissed her husband on the forehead.

'Natalie's had tea, Ma, and she likes a hell of a lot of sugar. Maybe she'd like some more.'

'I would like some more,' said their guest smiling shyly, and hastily adding the word 'please'.

When Minda came into the room, Hortense asked: 'Would you please bring a proper tray of tea with milk and a bowl of sugar. Mr Malone has thrown chicken legs on the carpet, I see. I did tell you he wasn't to be given chicken in here. He won't use a knife and fork unless seated properly at a table.'

Minda came back with a heavy tray carrying a tea set, with a silver teapot, a silver jug of milk and a large silver sugar container with a lid on it. Engraved on the lid were the words '*Je t'aime, Rex*' in minute italic script.

'It's very nice of you to help us, Natalie,' said Hortense. 'Rex has told me a lot about you already. He says you speak Russian.'

'Not only does she speak it like a native,' said Malone, 'she also taught herself and went to Russia alone. I've never seen such guts in my life.'

Natalie did not understand why he kept saying this. She also did not understand what was so extraordinary about speaking Russian. She had found it easier than French and German and it had only taken her six months to learn it. Malone had just left the room to go to a press conference in the office and Natalie looked in Hortense's direction, about to speak to her.

Dolores Murphy had come back. Natalie could not understand how this woman could triumph over the powerful, dominant and overwhelming aura of energy that surrounded Malone and remained in his house, even in his absence. She was convinced the intruder was real but tried to tell herself it was a hallucination.

Hortense did not see the Murphy sister, but Natalie was so certain she was in the room that she was not afraid of telling Hortense to ask her to go, and turned towards her with intent to do so.

The face was white like a skull's and the eyes sunken and menacing. The figure was covered in black lace with an extra black shawl covering the head and shoulders. Dolores was not put off by the presence of Hortense and walked closer to Natalie, who withdrew as far as she could until her head hit the wall.

'Please don't come to this house. Anywhere but this house,' she said in a voice scarcely above a whisper.

'I've brought my brother with me today,' answered the intruder, with the husky voice of the undead. 'You like it when I bring my brother, don't you?' The soft Irish accent would have been less menacing had it been louder and harsher.

'Please, I don't want to see your brother.'

She went over and clutched Hortense by the arm, thankful that Malone was not there to see she was capable of fear, which in his eyes would have been more worthy of reproach than prostitution.

'Please make her go! Get her out!'

'Who?'

'It's the sister again – the sister with the urn – she's back!'

'Whose sister?'

Natalie gripped the older woman more tightly than before. 'She's in the room and you've got to make her *go*!'

'But there is no one here. *Il n'y a personne. Je ne comprends rien du tout*!' Hortense always instinctively lapsed into French in a situation over which she had no control.

'The urn lies on the tray. It waits for you,' said the soft Irish voice. 'I put it there before the tray came by.'

Natalie tried to behave as if Malone were in the room. She ignored the sister. As she poured out tea and milk her hand shook so violently that she spilled more than she poured.

'Are you having sugar?' Hortense behaved as if nothing had happened but suspected there was something seriously wrong with her guest.

The words '*Je t'aime, Rex*' were no longer visible and Natalie seemed repelled by the silver container offered her.

'Papa says what a sweet tooth you have,' said Hortense, smiling, 'and now you've decided you won't touch the sugar. Surely you can't suddenly have decided to diet?' She continued to hold the sugar container in front of Natalie, partly out of kindness and partly because she was proud of the engraving that she had had put on it herself and which she feared Natalie might not have seen.

'Come to hell with us, daughter. There is no place for you in the land of the living.'

'Get out of this house, you ridiculous Irish woman!'

'Who are you talking to, Natalie?'

'My brother's waiting for you, daughter. Take him when the lady offers him.'

Natalie clutched Hortense's arm in another vice-like grip.

'That isn't sugar! There's no sugar, not in there, there isn't! It's something else. For God's sake make her go!' She screamed with increasing ferocity until she fainted.

* * *

The press conference held by Malone was rowdy. The reporters had become over-excited, interviewing this dashing, extroverted, controversial, entrepreneurial buccaneer who was wearing a tweed workman's cap incongruously combined with a white flannel suit.

'How's your Daimler, comrade?' called a *Morning Star* reporter wearing a black rubber mackintosh.

'My Daimler's going like a bomb, thanks, comrade,' retorted Malone. 'I bet your boy-friend likes your charming mackintosh.'

Laughter ensued. When it died down a *Guardian* reporter, wearing an ill-fitting brown suit and black-rimmed spectacles, got up, rattling a ream of notes in the air until he found the right place. Malone was reminded of an allegedly comic scene near the beginning of *Henry V* and waited with patient disdain.

'How do you reconcile your wealth with your egalitarian values?' asked the reporter.

'That's a silly question,' replied Malone, his voice raised in anger and frustration with human folly. 'Through my financial actions I've been able to give thousands of jobs to people who would otherwise be on the dole.'

The *Guardian* reporter flapped through his notes, letting some of his papers fall to the floor. He continued: 'You've been described as a gold-obsessed megalomaniac who . . .'

'By an idiot, yes,' interrupted Malone. 'I don't need what you call gold, now. By the time I was twenty I'd made all the money I needed to last for the rest of my life.'

'So, is it your lust for power and self-glorification that makes you go on?'

'No. I like people and I like helping them, and without my self-made capital I wouldn't have been able to help anyone. Because of my background I don't renounce my working-class origins and my sympathies have always been with the underdog, regardless of my respect for enterprise. The fact that I've made a bob or two on the way has nothing to do with it.'

The *Guardian* reporter was feeling in a vicious mood that afternoon because he had gone home the night before and found his wife in bed with his chauffeur, who was a smarter and better-looking man than he. He could not confess his misery to anyone without having to admit that he employed a chauffeur which, as he was a militant Left-winger, would have been intensely embarrassing. He couldn't bring himself to hit his wife or to sack his chauffeur, who would have given him away. His grievance had festered to a climax and was intensified by the fact that his chauffeur looked rather similar to Malone, whom he decided to use as a scapegoat.

'It's said you call yourself a socialist when the surroundings suit you,' he began. 'What have you to say about this?'

'I am a capitalist and I am also a socialist.'

'I didn't know you could be both. Can you?'

'Perhaps you should learn to talk less and listen more. I've just told you you can and I've also told you why,' said Malone patiently.

'What you say hasn't made me any the wiser.'

'The wiser, I dare say not. Only better informed.'

(Laughter)

'Well, perhaps you'd kindly explain *why* you are a socialist,' the man barked defensively.

When Malone replied he did not raise his voice in anger but spoke in a soft, low voice, suggesting that the words he chose were not as painful to utter as it was to witness the hatred and mindless resentment in the kind of person who took pleasure out of dragging such a traumatic confession from him. His audience consisted of some of the most hardened reporters, who had covered pub bombings, mass dismemberment and starvation in Third World countries. They were silent while listening, and even those who despised Malone were moved by what he had to say.

'I am a socialist because until the age of eight I had no shoes. Because as a child I could never forget the pang of cold and hunger. Because I was turned away from school for being too poorly clothed and only received three years' education. And because my father and brother spent most of their lives unemployed.'

The *Guardian* reporter had been educated at Harrow and Christ Church, Oxford, although he had put himself down for an invented comprehensive school on his job application forms. He had taken his comfortable boyhood days for granted. He was more preoccupied with himself and his wife's infidelity than Malone's words, which left him totally unmoved. He asked a below the belt question about Malone's wife and children. Malone was about to explode in a violent fit of rage when he was startled by his wife's hurried entrance. She looked baffled and worried. She whispered something in Malone's ear, gesticulating violently as she did so. He listened without interrupting her, leaning forward with his arms folded on the table.

'Blimey, Ma!' he shouted when she had finished, looking

equally as surprised as she. He turned to the reporters.

'You'll have to excuse me, gentlemen,' he said. 'Something's gone wrong.'

'An excess of fancy chess sets and not enough room to accommodate them?' asked the *Morning Star* reporter in the black rubber mackintosh.

'No,' said Malone, smiling, 'just an excess of chipped queens.'

Hortense had not explained what had happened very coherently because of the presence of the reporters and her description gave Malone the confused impression that their guest suffered from epilepsy.

When he returned to the drawing-room, he loosened his tie and took Natalie upstairs, carrying her in a purposeful manner devoid of emotion. A photographer seeking an opportunity to catch him in a Rhett Butler pose was held back by security guards.

Hortense followed after him as he mounted the stairs. 'But Papa,' she said, wringing her hands, 'she kept turning round and looking at something. It was all so odd. What do you think she was looking at?'

'How the hell should I know?' snapped Malone. He had become short-tempered because it meant having to free one hand to remove his cigar to speak.

'And then there was all that extraordinary business about the sugar. What does it all mean?'

'Bugger the bloody sugar! I'm going to the room on the far side. Get the doctor.'

He took Natalie into a room and left her in a horizontal position. She was beginning to regain consciousness, although she was not yet orientated.

'She has gone now, has she not?' she shouted, not aware that she was speaking to Malone.

'Yes, she's gone to get a doctor. You had some kind of turn. You'll be OK.'

'She won't bring the ashes back. You won't let her bring the ashes back, will you?'

'Don't shout. I've thrown the cigar away. I'm sorry if it bothered you.'

'You haven't understood. Please don't let her bring the ashes back. Anything but the ashes.'

'The ashtrays here are emptied twice a day. We Malones are clean. And keep your voice down. There are reporters downstairs who might think I was seducing you.'

'I'm talking about the other ashes.'

'What ashes, for Christ's sake?'

'The ones that dreadful woman brings.'

'If you're referring to my wife, you've being bloody discourteous.'

'No. I'm referring to the other woman who's always in black and who was here earlier.'

Crises had a calming effect on Malone.

'Epileptic turns are often precipitated by horrible hallucinations,' he said. 'If you've got epilepsy, the doctor will sort all this rubbish out. It's a physical ailment, not a mental one, and it is easily treated. I'm going to close the blind. You will rest until the doctor comes.'

'Will you stay until he does? I don't want her to come back when you're not here.'

'No one will come in here except Hortense, the doctor or me.'

'I want you to stay!'

Malone flew into a rage. 'Will I, hell! I've got a press conference still going on which I've had to interrupt because of this incident. I'm not sitting up here talking a lot of rubbish about ashes. Christ, woman, I'm trying to win an election, not run the bloody Salvation Army!'

'Please stay,' she persisted, undaunted by his quick temper.

'There's no need. Nothing's going to happen to you here. I've got to go.'

A *News of the World* reporter lobbied Malone as he descended the stairs.

'Rather a noisy household you've got here, Mr Malone. Do you keep a spare woman up there like Mr Rochester?' he asked impertinently.

'My daughter fell. We think she broke her leg. We're waiting for the doctor.'

'Your daughter's very attractive. May I go up and meet her?'

Malone loosened his tie again. A stray lock of black hair fell over his forehead, giving him the appearance of a harassed Spanish gypsy who'd just been asked to move his wagons.

'Shove off, guv,' he said quietly.

* * *

Dr Mutton was a long-winded, soft-spoken, mild-mannered man with a kind face and a natural smile. It was for his kindness and his sensitivity that he was most noted, but his inability to stop talking once he had started, particularly on telephones, exasperated anyone who had dealings with him. He had been the Malones' family doctor since the birth of their eldest child. The Malones were a healthy family so he seldom visited them except during flu epidemics.

Natalie Klein was reassured by the fact that Dr Mutton had never met the doctors she had consulted in the past, all of whom had described her as a 'pathological hypochondriac', although she did not regard herself as such.

'So you've had a fit?' said Dr Mutton softly.

'Something like that.'

'Is there a history of epilepsy in your family?'

'No.'

'Have you a doctor whom you attend?'

'Not really.'

'Either yes, or no. Who is your doctor?'

Her subsconscious told her it would not be wise to mention Dr Heineman so she said she had no doctor and that the doctor whom she had once consulted some years ago had died without her being able to remember his name.

'Have you had any similar attacks before?' asked Mutton.

'Often. Sometimes once or twice a week. Sometimes not more than twice a month.'

'Have you had them all your life?'

'No.'

'Have you had any head injuries – any accidents?'

'No.'

'When did the attacks start?'

'One year ago.'

'Are you taking any drugs?'

'Yes, a hell of a lot of stuff to keep me alive.'

Mutton looked puzzled. 'What are you taking?'

She listed about twenty different names, none of which struck Mutton as being harmful or likely to cause epilepsy, but all of which he considered to be unnecessary.

'Why do you feel the need to take all these pills?' he asked.

'I'd be afraid to go about my daily business if I didn't. I need to be sure I won't get ill. I'm never secure unless I can be sure I won't become ill.'

'You have a deep-rooted fear of illness, haven't you?'

'Who wouldn't fear it?'

'Your fear of it has reached obsessive dimensions.'

'There's nothing obsessive about looking after one's health.'

Mutton knew he had an extreme case of hypochondria on his hands but his instincts told him the condition lay deeper. Whatever the trouble was, it was psychological in origin and if the attacks were to stop, it had to be unmasked.

'What happened a year ago?' he said suddenly.

She wiped imaginary blood away from the index fingers of

each hand – the fingers she typed with. She opened her mouth to speak but her tongue froze.

'What happened?' repeated Mutton sternly.

'A man who hated me died on the road.' She was talking in fits and starts. 'He had the letter in his hand. I'd written him an abusive letter.'

'Was it suicide?'

'No. If he'd meant to commit suicide he wouldn't have got it right. He was Irish.'

'Did you hate him because he was Irish?'

'No.'

'Why, then?'

'It hurts.'

'Recovery is not brought about without pain. We must all be prepared to cross the barbed wire fence to get into the field where the green grass grows.'

'I would like to be able to answer you but I can't.'

Mutton leant forward. His voice was scarcely above a whisper. 'Why did you hate this man?' he asked.

'Because he called me a coward,' she replied in a low voice.

'What did the letter to him say?'

She couldn't handle the question and changed the subject dramatically.

'His – his sister's a Catholic!' she shouted.

'So what?' asked Mutton quietly.

'His sister put him under the earth. She did that because she's a Catholic. But his sister hates me so she had him exhumed so I couldn't visit him and then she cremated him.'

'The expression on your face suggest this horrifies you. Why does that side of it upset you so much? Are you a Catholic?'

'No.'

'Do you hold any religious views?'

'No. I don't need them as long as I've got my pills.'

'You can't help yourself unless you tell me the truth.'

‘His sister had it done so that I couldn’t visit the grave at night. I touched him after he died so she had him burned.’

‘I don’t understand what you mean.’

‘I had to because I knew he couldn’t say “no”.’ Her answer was gabbled and manic.

‘You talk like an infant going to a fun fair,’ he said, wiping his forehead with a handkerchief.

‘It meant more at the time. The sister bears an unnatural grudge against me.’

‘Unnatural behaviour sometimes provokes a natural grudge in the next of kin.’

‘I can’t see it from your point of view. His sister has stopped at nothing to persecute me. She follows me wherever I go, making sinister and terrifying threats and carrying the urn containing her brother’s ashes under her arm. Sometimes she wakes me in the night and shovels them down my throat until I wake up choking. She tells me her brother was right to think I was a coward. I wouldn’t mind so much if she attacked me when I was alone. She doesn’t. She does it in front of other people, now. She even got into this house today and started threatening me. Mrs Malone saw her.’

‘That is where you are wrong. Mrs Malone didn’t. That’s why I was sent for.’

‘My word has never been doubted in my life. I don’t understand why you should be an exception to this rule.’

‘Then how did this woman get past the security guards here?’

‘She can come and go any time she wants. She’s not like you or me, you see.’

‘I do not see,’ said Mutton. ‘What are you trying to tell me about this woman?’

She didn’t answer. There was a silence of about three minutes.

‘In what way is this woman not like you or me?’ he asked quietly.

'She's dead! I killed her. I took her to Bodmin Moor and put her down a shaft.'

'Were there accomplices?'

'No.'

'Did your action strike you as being morally wrong?'

'Of course not. The woman might have told the truth if I'd taken her to court on grounds of harassment, so I had to do her in.'

'Do you feel no guilt at all?'

'No.'

'Have you no conscience?'

'Of course I have. I wouldn't hurt someone who hadn't hurt me or mine. I wouldn't rob an individual, only an organization. I am loyal to my family and friends. I am compassionate towards those who suffer and I am kind to animals and children.'

'What about your victim's relatives? They may not have done you any harm but they are suffering from a bereavement caused by you.'

'I understand what you are trying to say. The woman had no relatives. No father, no mother, no children, nothing. She and her brother were the only survivors of that family.'

'The fear that you might one day be found out couldn't be a very pleasant thing for you to have on your mind.'

'I won't be found out.'

Mutton paced up and down thoughtfully for a few minutes with his hands clasped behind him, then he said: 'I'm not morally obliged to repeat what you've told me because a doctor is, in theory, if not in practice, immune from being an accessory to the fact. When you "see" this woman, all you really see is what little there is of your conscience, taking on a physical form. No one else here saw this woman. Only you. Your subconscious is trying to tell you you've committed a murder.'

'It wasn't murder. It had to be done. She knew I got carried away with her brother and interfered with him after he'd passed on. You won't tell Malone, will you?'

'Mr Malone to you.'

'I don't mind about the killing. It's the other thing I wouldn't want him to know about. It's just that I don't think he'd consider it a terribly conventional thing to do,' she said mildly.

'What you have told me is in confidence.'

'Good. So when Malone asks what's wrong, you will say epilepsy? Won't you?'

'Do stop calling him "Malone". Since you're staying in his house, it's damnably impertinent of you. No, I won't tell him about the nature of your association with the brother and sister. I know you want him to go on being your friend. He likes you, which is why I think you need a chance.'

'Will the woman come back?'

'She will. But the frequency of her visits will depend on how active your conscience is. It would be an understatement to say your scruples are fairly relaxed. Hence, you will find that the woman will pester you only occasionally, and her visits will become increasingly fewer and further between.'

'Doctor!' Malone's voice reverberated from the other end of the house. He came upstairs and knocked on the door.

Mutton was putting his instruments back into his bag and was about to leave.

'A word with you, Doctor,' said Malone.

'Yes, Mr Malone?'

'What the hell's wrong with her?'

'At this stage it's hard to say. It might be a complex condition, but I wouldn't go so far as to totally exclude a diagnosis of epilepsy or a variant thereof.'

Malone loosened his tie again. 'Can we cut the medical jargon? You're talking to a layman,' he said.

'It may not be epilepsy.'

'Then what the hell is it, for Christ's sake?'

'There are two things. First, although there's nothing physically wrong with her, she's a clinical hypochondriac, so obsessively preoccupied with her health that she feels the need to take thirty pills a day.'

'*Thirty*?'

'Yes. Sometimes even more. A hypochondriac does not know he is harming himself by tipping explosive cocktails of pills down his throat. He is convinced he is doing himself good and his condition is hard to treat. In her case, it's just possible that her fits are precipitated by excessive doses of pills.'

'Christ, what a bloody load of rubbish! You said there were two things wrong. We've heard the first. Now let's hear the second.'

'She had an unfortunate experience a year ago. She had a bad shock. I don't know the details but she feels she is a failure and, for some reason, a coward. Perhaps it's something someone said to her. I'm not sure. Also, she's been very over-worked recently. I don't think she's really suited to the kind of work she does. This causes her anxiety and that alone can precipitate such fainting attacks.'

'And the screaming when she recovers consciousness?'

'When one faints in unfamiliar surroundings, one is often terrified before becoming orientated. The brain is not fully primed and the sufferer may shout strange things that others can't understand.'

'Have you told her to chuck out the pills?'

'Of course. But convincing a hypochondriac is not easy.'

'I'll convince her!'

'In that case all I can say is good luck to you, sir!'

'Well, missy,' said Malone, after Mutton had left, 'there's nothing wrong with you at all except that you are tired and taking far too many pills, all of them unnecessary. Chuck 'em out. Also, you lack self-confidence. I could tell from seeing you earlier that you are not a failure, but you must prove that to yourself and not to me. You must stop the macabre work you are doing. I'll put some money into your business to keep it ticking over. Will you work for me full time during my campaign? Will you take the opportunity of proving you are not a failure?'

'I will take it.'

Malone shook her by the hand. The handshake was almost strong enough to break her fingers. 'I congratulate you,' he said, as if he had a million pounds at stake. 'You've made the right decision. But if you do canvass for me, you're going to have to mend some of your ways, not all of which are satisfactory. First, none of this zany talk about ashes or I'll chuck you in the pool. Second, you'll bring no pills into this house. Chuck them out. Third, you are not to speak abruptly or to bark at any of my constituents unless they give you cause to do so.'

'I'll do everything you say.'

'I'm sure you will. This is an important day for both of us. We are helping each other. You are helping me win and I am helping you realize that you are stronger than you know. You had some nasty shock, I heard. I don't know what happened and I don't want to know. But whatever it was, you're going to get over it.'

'Are you sure of that?' She asked this question to persuade herself that the power he wielded was supreme, omnipotent and inviolate.

'Of course you're going to get over what there is to get over. If whatever it was happened a year ago, you've got over the worst of it already. That was a silly question, Natalie.'

He stared at her reprovingly.

'You've given me a lot of reassurance. It's so nice of you. You talk to me like an equal.'

'You are my bloody equal!' The eyes that could have drilled holes in concrete a moment before were gentle and friendly.

'Is there something I can give you in return – a thing that has material value?'

'Yes, there is. A hammer.'

'A hammer. Whatever for?'

'To knock the last nail in your coffin of no self-confidence,' he said. 'We dine at eight. Hortense will have some things for you if you want a shower or bath first. Don't be late.'

* * *

As was his habit after his rounds, Dr Mutton dined alone in an Indian restaurant. He thought at length about his strange new patient while driving home after his meal. He was a fanatically religious man and did not think that anything justified the taking of another person's life. He had promised her that he would treat her confession in confidence. On the other hand, he regarded her act as a sin and believed, in the Victorian tradition, that a soul is better off, if punished by imprisonment on earth rather than after death. This view was not held by his patient but he felt that his obligation to save her soul outweighed his obligation to keep his promise. He became depressed and confused over having to make a decision. He decided to act on impulse and play the rest by ear. That way he would satisfy his own conscience. He pulled in outside a telephone box. He would not call the police, he told himself. He would call Malone and see how things went from there. It was only 10 p.m. according to his watch and he assumed that would not be too late an hour to make his call.

Natalie was sitting next to Hortense on a *chaise-longue*, while Hortense told her about the research she had been doing for her PhD in French Literary Studies. She spoke at length about the *Theâtre de l'Absurde*, its nihilistic themes, its aim to startle and shock, and its dominant flavour of black comedy. Hortense's knowledge was boundless and Natalie, who had opened the conversation by expressing an interest in black comedy, felt honoured to be listening to these revelations free of charge.

From the *Théâtre de l'Absurde*, Hortense moved on to *Crime and Punishment*, of which she had recently seen a theatrical production. She asked Natalie if she had seen it.

'Yes, I saw it, but why did they have to have such an old man playing Raskolnikov? I thought the sexual charm of Raskolnikov lay in his youth as well as his nihilism.'

Her own remark reminded her of Murphy. She felt an impulse to confess her crime and the circumstances leading to it, but checked herself.

'I didn't know that sexual charm lay in nihilism,' said Hortense.

'It does. The tortured expression of a death wish is erotic. That's what I think. I only say that because I am not like that myself and because I'm afraid I'm rather a voyeur of suffering. When reading the book I have an urge to take Raskolnikov from the printed page and drag him to bed.'

'I don't agree with that entirely. To be saddled with a man who has got nothing to live for is a bore,' said Hortense, and this further reminder of Murphy and the manner in which Malone contrasted with him so refreshingly, reassured Natalie and made her laugh out loud. It was not a natural laugh but the cackle that an obscure private joke so often provokes.

'For Christ's sake, shut up!' shouted Malone from another part of the room. He was wearing braces and shirt sleeves and was watching *Match of the Day,* chewing an unlit cigar, mesmerized by the game. West Germany were playing Czechoslovakia.

'Of course,' she continued in a quieter voice, 'I could not live with such a person twenty-four hours a day. The mood might become infectious after too long. I am only speaking in terms of one night stands.'

Hortense laughed out loud.

'Shut up, the pair of you!' said Malone. 'You're both being

mean. I want to watch my game.'

'I view *Crime and Punishment* in a different way,' Hortense continued in a lowered voice. 'Dostoevsky was a black humorist in his own right. It doesn't matter whether Raskolnikov was attractive or not. It is the whole tone of the book that is comic. I think that if we are to find any peace of mind, we must look for Napoleon within ourselves. Take Raskolnikov: he committed a trivial murder to see if he dared. He did it to prove he was as strong in his own world as Napoleon was in his. Here we see a man who started off seeking Napoleon within himself and ended up believing in God. Now, that is true black comedy. More so, because it wasn't even intentional on the author's part.'

Natalie admired and respected Hortense. Her path, strangely woven though it may have been in lies and guilt, had met fleetingly with that of the older woman. Hortense had laughed over a reference to a man who had killed. Her approach made the act of killing seem less haunting. Although Hortense was only speaking of fiction, Natalie realized that she herself must find Napoleon within, and that only when she had done so would she be able to shake off these ghastly visits from Murphy's sister.

'There's one thing you must remember, Natalie,' said Hortense, 'you cannot really identify with such a man yourself. Raskolnikov was a coward, and I know *you* are not a coward.'

You are not a coward. The words echoed in her mind and repeated themselves until she felt hypnotized by them. She thought of the appropriate lines from her favourite poem, which she repeated in times of adversity or extreme excitement. She leant forward as if in prayer and recited them to herself:

> *'And I said: She is warmer than Dian.*
> *She rolls in an ether of sighs . . .*

She has seen that the tears are not dry on
These cheeks where the worm never dies.'

'Are you all right?' Hortense asked suddenly.

Up to now, the conversation had been in French. Natalie would have found it peculiar and taxing to say such things in English. Although it was her mother tongue, she regarded it as a language in which only discreet and guarded sentiments could be expressed, which is why she kept herself to herself as much as possible.

The conversation had continued for an hour and a half. Natalie's mind felt freer but her tongue was unused to the unnatural movements that the speaking of French imposed on it, and it felt very stiff and her mouth excessively dry.

She got up slowly.

'I'm all right,' she replied, this time in English. 'I'm going to get a glass of water.'

Malone was still watching *Match of the Day*. It was a close game and the only form of entertainment, apart from opera, that could hold his attention. Natalie walked past him on her way to get the water.

A Czechoslovakian full-back was moving around by the goal. The camera showed his foot kicking the ball but she could not see where the ball had gone.

'Was that a goal?' she asked Malone, not because she was interested in football but because she wanted to flatter him by identifying with one of his interests.

'I'm afraid not. It hit the post.'

The telephone rang. Hortense answered it.

'It's for you, Papa.'

'Who the hell is it, for Christ's sake? This is the only relaxation I get.'

Hortense covered the mouthpiece. 'It's Dr Mutton.'

'Christ, Ma, not him again! I've spent the afternoon with him. What does he want?'

'Mr Malone's got someone with him,' said Hortense. 'I'll take a message if you like.'

'I need to speak to him about a very urgent matter.'

'He needs to speak to you about a very urgent matter.'

'Does it concern an illness relating to someone in the family or in the house?' asked Malone with a rasp in his voice.

Hortense repeated the question to Dr Mutton.

'No, but I *must* speak to him.'

Malone lurched over to the telephone, looking over his shoulder as another Czechoslovakian full-back tried to get a goal. His telephone manner had never been his forte and the idea of having to speak to someone as longwinded and verbose as Dr Mutton, who couldn't stop talking once he started, taxed his temper to the point of no control.

'Yes?' he snapped.

'I've just had a splendid Indian meal,' began the slow soft voice. 'I've been reading the Gospel of St Mark over the food. It was so enlightening. You should mention religious themes in your speeches. It's a great vote-catcher. I had to wait for ten minutes before I could use this kiosk. The woman using it before me was talking about the many different ways there are of cooking scrambled eggs. I never believed there were so many.'

Malone was exasperated by the flow of unsolicited information. He sighed heavily into the receiver which supported his chin. Natalie had no idea what was being said and knocked half a glass of neat whisky down her throat.

Dr Mutton suddenly realized that he had forgotten to identify himself and became confused, embarrassed and flustered.

'Oh, by the way, it's Mutton here.'

'B-a-a-a-a-h!'

Mutton was deflated. He completely forgot how to phrase what he had planned to say and hung up. He satisfied his conscience by telling himself that at least he had tried to expose Natalie Klein's guilt. As far as he was concerned, trying was as good as succeeding. He would give no further thought to the matter.

'What did Dr Mutton want, Papa?' asked Hortense, watching the glass that shook in the younger woman's hand.

'That man Mutton is a Jesus glutton,' said Malone and went back to his game.

'Did he say anything important?' Natalie forced herself to ask.

Malone didn't answer. He began to chant a strange, unearthly, melancholic dirge, slightly out of tune. To Natalie it somehow didn't sound like a song. It was a sound she had never heard before and it alarmed her.

It was the Czechoslovakian National Anthem.

'It's not possible!' Malone shouted, banging his fist on the table. 'It's just not possible!'

The empty glass fell from Natalie's hand. It broke as it hit the floor.

'What isn't possible?' she asked, as the bile rose to her mouth.

'The bloody goalkeeper's been knocked unconscious!'

* * *

The Malones had left for their constituency headquarters by the time Natalie came down to have breakfast. She had a hangover. The Sunday papers were on the kitchen table. The popular press had given more extensive coverage to the press conference than the more academic papers. Some newspapers ran such headlines as:

MALONE DRAMATICALLY LEAVES PRESS
CONFERENCE DUE TO DOMESTIC CRISIS

followed in smaller print by: Mystery Shouting Heard.

The *News of the World* was the crudest. The incident covered the front page. The headline read:

SINISTER SHOUTING AT MALONE HALL – 'SHOVE OFF, GUV' IS HIS EXPLANATION.

In the short time she had known the Malones, she had been a hindrance to their campaign. She told herself she would atone for the trouble she had caused. She would dedicate herself entirely to making him Prime Minister and had thought all night about the methods she would use to this end. She had decided what she would do and how, but the method she had chosen was not a method that Malone, in his rough and ready but pure and rustic honesty, would have approved of. She decided she would not mention the matter either to him or Hortense. It would take a little time to work it out but she was going to do it, and once she had made up her mind that she would do something, no matter how trivial, she always finished it.

The Malones were back by the time she was ready to leave. She thanked them and promised she would be back to help them as soon as her own domestic affairs were settled. Malone gave her a fifty pound note.

'You're to have this. Buy yourself a slap-up dinner at the Ritz. To work for me, you're going to need all the energy you've got.'

'Thank you.' She could think of nothing else to say.

'Goodbye, Natalie,' said Hortense. 'Remember you'll always be welcome here and I want you to have all the friendship that I can give you.'

Malone followed Natalie to her vehicle, which had been parked by his chauffeur who had collected it from the roadside. She jerked her thumb in the direction of the polished Austin hearse that looked like a glossy carrion bird, its elm-surfaced bier-rack newly waxed, its silver bier pins gleaming. 'You'll find this useful,' she said. 'I'll be able to drive at least ten of your supporters to the polls in this at a time.'

Malone frowned. It was the first time she had seen him look worried.

'It's your vehicle I'm not too confident about,' he said quietly.

'I don't understand. It's exceptionally reliable,' she replied in genuine innocence. 'Why aren't you confident about it?'

Malone stared at the ground.

'Because I want to become Prime Minister,' he said.

* * *

When she arrived Natalie told Elliott that it would be in their mutual interests for her to work on Malone's campaign. The opinion polls were all very similar. The Tories stood no chance of winning. The Malonist Party was in the lead, with the Labour Party only fractionally behind them. If Labour won, which at that time seemed unlikely but by no means impossible, they would have to carry out the pledge stated in their Manifesto, that the funeral industry would be compulsorily nationalized.

Elliott was swayed by Natalie's arguments and said he would manage the business in her absence. Although it belonged to her, she had become bored with it. The only side of the business that interested her was fiddling the books and counting the money.

Elliott had felt over-burdened at first but accepted her suggestion that he get another obsequious assistant to handle the administration and occasionally pacify the bereaved.

She would return to the maisonette over the shop each evening, but would have no active part in the running of the business any more. Her decision to relinquish her responsibilites and spend time away during the day was a welcome relief to Elliott. Her continual nagging about untidiness, her permanent preoccupation with her health, her obsessive habit of washing things that had already been washed, cleaning things that had already been cleaned, her bizarre tastes, her peremptorily expressed demands, such as waking him up during the night and saying 'sex please' – all these things, combined with her violent temper, were taking their toll on him and on his peace of mind.

'One of these days I'm going to build a boat and put to sea,' he would threaten when the nagging became too much for him. But in spite of her faults he adored her and would have done anything for her. She knew this and his feelings for her were reciprocated, if not always shown.

Natalie took up Malone's offer the night before she was due to turn up at the Malonist Party headquarters, a big red brick building used at other times as a bingo hall. She went to the Ritz in Piccadilly and ordered two 'white ladies', a pot of tea and caviar sandwiches.

She drank the two 'white ladies', after which she felt a sense of well-being. She started to pour out the tea but the pot fell from her hand.

Murphy's sister was back.

'You thought you were safe from me,' said the hideous figure in black lace. The part of Natalie's personality operating at that moment was the part that had no idea the sister was dead. When she was with the Malones she knew at least that she had taken someone's life, and her fear of being found out was the only unpleasant emotion she experienced. She felt no guilt at all.

The Malones were not with her now. The sister was real.

'You've punished me enough, haven't you?' she said in a raised voice. The tea-room was crowded, mostly with a group of American tourists, few of them the better for liquor. They stared at Natalie, fascinated by this pretty but strange young woman, addressing the air with her quaint English accent.

Among the people staring at her was Harley Street's wealthiest and most disreputable psychiatrist, Humphrey Buttercrow. He had been hired by Hank Donleavy Jnr, a flashily dressed, well-built, middle-aged man who owned two five-star brothels in Texas and a casino in Los Angeles. Like many Americans, Donleavy felt insecure in Europe and was noted for his eccentric habit of hiring an analyst in every European city he visited. Dr Buttercrow was his London man, prepared to see him over tea at the Ritz at his patient's request, rather than in his austere consulting rooms, provided the patient paid treble the consultation fee and the price of the tea as well.

When he heard the shouting, Donleavy had already become bored with making his own confessions about his inadequacy in what he called 'cultural joints'. He turned his attention to Natalie, in whom he had developed a voyeuristic interest.

'Hey, lady, someone bothering you over there?' he called.

She didn't know he was joking and accepted his offer of help.

'You've got to help me! It's the woman who's trying to shovel her brother's ashes down my throat!'

'Ashes! Nuts! I can't see no one doin' that to ya, lady,' said Donleavy.

'You must be able to see her. For Christ's sake get her out of here!'

Donleavy laughed. Dr Buttercrow looked passively amused.

Dolores pushed Natalie to the floor and sat astride her. She prised open her mouth and shovelled the ashes down her throat. Natalie started choking. The air wouldn't get to her lungs. She screamed and sobbed hysterically.

Donleavy suddenly felt guilty about his teasing.

'Hey, I didn't mean to joke about that dame, Doc,' he told Buttercrow. 'I feel real bad about it. I want you to give her whatever treatment you consider necessary.' He handed Buttercrow a thousand pounds in fifty pound notes.'

Buttercrow was aghast. 'I'd do anything for that sum,' he said, shaking Donleavy's hand warmly. 'I'm due to go to the Bahamas for six weeks in a few days. Obviously, I can't have her followed up as an out-patient, so I'll put her in my clinic. She can't come to any harm there.'

'What's your clinic?' asked Donleavy.

It was in Buttercrow's interest to lie.

'It's a beautiful place, like a five-star hotel surrounded by glorious countryside,' he said sentimentally and waved his arms. 'It's such a lovely place that our only problem is persuading our patients to leave it once they're better.'

'Well, am I proud!' Donleavy exclaimed, slapping Buttercrow on the back. 'I feel I've done someone a good turn and that sure is good therapy for a drunken brothel-keeper.'

A police car and ambulance came. Buttercrow produced his identity card, which looked perfectly respectable. He knelt over Natalie out of morbid curiosity, fondling the notes that Donleavy had pressed into his hand. A hypodermic was pushed into the main artery of her left arm. She did not regain consciousness for a very long time.

* * *

Dr Buttercrow had founded the clinic on the proceeds of the soaring consultation fees extracted from his Arab clientèle. Ironically, it was situated on Bodmin Moor. It was a mental institution for women, and the majority of its inmates were the adulterous wives of Arab sheikhs who paid psychiatrists such as Humphrey Buttercrow to have them appropriately punished.

The clinic was a granite-walled building with small barred windows and a slate roof. It was indeed, as Humphrey Buttercrow had said, surrounded by beautiful countryside, the charm of which lay in its wild and desolate appearance.

Dr Buttercrow had his own office in the clinic. He used a lavishly decorated dining-room with stained glass windows in a wing sealed off from the inmates, who were confined to their padded cells and fed on gruel twice a day through a hatch.

When Buttercrow was not there, he was in his London consulting rooms. The clinic was manned during his absence by two sexually frustrated, powerfully built matrons, aged about forty, both of whom were karate black belts. They were from Yorkshire and were known by their surnames, which were Blarmey and Sykes. Sykes was the tougher of the two. She had demonic eyes, closely cropped greying hair and a wicked, but at the same time, faun-like face.

Blarmey, who was almost as tough, had a menacingly large, hawk-like nose, moulded into that shape by a plastic surgeon to make her appearance more deadly. Neither Blarmey nor Sykes had had heterosexual relations since they were given control of the clinic fifteen years before. They were both highly sexed and when the going got rough they used each other with bestial urgency on the floor of the room they shared. They wore stiff khaki overalls and wide, silver-studded leather belts. They never bothered to remove these uniforms when satisfying their sexual needs: they were so overpowering that they simply didn't have time.

When Natalie recovered consciousness she found herself in a room ten foot square with padded whitewashed walls. There was a mattress on the floor but no bedding. The first thing she was aware of was the fact that she could not move her arms. She had no idea that strait-jackets were used in the second part of the twentieth century and was afraid of moving her fingers in case it meant her having to find out that her arms had beem amputated. During her confinement she would scream in terror, and every time she screamed either Blarmey or Sykes would hit her with a belt and give her an intravenous depressant. Instead of being cocky and over-confident as she had been on her first day, she grew to fear the two women and cowered whenever one of them entered the room. They frightened her more than Murphy's sister.

Dr Buttercrow visited her once a week. He was a disproportionately tall and thin man of forty-five, nicknamed 'Buttock Row' because of his penchant for sodomy. She hated his oily manner and shifty eyes. When he visited she screamed filthy abuse and spat at him.

'We are all here to help you,' he would say, patronizingly.

'You're not trying to help anyone. You get kicks through gaping at people like me, the same way as the ghouls who stared at nuts in Bedlam!'

Buttercrow loved these outbursts. One of his greatest pleasures, apart from skiing and frequenting his villa in the Bahamas, was watching Blarmey and Sykes beating the inmates with their studded leather belts.

'Like a jolly good glass of port, what!' he would exclaim if watching a particularly violent beating, preferably of victims who had not been drugged first, because the anaesthetizing effect of the drugs on the brain stifled the screams that so delighted him.

After her beating, Natalie tried to remember her first consultation with Humphrey Buttercrow before she had been committed. His Harley Street consulting rooms, their walls covered lavishly by Van Goghs and a Matisse which he had splashed up and signed himself, gave an impression of opulence, success, distinction and expertise in a chosen field.

When meeting patients for the first time, Buttercrow liked to address them as children. He would humour them by boasting about his treacherous lack of ethics, partly to ease their own guilt by dwarfing their comparatively minor misdeeds, but mainly because he was proud of the ingeniously dishonest methods with which he had accumulated his vast fortune. Naturally, he said nothing about his clinic, but he loved to tell his patients about wealthy Arabs whom he had befriended and to whom he had given depressants instead of antidepressants, hoping they would commit suicide and with luck leave handsome sums to him in their wills. The people to whom he boasted could prove nothing if they ever got round to reporting him.

Occasionally, this method gained the trust of some of his less intelligent patients. A spirit of merriment sometimes gives a vulnerable person confidence. Some of his patients found him repellent and only consulted him once, but these were outnumbered by patients who found him twistedly attractive. Natalie hated him from the start. His refined, genteel mannerisms, his unnaturally courteous behaviour, and his simpering namby-pamby voice enraged and nauseated her.

'Why were you screaming in the tea-room?' he asked gently.

'I had a fit, an epileptic fit.'

'That was not an epileptic fit. I know because I saw it.'

'Epileptic fits are precipitated by hallucinations,' she said repeating Malone's words, which gave her confidence. 'I've had them before.'

'But you did not lose consciousness as in the case of epilepsy. You saw visions and you heard voices.'

Although she had no idea at that moment that she had killed Dolores Murphy, her instincts told her to stick to the cover of epilepsy to survive.

'I saw no one and I heard nothing.'

'You saw a woman carrying her brother's ashes and you felt her putting them down your throat.'

She did not remember what she had shouted and Buttercrow's revelation terrified her.

'I said I saw no one and I heard nothing!'

'Did you kill the person whose ashes were put down your throat?' asked Buttercrow. He had guessed blindly and his closeness to the truth was coincidental.

'No!'

'But you did kill the woman whom you saw, did you not? Had you not done so, she would not have become manifest.'

'I saw nothing and killed no one!'

There was a long silence. She looked at a vulgar-looking gold clock on the mantelpiece which had struck 1.15. Plump-legged, winged cherubs clung to a gold carved rock serving as its base. It was contained within a glass dome which muffled its chimes at fifteen-minute intervals.

'A charming clock, isn't it?' said Buttercrow, diverting from the heavy questioning to small talk and boastful exhibitionism.

'An Arab with too much money and a recurrent depressive illness killed himself and left it to me in his will. It's worth two thousand pounds. It's solid gold.'

'Why couldn't you cure the Arab? That complaint is very easily catered for.'

'I could have cured him easily, my dear. Lithium salts cure recurrent depression within two weeks.'

'Why didn't you give them to him?'

'I'm not a fool. A patient cured is a patient lost and a patient lost means I have to travel economy when I fly to the Bahamas.'

'A patient in your filthy stinking hands is as good as dead,' she said and uttered a stream of obscene abuse.

Buttercrow drummed his fingers on his desk. He listened until she finished, his face serene and unruffled, his eyes complacent.

'Why do you feel the need to use such words?' he asked quietly.

'Because you're detaining me against my will when you've no right, either legal or moral, to do so. There's nothing wrong except epilepsy.'

'It is not epilepsy. It is something entirely different and it is a condition that I am going to treat.'

'Let's have it then, you stinking gutter quack. What have I got?'

'In layman's terms, it's a form of madness. We, in our profession, call it schizophrenia.'

Schizophrenia. The only knowledge she had about this condition had been gained from seeing the film *Psycho*. She remembered a ferret-like, frightened little man dressing up as his mother and attacking people with a carving knife. Schizophrenia. The word was definitely offensive, whatever it meant.

'I haven't got it and your detaining me is unlawful. Malone's expecting me and I promised him I'd work for him.'

'Who's Malone?'

'If you haven't heard of Malone, you're the one who suffers from schizophrenia.'

'Who is he?' repeated Buttercrow.

'He's only your future Prime Minister and he'll soon put a stop to your shit.'

'Do you mean that man who calls himself Rex Malone?'

'That's who I mean and that's who I'm working for.'

Buttercrow would not only be deceiving Hank Donleavy Jnr, for whom he held a deep affection, were he to release his patient. He also knew his practice would be in danger. He decided to try to shake his patient's loyalty, knowing there could be a risk of a vicious rather than compliant reaction.

'Are you English?' he asked.

'Yes. What of it?'

'Are you a patriot?'

'Why should I be? I don't ask what I can give this country. I only go out of my way to get what I possibly can out of it. My loyalty goes to my family and my close friends. My roots lie in this country and so do all my social and family ties, but patriotism is an emotion I have never experienced. I leave all that to the military and preoccupy myself with my own business.'

'You do realize Malone is a crook and a fraud as well as an alien?'

'You're sick! What the hell's an alien, anyway?'

'A foreigner.'

'What's wrong with that, you racist bastard?'

'He's not really part of our culture although he claims to be more English than the English. But he's a phoney. Even his wife's French.'

She flew into an orgasmic, bull-like fury. She thought of Hortense, of her love of life and her allegiance to the spirit of the French culture on which she had been raised. Her shouts could be heard the other side of the street.

'You! You, who live off the suffering of others! You sick whore! Who are you to dare to call someone a fraud or a crook?'

It was not usual for patients to kick his Achilles' heel and he was taken aback. He diverted the conversation to a more gentle theme.

'What do you think of my charming clock?' He lifted it from the mantelpiece as an automatic reflex, in the way he did when showing it to admiring dinner guests. He was so preoccupied with her personal accusations that he forgot to consider the consequences of his action.

She took it from his hands and looked at him with a hate so vicious that a spurned alley-cat might have had trouble competing with it.

'Ro-co-co and a bottle of scum!'

She threw it at his head despite its weight, cutting him above the eye. He overbalanced and fell, spraining his right wrist and he was right-handed.

His reactions had never been quick. He took a few minutes to recover his senses before he pushed a button, summoning three nurses in white overalls to hold her down before inserting the needle that would switch her off at the mains.

Buttercrow needed the signature of a second psychiatrist to

get her certified. Blarmey and Sykes refused to admit any patients unless there were two signatures on the form of committal. Although they were fanatical about the laws of psychiatric admission, Buttercrow had never resisted them because of their physical strength. He had invariably managed to produce a second authenticated signature to avoid a confrontation with them.

He called his secretary, Elma, a timid, twenty-year-old coloured lady, on the intercom. His behaviour towards his employees lacked the obsequiousness he used to beguile his patients. He found it a refreshing contrast to treat his subordinates as muck-raking lackeys.

'Get Dr Morganton-Bradshaw on the telephone,' he commanded.

He had deliberately hired her on a permanent/temporary basis which meant that she could never take sick leave and could be fired at five minutes' notice, although she had been there for five years. The Health Service cuts had prevented her getting a more secure post in a public hospital. Her colour would have restricted her chances of re-employment in private practice, and it was through necessity, not choice, that she worked for Buttercrow. She needed the high wages a temporary medical secretary earned doing a forty-two hour week to support her sick mother in Birmingham, and to finance her journeys to and from that city twice a week. Elma was depressed and worried about her mother's illness and her thoughts had wandered.

'Anything the matter with your hearing?' said Buttercrow.

'No, sir.'

'Then get him on the line. With the amount you're being paid, I don't expect to have to tell you twice.'

'Yes, sir.'

* * *

Dr Morganton-Bradshaw was only fractionally less unethical than Dr Buttercrow. He had cancelled his afternoon surgery and was sipping brandy in the dining-room adjoining his consulting rooms. He had been lunching with Professor Bollard, who was completing his two hundred thousand word illustrated thesis on tertiary syphilis, and Dr Bumble, a specialist in sexual deviation. They were blind drunk by the time they had finished eating, but before alcohol had taken its toll on this merry trio, they had been talking shop.

'There is a popular but unsubstantiated theory that syphilis originated from Arabs having sexual intercourse with sheep,' remarked Professor Bollard, his speech slurred.

Dr Bumble interrupted him. 'No, no, my dear fellow, according to an article I read in last month's *Lancet* . . .' He hicupped and couldn't complete the sentence. 'According to . . .'

'Do get on with it,' muttered Professor Bollard impatiently.

'Well, according to an article I read in last month's *Lancet* . . .'

He stopped speaking. He pushed his chair away from the table and was sick on the carpet while Bollard and Morganton-Bradshaw laughed convulsively like educationally subnormal children.

'I say, chaps,' suggested Morganton-Bradshaw after a five-minute interval, 'how would you boys like a bit of music?'

'Jolly good show, what!' said Bollard.

Morganton-Bradshaw staggered over to a record player and took Rachmaninov's 'Second piano concerto in C minor' from its sleeve and put it on the turntable. The pure, mysterious silver notes wafted through the room like an antidote to the pollution therein.

'My cleaner's off sick. Uterus gone for a burton, blast it!' said Morganton-Bradshaw. 'Would you boys mind giving me a hand, piling up all these plates?'

'All right, old chap,' said Bollard. 'Jump to it, Bumble! It's Stackers, Harry Stackers.'

'That's right,' boomed Morganton-Bradshaw, 'it's Harry stackers and Sergei Rackers!'

It was after the plates had been taken out and the guests departed that the telephone rang. Morganton-Bradshaw was lying in a semi-stupor on the couch his patients used. Although he thought its overall structure was disorganized and rather untidy, he loved the concerto so much that he played it a second time. He picked the receiver up and held it close to his ear. Heavy drinking sometimes made him deaf.

'Who is it?'

'William, old man. I need your help and it's damned urgent,' Buttercrow pleaded. 'Would you mind coming to see me right away?'

'Not a chance. I'm so damned drunk I'd never be able to bomb my Ferrari round the block.'

'You're only one block away from me. Come on foot, for God's sake!'

'A man in my position couldn't be seen staggering up Harley Street, holding the railings.'

'What the hell are you doing?'

'Having an absolutely spiffing time, lying on my couch, listening to rollicking old Rackers.'

'Do you mean Rachmaninov?' barked Buttercrow.

'Yarse, and I'll tell you another thing, old man. Something damned funny. Do you know that this was Beria's favourite music, and before raping little girls he used to put them at their ease by taking them on his knee and telling them that the music made him cry if he listened to it alone. Ha! ha! ha!'

'I couldn't give a bugger what blasted Beria did!' bellowed Buttercrow. 'I've got a paranoid schizophrenic here, who's just smashed up my consulting rooms and all I need is your signature along a dotted line to say you've seen her and considered her to be insane so that she can be committed.'

'Why don't you bowl over here, old man? Lot easier, what! I'm prepared to sign a document saying I've seen this patient, but I'm not moving because I can't stand up.' As he spoke, the hand not holding the receiver conducted with languorous movements and when he had finished speaking he sang loudly in time to the music.

'Turn the bloody music down!' shouted Buttercrow, 'and stop that damned silly singing. I'm trying to talk to you.'

'What is it, my dear chap?'

'You've got to come. I can't leave the patient alone with my staff.'

'Is the patient male or female?'

'Female.'

'What's your problem, then?'

'You don't understand. I don't trust a single member of my staff.'

'Why can't you just let her go? Is she armed or something?'

'No.'

'Then all she could do would be to roam the streets. No harm done. Not to herself. Not to anyone.'

'Who cares if she's a danger to herself? She isn't. As long as she goes free she's a danger to us.'

'Why to us?'

'She's dangerous because she's a friend and supporter of Rex Malone. She won't hear a word against him or his wife. That's what made her smash up my consulting rooms.'

Morganton-Bradshaw thought for a few seconds and sat bolt upright. He felt a wave of nausea and dizziness which affects many people when they are drunk.

'Malone? Malone? No!'

'I'm afraid so. Do you know what that's going to mean to people like us? It's not so bad for you with your disciplinary clinics ticking over in Jersey. You're safe. My clinic's on Bodmin Moor. A man like that could put a stop to my livelihood.'

'Your clinic sounds much more seriously threatened than my two. I don't think the position concerns me at all.'

'You owe me the favour as an old colleague.'

'We're not freemasons and I owe you nothing. Rex Malone won't interfere with Jersey. I'm drunk and I'm not coming. Solve your own problems!'

'For God's sake, William, we're friends, aren't we? I have quite a lot of letters from you on my files. May I forge your signature on this document? Dash it all, old man, I can't have a paranoid schizophrenic let loose after what I've told you. I'm due to go to the Bahamas the day after tomorrow, so may I imitate your signature, *please*?'

'I suppose so,' said Morganton-Bradshaw and rang off. His liver couldn't take the strain he had imposed on it. He needed to get to the bathroom fast.

* * *

It was five o'clock in the afternoon. Elma was about to lèave with her suitcase. She had just received a call on the second line to say that her mother's condition had deteriorated and become critical. There were only twenty minutes in which to get the next train to Birmingham.

Buttercrow heard the door opening and caught up with her.

'Sorry to disappoint you. I know how much you enjoy your jaunts to Birmingham. This evening you're putting in overtime because in the past I've paid you falsely for hours you said you'd worked when you'd been absent from the office.'

'A message has just come through to say that my mother is critically ill.'

'I thought you'd been told not to receive personal phone calls?'

'My mother is *dying*. If I don't go now, I may never see her.' Elma began weeping.

'Don't burden me with your personal problems,' said Buttercrow. 'Unless you're prepared to pay fifty-four guineas for me to listen.'

Elma's first instinct was to slap him, but another wiser idea suddenly entered her head.

'Have you no charity?' she asked.

'I do not invest in charity. Either you come back and do as you're told or your jaunts to Birmingham will be financed by what you earn on the streets.'

Elma had never been particularly brave. It was not in her nature to take a vicious stand against injustice, not because she lacked vindictiveness but because she lacked courage. She returned to her office, unlocked her drawer and took out a notebook and pencil.

As he cradled his bandaged right wrist in his left hand, Buttercrow showed her a letter addressed to him, signed by Morganton-Bradshaw. The signature was easy to read. The handwriting was markedly italicized and the Es Greek. The person holding the pen had either been to a grammer school or a public school.

'Have you ever seen one of these before?' asked Buttercrow, handing her a fountain pen with an italic nib.

'No, sir.'

'I thought not. I bet you've never used anything other than a biro in your life. Try and write with it.'

As she did so, the ink got onto her hands and on the notebook. The pen wouldn't write straight.

'You hold it at this angle: now try.'

Elma wrote her name.

'Now, you will write Dr Morganton-Bradshaw's name just as he has written it.'

'Why?'

'People of your social status don't question orders given by their betters. They obey them.'

'I'm not forging his signature. It's against the law.'

'If you're not prepared to break the law in this instance, you will be earning your living as a tart, starting on Monday.'

'I will do it.' After practising it for an hour, she got it right. The imitation was perfect. She transcribed it on to the document that was to have Natalie Klein legally committed to a mental institution.

'Good,' said Buttercrow. 'Now you can go and see your mother. It is more likely than not that she will last until the small hours of the morning, because that is when blood pressure is at its lowest.' As he walked down the stairs, he leant over the banister to add a sadistic amendment to his repertoire: 'Do have a nice weekend,' he said.

She left her suitcase where it was and went up to him as if to shake his hand. In so doing she gave it a violent wrench. The pain was so intense that he fainted.

Elma had gone by the time he recovered consciousness. He did not know that she had put a bugging device on his telephone and was carrying the tape of his conversation with Morganton-Bradshaw in her bag, as well as a tape of her conversation with him about the forgery. Nor did he know that she was an active supporter of Rex Malone.

There would be little likelihood of finding her mother alive, but on her last visit her mother had told her that she would only rest in peace if she, Elma Jessie Halifax, were to help Malone become Prime Minister. Her mind was at rest and her conscience clear. She would find other work on Monday. She did not need such a high salary now. Her visits to Birmingham would no longer be necessary.

* * *

Buttercrow's consulting rooms were on the first floor of a four-storeyed building. Mr Fergus McKenzie used the rooms on the ground floor. He was a respectable, clean-living Scotsman who neither drank nor smoked. He worked for three days a week in a National Health hospital and saw private patients on Monday and Wednesday afternoons. He knew nothing of Buttercrow's corrupt practices and the only connection between the two doctors was the austere oak-panelled waiting-room their patients shared.

Mercedes Caja was a regular and unwelcome patient of Mr McKenzie's. Born in Madrid, she had lived most of her life in London. She was noisy, aggressive and hysterical. To atone for her defiance of the staunch catholicism on which she had been raised, she ordered McKenzie to fit a coil without an anaesthetic. He had to put cotton wool in his ears so as not to be deafened by her screams. He told her not to indulge in sexual activity for at least two days.

'What about this evening? I shan't mind the pain.'

'Let me give you a wee word of advice,' said McKenzie conspiratorially. 'If your front entrance is indisposed, you need feel no qualms about using the tradesman's entrance, but be sure to grease your partner's member if you've just passed a motion.'

The door was suddenly thrown open, so violently that it knocked over a side table on which seven gynaecological textbooks written by McKenzie were lined upright, with his name on each of them in bold letters. The books fell over one after theother like a pack of cards. McKenzie abandoned what he was doing and stared at Malone in shock.

'Is your name Buttercrow?' said a voice, the pitch of which was so deep that it frightened McKenzie.

'You might have waited and given the door a wee knock before you came blustering in,' he stammered.

Malone clutched McKenzie by the arm. 'Bugger the eyewash, guv,' he rasped. 'Don't think I'm deceived by the sound of a woman's screams. I know what you're doing.'

A cry came from the other end of the room.

'Help me! You've just left me here! Who is this man? It's neither in nor out!'

'What is neither in nor out?' asked Malone and walked over to the corner of the room where he ripped down the curtain dividing him from McKenzie's patient. Her legs were in stirrups. She was throwing her head from side to side, screaming.

Malone was unfamiliar with matters such as these and concluded that the woman was being held against her will and tortured. The pain was so violent that she screwed up her eyes and lashed her arms in the air, hoping to grab McKenzie by the arm.

'There you are! Where have you been? Who were you talking to out there?'

Malone became acutely embarrassed. It dawned on him that McKenzie was a specialist in women's matters. He stared at the floor in bewilderment and then looked towards McKenzie with his head raised while the woman dug her nails into his flesh.

'Please take it out!'

'Blimey, madam! I haven't got the right kind of authority. I came here by mistake. I apologize.'

McKenzie attended to the woman while Malone turned away, waiting for it to be over.

'Where are Buttercrow's rooms?' he asked McKenzie.

'A few wee manners would be the very making of you, mon. They happen to be on the first floor but he's away at the moment.'

'Where is he?'

'I don't know. I hardly see him. He doesn't tell me his business. He's a psychiatrist and I'm a gynaecologist. Our paths don't meet.'

'A gynaecologist? In that case I must apologize very sincerely for what happened. I wasn't to know.'

'If you'd had a wee look instead of stampeding about, you'd have kenned that as soon as you came in.'

'I'm bloody sorry, sir. Perhaps you would be good enough

to give me that lady's name and address. I ought to send her some flowers.'

'You leave them with me and I will have them sent to her residence.'

'Good. So you know nothing about Buttercrow's whereabouts? This is important.'

'Now you mention it, the husband of one of his patients, an Arab, was in the waiting-room. He was talking about a mental hospital somewhere on Bodmin Moor in which he has a holding, but that's all I know.'

'Thanks, guv, and once more, I'm sorry.'

* * *

Natalie Klein had lost track of the time she had spent at the clinic. Because of the beatings administered regularly by Blarmey and Sykes, she had forced herself to behave meekly and submissively. The intravenous drugs had weakened her so much that she had temporarily lost the use of her legs. Sykes had asked Blarmey to remove the strait-jacket and tied her hands behind her with bandages.

One morning she was woken from a drugged stupor by workmen repairing the roof. Some slates had fallen off under the pressure of the moorland winds. The acoustics of the building were such that noises from the cells could be heard from the roof but not from the other cells. Blarmey and Sykes had taken this into consideration and had drugged the inmates more heavily that day to ensure that their cries of misery would not be heard.

Natalie could remember little, if anything, about the three weeks before her confinement. Sometimes she was comforted by dreams about some people who had met her and been kind to her. There was an occasional flashing association in her mind between reality and dreams, but it only lasted for a few seconds and left a dead feeling of oblivion in its wake.

She went on her knees, and raised herself, only with great effort, to the level of the six-inch-square barred window. Through it she saw a grey-black sky and the mists rising from the moor, as if to make the sky greyer than it already was.

One of the workmen on the roof was whistling. Whatever the tune was, she associated it with something inexplicably pleasant. As the man continued to whistle, the grey-black sky miraculously cleared and was lit by a glaring mediterranean sun that radiated an unexpected feeling of hope.

Her first suspicion was that she had been injected with an opiate, but because she had been injected four hours ago she thought that, for some reason, it was the whistling that was responsible for her sudden change of mood. Her spirits had risen as soon as the whistling had started.

She tried to work out what tune was being whistled. She wondered why she had heard it so many times without recognizing it. She forced herself to recall occasions when she had heard it. She had heard it sung in an Irish public house but could not understand why it gave her hope.

The whistling continued. Suddenly, she remembered it was the tune of a song called 'Cockles and Mussels' about a woman selling shellfish. Why did a woman selling shellfish remind her of Empire furniture, musical instruments or Napoleon? Why did it fill her with an unexplained sensation of self-confidence and personal glory?

The words of the song gradually came back to her as the man continued whistling. *Mollie Malone!* That was another name for this famous song. She repeated the name to herself and remembered a recurrent dream about two characters called Mr and Mrs Malone who had gone out of their way to befriend her. She wondered if this was only a dream about an ideal that became manifest in her subconscious to ease her misery.

A familiar, rounded baritone voice raised in anger reverberated down the narrow corridor. She thought this was an auditory hallucination.

'. . . the lavas that restlessly roll
Their sulphurous currents down Yaneek
In the ultimate climes of the Pole . . .'

She was grateful she was still able to recite out loud. It eased the fear and confusions. It was the only antidote to the absence of liquor that she knew.

* * *

Blarmey and Sykes had been clearing up administrative work in their office, a room with a glass-paned wall which served as a treble-glazed, bullet-proof window, covered by horizontal and vertical bars. From it, one could see everyone who entered and left the clinic. The two women were expecting a new senior consultant to whom Dr Buttercrow was going to show the layout of the clinic so that it could be visited during his absence. The man he was waiting for had just been disinherited by his millionaire father and would have sunk even to selling heroin to maintain his lavish life style. He had no sense of ethics and was ideal for Buttercrow's purposes.

A chauffeur-driven Daimler swerved up to the gridded doors, churning up the gravel in the drive. Its passenger was leaning forward, asking the driver to go faster, and seemed angry and impatient.

As the white flannel-suited passenger got out, he carried with him an aura of authority that impressed and excited Blarmey and Sykes, who were convinced he was the new consultant. Sykes was attracted to him instantly and stared at him through a pair of binoculars.

'Never seen such a nice piece of work in my life,' she said. 'I hope he's a dab hand with the whip.'

'Give over!' said Blarmey, as she snatched the binoculars from her colleague. 'I want to have a look. I hope he's for the taking. It'd give us a change from each other.'

'If he's for the taking, I'm to be first because I'm the boss.'

Sykes was about to operate an electronic device which opened the outside grid and the inner grid six feet away from it. The newcomer did not come to the front entrance. He went straight to the washrooms in an annexe attached to the building.

Buttercrow was using the washroom when Malone entered. He was in a heartier mood than usual that day because he had just witnessed a particularly sadistic beating. He did not look at the mirror covering the wall in front of him. Nor did he look at the newcomer, but he noticed through the corner of his eye that the man was smoking a cigar and wearing a white flannel suit. His air of nonchalant self-confidence impressed him. The man was obviously the new consultant, who seemed to have a far greater air of authority than he had expected. He decided to go out of his way to impress him.

'Take a tip from me, old chap,' he said, slapping his thigh with a swagger stick and filling the air with a whiff of stale brandy, 'here's what I say to 'em the first time I meet 'em, to put the damned blighters at their ease, if I think they're clinic meat. I swan into the room where they're lying down waiting for me and I say, "Absolutely strapping stuff, sex, hey what!" Do you know what I do afterwards? I bung my stinking carcass out of bed, wipe the spunk off my hampton, crash into a bath, go for a smacking good run round the block. Then I burn up to the kitchen where I make four socking great crumpets, all of them absolutely *squelching* with butter. Then I bowl upstairs and start all over again, what!'

Malone dropped his cigar. He concluded his companion was a patient and decided to be as kind to him as possible. 'Blimey, guv, some like it hot,' he muttered.

Buttercrow recognized his voice. He looked in the mirror and was staggered to see a man who couldn't be anyone other than Malone. He wondered how he knew of the clinic's existence. His reactions were slow. Instead of pursuing him from the water-closets, he stared transfixed at his own deathly pale reflection in the mirror.

* * *

Malone walked to the main entrance of the clinic which he entered as the electronic grids were opened by Sykes. She and Blarmey had buttoned their khaki uniforms, straightened their hair and tightened their studded belts. Blarmey was so excited by the appearance of the new visitor that she inadvertantly put her hand on Sykes's bosom.

The gesture enraged and revolted Malone, who marched up to Blarmey and pinned her against a wall. Blarmey had always had sado-masochistic tendencies. She hoped he would drag her into a corner and violate her after roughing her up first.

'Natalie Klein,' he said.

She stared vacantly ahead. Part of her wanted him to hit her. The other part was afraid.

'Direct me to Natalie Klein who is interned here.'

Sykes handed a bunch of jangling keys to Blarmey, who escorted Malone to a room at the end of the long corridor. It took her a long time to find the right key. Malone had lost patience by the time she had tried ten different keys. The door was six inches thick but he heaved his weight against it until it gave way. It was only then that Blarmey realized he was not a doctor. It took her a few minutes to come to her senses before she went back to tell Sykes.

Natalie was sitting in the corner of the small cell when Malone broke in. She was exhausted by the drugs and so engrossed in chanting about the sulphurous currents of Yaneek that she didn't notice him.

'What the hell are you doing here, you bloody idiot?'

The rough words gave her courage. A soothing approach would have reduced her.

'They put me under. Then they brought me here.'

'Who did?'

'I don't know. I think his name's Buttercunt.'

Malone laughed. 'You must mean Buttercrow.'

'That's right. He came at me with a hypodermic and knocked me under.'

'Had you had one of your funny turns?'

'Yes.'

'Where was all this, for Christ's sake?'

'The Ritz.'

'Were you conscious when he approached?'

'Yes.'

'When someone comes up to one with a needle, with intent to inject, one automatically puts up a fight, if one is a friend of the Malones. We Malones are tough!'

'I did put up a fight but two others held me down. Then I found myself here.'

'Have you got a doctor of your own in London?'

'Yes.'

'Does he know about these turns?'

She said he did, which was untrue, and added: 'He says there's something wrong with the brain waves.'

'He's damned right. The sooner you get all this rubbish fixed, the better.'

'I'm going to London to see him as soon as I get out of here. Then he'll give me the results and tell me what to do next.'

'Good.'

Malone took a knife from his pocket and cut the bindings off her wrists. 'Come on, get up. We've very little time.'

'It's the injections. I can't move.'

He ignored her. She tried to get up. He didn't help her so

that she would regain confidence through getting up alone. She clawed at the padded wall and got to her feet.

'Good. Come with me.'

Her legs gave way and he gripped her roughly under the arm. 'Your eyes are out of focus so look down to the floor. That way we'll look like old friends visiting.'

While he was walking her away from the room, she wondered if he had ever been afraid of anything. After all, on the field of battle, he had astounded his comrades by walking straight in front of enemy cannon, saying he didn't care if he got killed as long as he won the MC. She believed in her state of confusion, that he could walk on water and feed five thousand on a loaf and two fishes.

'Yea, though I walk in the valley of the shadow of death, I will fear no evil, for you are with me and your rod and your staff comfort me,' she said out loud, remembering lines she had learned in childhood.

'Shut up, you bloody idiot! I don't want a load of crap from the scriptures. I get enough of that from Mutton!'

Blarmey, Sykes, Buttercrow and Morganton-Bradshaw were standing at the reception desk. Morganton-Bradshaw had felt morally obliged to come and interview Natalie to make sure she really was insane. He and Buttercrow had arrived at the desk together.

'Excuse me, sir,' said Buttercrow, 'that's my patient you've got with you. You are not lawfully entitled to take her off the premises.'

'Bugger the eyewash, Doc. She's not officially certified.'

'I have a document here with two signatures on it to testify that she's a schizophrenic.'

'Balls! One of those signatures is bona fide. The other's a forgery. I've been given the evidence. You're a liar, a sadist and a quack.'

'Publicized reports do not account for you as being particularly honest, either,' said Buttercrow.

'The reports you refer to are libellous and I have sued successfully. Get out of my way or I'll have to force you.'

Buttercrow produced a Colt .38 given to him by Donleavy as a birthday present. 'You're not leaving.'

He pointed the Colt .38 at Malone, who kicked it from his hand and unloaded it before handing it back to its owner. Buttercrow tried to hit him but missed. Malone knocked him down and Morganton-Bradshaw picked up a lead club from behind the desk. He was about to hit Malone with it but was kicked in the stomach. Sykes intervened, making karate chopping movements and uttering frightening sounds. Malone knelt down and picked her up by the ankles like a sack of potatoes and slung her over to the other side of the hall. The last person to deal with was Blarmey, who was mesmerized by him and about as useful a combatant as Ferdinand the Bull.

Malone wrenched Natalie to her feet. 'Come on, missy, we're getting out of here.' He took her outside to the Daimler, the door of which was held open by the driver, a very fat man, ironically called Mr Tonky which is the Russian word for thin.

The moors were misty and Tonky drove slowly.

'Step it up, guv,' ordered Malone impatiently, 'otherwise we'll be in the same place this time tomorrow.'

Tonky continued at ten miles an hour. Malone hit him on the ear with a rolled-up copy of the *Malonist Voice* but regretted his action. He explained that he was swatting a wasp about to sting Tonky. Natalie laughed hysterically while Malone called the police from the telephone in the Daimler. He exposed the unlawful use of the clinic on Bodmin Moor and stated that he possessed a tape to prove that two such clinics existed in Jersey.

The inmates of all three clinics were discharged. There was a long case at the Old Bailey. Buttercrow and Morganton-Bradshaw were branded as neo-Nazis and jailed for life. Not all the inmates of the three clinics were English but those who were and who had never voted before in a General Election voted for Malone in the forthcoming election. His involvement in the unmasking of the evils of perverted psychiatrists gained him a smattering of nationwide votes that would otherwise have gone to Labour.

* * *

Hortense was waiting in the hall, when Malone, Natalie and Tonky arrived. Malone got out of the car hurriedly and went in with Natalie following in his wake.

'I'm afraid Natalie's been very naughty, Ma!' he said.

'How?'

'She allowed herself to be binned without putting up a fight.'

'But I did put up a fight!' retorted Natalie.

'Putting up a fight on its own is not good enough. When we Malones fight, we win!'

Hortense embraced Natalie as if she had been her own daughter, and ordered tea to be brought into the room where the musical instruments were. She made a point of asking the maid not to bring the big silver container and requested that the sugar be brought in a receptacle without a lid.

'I'll have mine upstairs,' said Malone, who was in a very bad mood. 'I'm washed out. I've had to knock out two quacks and lift a hermaphrodite as heavy as Fatty Arbuckle's coffin, plus call the police. My shoulder's hurting again. You can't even get a decent osteopath these days. The only really good osteopath was so much a victim of reactionary Victorian values that the idiot topped himself in 1963.*

Hortense had never heard Malone talk at such length when

* Reference to Dr Stephen Ward, a high society figure, extensively involved in the Profumo Affair.

he was tired, and the flood of unsolicited information only vaguely related to his complaints puzzled her.

'Go on, Papa,' she said, with an impatient wave of the hand, 'the longer you talk, the less you'll sleep.'

Later that evening, Hortense played the 'Moonlight Sonata' in a complex key with a lot of sharps. She asked Natalie if she knew how to play it.

'I can but not as well as you. I'll play it if you want but I can't guarantee you'll think it very good.'

She played it in a beginner's key but was hit unexpectedly by an anxiety attack. It was caused partly by another surge of the fear of illness. Her pills which catered for every part of the body were in London, and she only felt mentally secure if they were within reach. She was also suffering from delayed shock resulting from her incarceration.

She decided she would have to go back to London as soon as possible to get her trunk load of pills. She played at an absurdly galloping pace with her foot on the loud pedal. In her subconscious she felt she was running away from an army of illnesses that would catch up with her, however fast she ran.

Hortense was amused but puzzled by her outward appearance. 'That's much too fast! And you look so worried. I've got something to show you that might cheer you up. Do you remember our labrador?'

'Yes.'

'She had some puppies while you were away. They're in the kitchen. I'll show you them. Would you like that?'

'Yes.'

The kitchen was an airy, open room. The only thing that wasn't open was its larder, which had a combination lock on the door to stop Malone getting in when Hortense put him on a diet. A wooden partition with family photographs clipped to it divided the room between the cooking area and the eating area, which had a television on a shelf on the wall and a round table with a smaller rotating table in the centre called a 'lazy Susan'. A telephone with several lines lay on a side table. To the right of the television was a small enclosed area between two doors, one of which overlooked the lawn. Six puppies small enough to sleep in a man's shoe played on a rug, surrounded by wire netting. Hortense picked one of them up.

'This is a present for you.'

Natalie was touched by the gesture and thanked her, using confused, exaggerated, rather antiquated language that, although intentionally sincere, sounded unnatural.

'Don't you want it? We've got five others.'

'What's his name?'

'We call him "Ballie" because he is always rolling.'

Natalie gripped Hortense by the arm. The gesture was so impulsive that it startled her. 'You are such a very *worthy* lady!' she said in an obscure, ponderous tone that to her companion was totally incomprehensible.

An eight-year-old girl interrupted the two women and ran through the kitchen from the hallway and out to the lawn. She had Malone's looks, the same dark hair, upward-slanting Slav eyes and high cheekbones. She wore blue jeans and a white T-shirt which bore the words 'Rexy's your Man'. Her hair was tied back in a pony tail.

'Arianne!' Hortense called after her. 'Arianne, come back here at once.'

But Arianne had run off.

'She's our youngest,' Hortense explained. 'She's rather a naughty young lady because Rex spoils her.'

Hortense pointed to a framed picture of a girl, aged about eighteen. She was the only one of the Malone children who resembled her mother.

'That's Sarah. She's our eldest. I think she's Rex's favourite.'

Natalie examined the picture closely. She found it appealing that Malone's favourite daughter should resemble his wife and not him.

'Sarah is more vulnerable than the other children, I feel. The cruelty she had to suffer at school makes me ill to this day. There is so much evil and resentment in the world, particularly against Rex. Petty-minded people envy him because he is self-made. One of the girls in Sarah's class told her that the daughter of a 'slicker' like her father was incapable of understanding the suffering of others.'

'How very unkind.'

'It was. The whole thing blew up during a German lesson. The woman giving the class was giving the German words for different cooking utensils. One of the girls got up and said: "There's no need to tell Sarah. A Jewish spiv's daughter would never need to do her own cooking." '

'How appalling! What did Sarah do to the girl then?'

'She was so dignified. She smiled sadly and turned away.'

'But afterwards, didn't she *do* anything to the girl?'

'She said: "It makes us look weak and cowardly to hit others below the belt." '

Natalie felt nauseated that that was all Sarah had done. She began to shout passionately.

'I believe in an eye for an eye and a tooth for a tooth, and more than that, an eye for a tooth and a limb for an eye! My vindictiveness would have known no bounds, even if I'd had to go to jail for it.'

'I know how you feel, but I'm not sure you are right. To forgive others in a cruel and callous world is the only way to punish them.'

'Why?'

'Because spite excites but forgiveness deflates.'

'I wish I could think like that. You must be very strong.'

'No, Natalie, not necessarily strong. Suffering and being at the receiving end of unkindness teaches us subtletly.

'I have no control over my temper when I am wronged.'

'I admire you for that. So does Rex, but you must try to understand that the only way to conquer your enemies sometimes is to be kind to them.'

Natalie did not agree but thought it would be discourteous to argue. Hortense suggested that she go outside and introduce herself to Arianne who was on the waste land behind the tennis court with her horse.

Arianne was a happy-looking child. She was shovelling a gruel-like substance into the horse's mouth. It was a white horse with rust-coloured markings on it.

'Hullo. Natalie Klein's my name. I am a friend of your father and mother,' she said, trying not to sound too stilted, 'and you're Arianne, aren't you?'

'That's me.'

A long and awkward silence ensued. Natalie had never got close to a horse before and she was afraid of patting it because she thought it would bite her. Arianne was the first to break the silence.

'Do you like my horse?'

'Yes. I think he is very nice. Does your father ride?'

'Not now he doesn't, but he did in the war.'

The answer confused Natalie. 'Cavalry, then?' she asked in a staccato voice.

'My father won the MC and when he rode into battle, he pranced on his snow-white steed and flashed his sword in the shining sun as he galloped fearlessly to glory like Agamemnon the warrior!'

She waved her arms theatrically in the air and Natalie found her choice of language comical. 'No one fought with swords in the Second World War. They used bombs and guns.'

'Others may have used bombs and guns but my father is not like other men. When my father rode into the enemy's ranks, by Crikey he used a sword!'

'Well, I . . . wouldn't doubt your word for one minute. But

I've got to leave you now. There are some things I have to do in the house.'

Arianne had taken a liking to Natalie and followed her, leaving her horse untied. It wandered onto the tennis court where it left mounds of manure in its wake and it had eaten much of the net by the time Malone saw it.

'What's your horse doing on the tennis court?' he asked mildly.

Arianne frenziedly passed her lighted cigarette to Natalie.

'How can I help it if some idiot leaves the gate open?' she said. Malone was annoyed. Natalie started laughing and her laughter turned to hysterical giggles. Malone softened.

'I don't mind so much the fact that it got onto the court,' he said, 'but in future I'd rather it didn't leave its visiting card.'

Natalie told the Malones she was going to London to get a medical check-up and fetch the remainder of her luggage. Apart from a change of clothes, all she really needed was her aluminium trunk of pills. These she intended to keep in the grey Citroën escort which Malone had lent her. She visited Dr Heineman and told him she suffered from fainting fits brought on by guilt over infidelity about which she felt embarrassed. She told him to tell anyone who rang him that she suffered from epilepsy. He promised her he would do anything she asked, but told her to ask Malone not to put any more calls through to his office as he had spoken to him more than five times already.

After her visit to Dr Heineman, Natalie visited an all-night chemist in Kilburn to collect further medical supplies. It was 10 p.m. The woman behind the counter in the uncrowded chemist told her to come back in half an hour. Natalie was bored and unfamiliar with the drab area she was in. She decided she might as well get drunk.

She left the Citroën in a side street and took a book with her to read while waiting. The book was Hortense's satin-bound copy of *Les 120 Journées de Sodome*, which she said she wanted back when Natalie had finished with it as it was part of a set. She was intrigued by the sound of loud traditional music coming from a public house near the chemist. Fifes, pipes and drums accompanied noisy singing. The music was attractive and had a hypnotic effect on her. She entered the building, where she approached the bar and ordered two measures of whisky.

The place was full. A heavily built, grey-haired man of about fifty was rattling a tin, calling across the room for donations to the Catholics of Ulster in their fight against British occupation. The man, a cell-commander with three men working under him, was not yet drunk but was certainly tight. He wore ill-fitting grey trousers and a blue anorak and was accompanied by a younger man who was equally well-built but more neatly dressed. It was only then that Natalie realized this was an IRA pub. She ordered two further measures of whisky and hurriedly opened the *120 Journées de Sodome,* pretending to be immersed in it.

A voice suddenly blasted in her ear. It was the younger man, who had been reading over her shoulder. 'This man, the Marquis de Sayde, did he ever do any good for Ireland?' he asked.

'I'm afraid he spent most of his time in jail so he didn't have a chance to go there, but had he not been in jail I feel sure he would have buckled down and done his bit for the place.'

The drink had made her accent markedly Welsh which, combined with the hearty, old-fashioned terminology, sounded very odd indeed. The older man went on rattling his tin and stood two feet away from Natalie, who was frightened and knocked back the rest of her drink, ordered another two measures and offered to buy the barman a drink. Then she returned to her book.

'So what was he in the jail for?' queried the older man.

Natalie hiccupped. She was amused by the man's reference

to 'the' jail. 'He lived in the eighteenth century when justice was even harder to come by than now, and he was jailed because he . . . sort of fought for the freedom of people in general, the human race in other words,' she replied.

The older man became more friendly. 'Oh, did he now?' he said. 'He sounds as if he had the makings of a fine Catholic fellow! Your book's in French, isn't it?'

'Yes.'

'I'd like to be hearing the sound of a foreign language, especially if it's the writing of a freedom fighter.'

There was an uncomfortable silence. Everyone in the room had been listening to the man. The drinkers thumped their glasses on the counter and turned towards Natalie, who asked for another drink which she threw down her throat before the man offering to treat her paid for it.

'Would you be reading it out then, so that the lads can hear?'

Natalie swallowed the drink and read aloud in French for about three minutes. The passage which she selected at random described a hideous sexual perversion involving an old man, a small boy and some excrement. She wasn't sure when to stop reading and was interrupted by the man with the tin.

'That sounds fine Catholic stuff! It's the first time in years I've heard a foreign tongue. Would you care to translate that into English for the lads?'

Natalie hiccupped again. 'I'll try,' she said, and the tin-rattler hissed for silence.

'It says . . . "Man is as free as the noble beasts of the field but his oppressors force him to walk in fetters. His hands are in fetters . . . His feet are in fetters . . . Even his soul is in fetters".'

The older man had been looking over her shoulder at the text as her hand traced along each line, simulating translation. He pointed to a word which recurred.

'*Merde*?' he said, pronouncing the word as murder. '*Merde* . . . does that mean fetters?'

'Yes, that's right. It means fetters.'

'Worthy Catholic stuff!' said the man, with a glazed look in his eyes. 'I'm sure the Marquis de Sayde, whoever the blessed lad was, is resting on our holy Virgin's breast, praying his guts out for Ireland.'

Natalie burst out laughing and spat a jet of whisky over the counter.

'I'm afraid I'm not very practised at holding my liquor,' she said.

'Never mind,' replied the man, who went on rattling the tin, which had a shamrock painted on its side and a notice in small letters which read: 'Help our Catholic poor shake off the chains of British imperialism.'

Many of the customers put donations into the tin. Natalie found a twenty-centime coin among her small change. The coin was worth about a penny, if that.

'Fine girl!' said the older man. 'I'm sure you've heard many a bad tale of the evils of the Black 'n' Tans.'

'Can those be melted down and injected into an artery like heroin?' she asked in genuine ignorance.

The question was so obscure and incomprehensible that the IRA man decided to let it ride and turned towards his friends.

'Come on, now, everybody, let's have a song and give a thought to our beloved Erin.'

The customers positioned themselves around Natalie, who was the only female customer. They sang a song called 'The Death of Kevin Barry' which had a funny, tuneless tune, alternating between very high and very low notes. There are several versions but the words are similar in each. The words sung that night were repetitive and easy to memorize. They sounded much better to the tune of 'Clementine' and Natalie had become so drunk that she did not fear her companions any more. She drowned their voices and sang it loudly to that tune. Passers-by in the street could hear the famous refrain:

'In Mountjoy jail, one Monday morning,
High upon a gallows tree,
An Irish martyr gave his young life
For the cause of liberty.

'For the names of his brave commrades,
And other things they wished to know,
British soldiers tortured Barry;
Kevin Barry answered: "No!" '

'I've never heard it sung like that,' said the older man, rattling his tin again as a nervous reflex action. 'I can tell you're not a Brit by your funny accent and I also know when someone's soul belongs to Ireland, so how about giving us your hand?'

'My hand?' Natalie extended her hand for a handshake and smiled to hide her anxiety.

'B'Jaysus, no! I didn't mean that. Here, take this. It's a form. Fill it in.'

Natalie examined the piece of paper. Although her brain was befuddled with drink, she recognized it as an application form to join the IRA. The fear and nausea that Malone had taught her to overcome returned. She wanted to get out and go back to the Malones. She held the form in front of her mouth like a napkin and knelt on the floor, clutching her stomach as if it contained bullion that was not to be ejected from its hiding place. The man bent over her, almost devotedly, and asked her what the matter was.

'Flu. That's all,' she said and was sick. The man, who was also very drunk, stood and stared. He momentarily forgot he had invited her to apply to join the IRA and brought her a glass of water. Then he turned towards the younger man. Tipsiness impaired his discretion. He spoke in a lowered tone, but unintentionally within earshot of Natalie.

'You've orders to go to Belfast first thing tomorrow,' he said. 'You'd better go and get some sleep. Where are you staying?'

'Number 60 Brondesbury Villas. My landlady's a Negress called Mrs Oates. I had to throw one of her saucepans away once when I mixed explosives in it. But I replaced it. She's safe.'

'You're supposed to change addresses every two or three days. You were told that on your training course.'

'I said Mrs Oates is safe. She and I get along. She can't recognize my accent. Tomorrow's also short notice. Can I make it the day after?'

'Not a chance. McKearney's orders.'

'Who's McKearney?'

'Even in the Movement, there are few who know exactly who he is or where he operates, except that he has his own built-in arsenal of arms that he organizes the importation of, from the States. It's said that the offensive side of the Movement's operations would be nothing without his organizing skills,' continued the older man, increasingly the worse for liquor, which seldom got the better of him but which made him dangerously careless on this occasion. 'He's our best co-ordinator and even carries out his own executions, despite his high rank. He's by far our best marksman,' he added.

'Where do I come in?' asked the younger man in a much more discreet voice which could scarcely be heard, even by his companion.

'McKearney will be carrying out the execution of Rex Malone, who appears to support the British presence. It will be carried out on his exit from a Belfast orphanage on Christmas Day. Your job is to create a diversion. You will be fixing explosives in the hotel with the other two lads. Liam McKearney, who's almost as expert a marksman as his father, will understudy him in case of obstacles.'

'Where does McKearney get big enough funds to finance the import of arms from the States?'

'I don't think anyone really knows. Maybe he bets on a big scale.'

'Does anyone know where he lives?'

'They are few that do and even they don't say. He may use another name. He may also have an underground hide-out.'

'So, where's this orphanage?'

'An agent of McKearney will tell you ten minutes before the execution. It's time you were off.'

When the younger man had gone, the older man returned to Natalie, who he thought had not overheard the conversation. He was too drunk to walk without supporting himself against the wall.

'Had too much liquor, have you, daughter? How did you like the song about Kevin Barry? I liked the tune you sang it to better than the one I know.'

Now that her stomach was empty she felt happier and more reckless.

'I don't know who the hell this man Kevin Barry was or what he did, but whoever he was, I'd like to think he wore tight-fitting black leather jeans when he mounted the scaffold and that he had a hard-on when the rope tightened round his neck!' she said in a passionate voice that echoed round the room.

* * *

Natalie had no recollection at all of what had happened. She woke up in hospital. X-rays showed a fractured skull, caused by a single blow on the back of the head, inflicted by a blunt instrument, possibly a bottle. It wasn't serious. Her family visited her. So did Malone. He stood by the bed for some minutes before she recognized him.

'What the hell were you doing in an IRA pub?' he asked.

'I was passing by. I didn't know it was an IRA pub until it was too late.'

'What happened? Can you remember?'

'There was a man of fifty rattling a tin and everyone sung a song called "The Death of Kevin Barry".'

Malone was bored stiff but because memory is comprised of a chain that must be worked through link by link, he went further. 'Sing it!'

Natalie sang it very loudly to the same tune she had sung it to before. A nurse interrupted her and asked her to be quiet, but she ignored her.

'Then what?'

'The man asked me if I wanted to join the IRA.'

'What did you say to the man?'

'I was sick.'

'What the hell do you mean, you were sick?'

'What I say. Then he gave me some water and asked me what I thought of the song.'

'Yes! Yes!'

'So I said I would like to think that Kevin Barry had a hard-on when the rope tightened round his neck.'

Malone swore. 'Then what?'

'Well, I don't really know what happened. It was hot. I was quite drunk and I think I must have been taken ill. I fainted and hit my head on something.'

Malone chewed his unlit cigar.

'Has it by any chance crossed your mind that someone might have found your remark offensive and hit you on the head?' he asked.

'Why, no, not at all.'

He sighed heavily, bit the end off his unlit cigar and spat it into a wastepaper basket. 'Does it strike you as being a particularly sensible thing to say to an IRA man?' he asked mildly.

'I suppose not, if one is sober. But there is something else you should know, which is far more important.'

'What, for Christ's sake?'

It took Natalie ten minutes to repeat the conversation she had overheard. She implored him not to visit Belfast. He did not indicate whether he would take her advice or ignore it. He regarded her with the look of non-committal serenity for which he was famous and quietly left the room.

* * *

Malone's other children were introduced to Natalie before going to the constituency the next day. They had been strictly brought up and had good manners. They treated Natalie like a sister.

Malone, Hortense, Miss Bechtold and Natalie went in the Malonemobile. The rest of the family and Malonist supporters followed in other cars.

The day-to-day work in the Malonist Party headquarters was routine. In the mornings, workers would sit in rows on either side of a long table, occupying the full length of a big rectangular hall. The workers' tasks were menial. Most of the work was putting election notices into envelopes and ticking off names on each canvassing sheet covering a single street.

Natalie helped to work a printing machine called a 'Malonograph', which on the turning of a handle produced a 'Malonogram', a sheet of paper showing a photograph of Malone and his family with the policies of his Party outlined underneath.

The Malonograms were transferred to another machine which folded them before they were put into envelopes. The folding machine often went wrong and the workers had to fold by hand. There were four Malongraphs each side of the table and the workers would operate in groups of three and four. Natalie sat in the same place every day between a vivacious woman aged about sixty and her daughter. The daughter, like the mother, was noisy, giggly, energetic and aggressive and her hair was dyed red. They were known as Old Hilda and Gladys Bingo because the daughter had won a fortune in one of the bingo competitions sponsored by the *Malonist Voice* and lived with her mother in a luxury house on the proceeds. The day she won, the *Malonist Voice* carried a front page headline:

CHEERFUL HARDWORKING GLADYS
STRIKES LUCKY

with a picture underneath of Malone toasting her with champagne.

Old Hilda and Gladys Bingo talked incessantly across Natalie, who found them irritating at first but soon grew to like them. Like the other workers on each side of the table, the three women operated in factory fashion. Gladys Bingo would take the Malonogram from the Malonograph and push it towards Natalie, who would fold it and pass it to Old Hilda who would then put it in an envelope. Old Hilda and Gladys Bingo would sing discordantly while working. Other times, to ease the monotony of the work, Natalie would crack jokes which were of a predominantly sick nature and Gladys Bingo would react with a lusty cook's laugh which would develop into a hacking smoker's cough.

The workers were suddenly startled by Malone's voice on the tannoy.

'Shut up, Bingo,' the voice reverberated. 'I can hear you cackling from my office.' Then the workers would start laughing and work would be delayed for up to ten minutes.

After things had calmed down, Natalie told another joke. Gladys Bingo made a noise like a horse with a twisting carving knife in its guts, and Malone stormed into the room in shirt-sleeves, chewing a cigar.

'Christ, I wish you'd shut up, Bingo,' he bellowed, and dragged the chair she was occupying to another part of the table, while she remained on it. He replaced her by a quiet, hard-working man called Jim and dragged Jim's chair (with Jim on it) over to Natalie. Neither Jim nor Gladys Bingo realized they had been moved until they found their new working companions.

Apart from the work on the Malonograms, uncanvassed street sheets were drawn up, once the names of the people to whom the Malonograms had been sent were ticked off. The sheets would be assembled in piles, according to district, and at the end of the day, canvassers would go in groups to each district.

Natalie would go with Hortense, Old Hilda and Gladys Bingo. While mother and daughter did one house, Hortense and Natalie would do the next, covering each side of the street.

Hortense and Natalie did their work quickly. Hortense, as the candidate's wife, said more, but for Natalie it was just a question of saying: 'I'm canvassing on behalf of Rex Malone, your Malonist candidate. Can we could on your vote? Will you need transport to the polls?' etc.

Old Hilda and Gladys Bingo were still working on that street, but Hortense and Natalie had finished their houses and sat down on the pavement to have a flask of black coffee. They got into a heated argument about whether or not the 1787 edition of *Justine* had more or fewer merits than the 1797 edition: Natalie argued in favour of the 1797 edition, saying that virtue does not bring about good fortune, but Hortense thought that the 1787 edition had more merit because of its conclusion that good fortune is achieved only by decent conduct.

'That has always been Rex's belief,' she said firmly, 'and it's mine as well. Take his case, for instance. Look where he is now, from nothing, and I don't think he would know how to tell a lie even if he tried.'

Natalie was moved by Hortense's argument. 'I think he's

an exception to the rule. What I say applies to a majority, but he is unique,' she replied.

The two women were interrupted by furious shouting, accompanied by the sound of a cooking utensil hitting the ground, followed by a woman's tears. The trouble had been started by Gladys Bingo.

'Who did you vote for before you'd heard of Malone?' she asked, in a bullying way, while a harassed woman at the door held a heavy saucepan of burnt eggs and beans.

'Sometimes Tory. Sometimes Labour,' said the frightened little woman, trying to ignore the gruff complaints of a man in the background complaining that his tea was late again. 'It depended who picked me up to take me to the polls first.'

'Don't you know one from the other?' barked Gladys Bingo, like a barrister prosecuting a heroin dealer.

'One's as good as another.'

'Oh, it is, is it? So that's your attitude! I think it's time I told you a thing or two about Mr Malone!'

The housewife tried to close the door but Gladys Bingo kicked it open before she had a chance. It was then that she dropped the saucepan, and let out a terrified cry which attracted Hortense's attention.

'*Beengo*! I think you'd better come away and sit in the car,' she ordered sternly and apologized to the housewife.

'Are you really Mrs Malone?'

'At your service.'

'I know of your husband, of course. He's very attractive. My husband forces himself on me every night and the only way I keep my sanity is to close my eyes and pretend he's Mr Malone.'

'How charming of you to say that! Can we count on your vote as well as your kind nightly thoughts?'

'I'll vote for him. The other parties are wankers. Will you send a car to pick me up?'

'Certainly. Natalie, will you mark "car" on the sheet, please?'

'Thank you so much for calling, Mrs Malone. I didn't know Mr Malone had such a nice wife.'

'Then perhaps you should write a letter congratulating us both on our choice of partner.'

The housewife smiled, for the first time in months.

The canvass sheet for that street recorded a 20% Tory preference, 41% Labour and 39% Malonist. Many of the streets in the cities of Barfax East had the percentages of the two favourites reversed. On a nationwide scale, the Malonists and Labour were equal in popularity.

'Bingo is not to go canvassing for me again, Ma,' said Malone at dinner. 'We'll have to keep her at headquarters on paperwork.'

'Who told you about Bingo's canvassing?'

'Just other canvassers. I'm not going to give names.' He turned towards Natalie. 'Tomorrow I want you to try on your own,' he said, 'without Hortense standing by you.'

She covered about six houses in a mainly Labour street, its inhabitants provincial and hostile on grounds of race as opposed to class. She said the same thing each time: 'I am canvassing on behalf of . . .' etc. The seventh house was opened by an unshaven man in his twenties wearing an imitation leather jacket.

'Inviting me to vote for a foreigner, are you?' queried the man.

'A foreigner's as good as an Englishman and in your case better.'

The man began to lose his temper. 'Not when a foreigner takes jobs that are supposed to go to British workers.'

'We are judged by our personality, our wit, our industry and our brains, not our nationality.'

'Do you want me to rough you up and give you a good shag?'

Natalie thought of the triumph she would feel if she returned to Malone with a black eye. The idea stimulated her.

'I'd like to see you try, but I don't think you'd be able to get it up.'

The man hit her across the face with the back of his hand. She kicked him in the private parts and bit her tongue in concentration. The blood from her tongue made her 'injury' look worse than it was. She made a note of his name and address, adding that she hoped he liked the taste of prison food, before returning to headquarters.

On entering the building she bumped into Miss Bechtold.

'Why, you're hurt!'

'It's nothing.' But she deliberately walked with a lurch towards Malone's study.

Malone was sitting at his desk, smoking a cigar. He looked up from his papers, his eyebrows raised. 'What happened? You've been injured. We'll get a doctor.'

'It's not necessary. I've got the son of a bitch's name and address. He told me he was a National Front supporter and that Hitler didn't torture his victims enough. He also said women who canvassed for foreigners were fit only to be tied up and raped. I told him his ideas were racist, but politely of of course.'

'Politely? What the hell do you mean – politely? We Malones don't talk with our tails between our legs.'

Natalie regretted her lie.

'What did he say next?'

'He grabbed me by the arm and said he was going to rape me.'

'Christ! What did you say then?'

'I said: I dare you to try, you wouldn't be able to get it up!'

Malone looked at her closely but he did not blush because Cossack blood flowed through his veins.

'Then he hit you?'

'Yes, but it's nothing. I'm only worried I may have lost you a vote.'

'It wasn't there to have been lost. Someone called you a coward once, didn't they?' he said.

The question startled her and she didn't answer.

'Well, did they?'

'Yes.'

'Has it not occurred to you that that person might have been speaking in extreme sarcasm?'

'No.'

'Well, I'm telling you they must have been. You've got more guts than anyone I've met outside my family. I'm very proud of you. Are you taking any action?'

'It's not worth it.'

* * *

The Irish ghetto in the principal city of Barfax East was about the size of Battersea. Its population consisted mainly of Catholics who had emigrated from Northern Ireland and married English Catholics, although some marriages were mixed, enabling an increase of Protestants in a Catholic-dominated community.

Carol Kelly was an example of a mixed marriage. She was an English Protestant by birth and married to Tom Kelly, a navvy. She had one son. The boy was reared as a Protestant and left home to find work, aged fifteen. Carol Kelly's health had always been poor and deteriorated when her husband died at the age of fifty-two. She had been widowed for six years when Rex Malone called at her house one Saturday morning. Natalie was with him. She had asked to see how he advertised himself, to improve her own technique.

Mrs Kelly opened her front door looking tired and haggard. She was wearing a dressing-gown and slippers. A scrawny border terrier followed her to the door and barked around her heels.

'Mrs Carol Kelly?' asked Malone, smiling.

'Yes.'

'Rex Malone's my name. I'm so pleased to have met you at last. I couldn't get an answer when I called before. A charming Bassett you've got there. What's his name?'

'He's a border terrier, not a Bassett, and his name's Jeff.'

'As you know, I'm your Malonist candidate and I'm calling to see whether you'd care to give me your hand. I'm offering a decent alternative to what the Tories and Labour have to offer.' He handed her a Malonogram, a copy of which she'd received already. She didn't say anything because she was a little deaf and only heard half of what he said.

'May I give you a day or two to think it over? And if you do decide you want to support me, I can arrange for a car to take you to the polls.'

Carol Kelly's concentration had wandered. She had not taken his identity in. Her ill health occupied her thoughts for eighteen hours a day, so she assumed in her subconscious that he was either a health visitor or her doctor's new registrar on his rounds. She associated his friendly behaviour with her ideal of a caring doctor's bedside manner. Suddenly .and without warning, she harangued Malone with an intimate description of a disgusting gynaecological condition that affects some older women. Before he could interrupt she took him through five detailed operations, a description of what the surgeon did, followed by what the surgeon said he'd done, followed by what the consultant said. She continued in a ranting monotone for ten minutes, while amused neighbours pulled their lace curtains aside to listen.

As she rounded off her tirade and brought it to a climax, the inhabitants of the street had formed an audience, while Natalie stood behind Malone, convulsed with giggles.

'He gave me a packet of medicine he said'd stop the pain.' Her voice rose to a startling crescendo. 'And I looked at it and I said to 'im as I says to you, too, "I'll be buggered if I'm going to use a suppository!" '

'Blimey, madam!'

'And them doctors, they're all the same. All crooks the lot of 'em.'

'That's just what the Malonist Party is going to stamp out, Mrs Kelly. We're going to put a stop to these doctors who don't care about their patients, their feelings, their loneliness. We're going to make wealthier people join insurance schemes to pay for private medicine so that more people who are less fortunate can use our Health Service, so that each doctor can give each patient more personal care and attention.'

Mrs Kelly was too deaf to hear the whole of that but she could tell she was talking to a man who wished to help her. His sympathetic tone had touched her and she began to sob. 'I won't use the filthy things!' she cried. 'I'd do anything but that . . .' and her voice diminished into a tight snuffling sound.

'Rexy's yer man!' said Malone.

'You must understand. I will not use them! I won't!'

'You're never alone with Rexy Malone!' Then he withdrew, smiling and waving. She would have liked to see the same charming smile on the faces of the many bored, disinterested doctors she had consulted.

'Mark "Nutcase" on the sheet,' he told Natalie, 'but make a note to send someone out to talk to her as there's a good chance she could vote for us.'

'I'll do that.'

'Now you see what they mean when they say I cater for all sorts.'

Malone, Miss Bechtold and Natalie went in the Malonemobile to another street in the Irish ghetto about a mile away. Malone did not like women shouting at him about gynaecological matters. It confused him and made him very bad-tempered. He was about to sound the horn as a young man and a middle-aged woman stood in the middle of the street, arguing.

'Your hand is hovering over your horn again, Mr Malone,' said Miss Bechtold.

'Sorry, matron. I've had it rough.'

'Nevertheless, it is something you have to be reminded of, Mr Malone.'

Malone ignored her but stared straight ahead with a look of composure worn as a mask to hide the frustration beneath it.

A woman in her late forties, wearing nothing but a bath towel, was running in circles around her son, gabbling like an agitated hen. This was Biddy McKearney, a nervous, dotty, bossy woman with red hair. She was five foot tall, young-looking for her age and was massaging herbal nourishing cream into her face with a cosmetic smoothing iron as she spoke. Her son, Liam, looked as dotty as his mother. He was wearing an ill-fitting leather jacket and green needlecord jeans two inches too long for him. He was clean-shaven, but his dark hair was long. His skin was olive green, his eyes dark grey like his mother's, his nose aquiline and his gait unsteady because he had a hangover. He was carrying a few unfastened bags, their contents spilling out of them. As he stooped to pick something up he dropped something else, continually distracted by his mother's shrill voice which showed a thick Irish brogue.

'Now, you won't be eccentric in Belfast, will you, dear?' said Mrs McKearney.

'I'm not eccentric,' retorted the boy, whose Irish accent was less obvious than his mother's.

'Yes, you are, dear, you're the most eccentric volunteer the Provos will ever have among their ranks. I want you to remember you're going across the water to help your father in an operation on Christmas Day that is vital to the cause.'

'I know, Mother.'

'So don't go round looking an oddity or you'll be stopped and searched.'

'I don't look an oddity.'

'You *do* look an oddity and you *are* odd and the boys will be laughing at you. You can't even pack a bag, let alone manage a marksman's cover.'

Mrs McKearney bent over and repacked her son's bundles still in the middle of the road, while Malone waited, hoping they would move on to the pavement. Mrs McKearney found a thick, elegantly bound book in her son's luggage.

'Fine book! Is this a history of Ireland?' she asked as she opened it. It was *The Lord of The Rings*.

'Tolkien!' she shrieked at the top of her voice. 'Tolkien! What's a big boy like you want to read Tolkien for? All he ever wrote about was pixies!'

'It's to help me relax, Mother.'

'You don't join the IRA to relax, nor to be eccentric either. When one of the boys gets eccentric, the person blamed for it is the mother. It all comes back to her. I know because I remember how it was in your father's day.'

'Mother, keep your voice down. You're slap in the middle of a British street and there's someone wants to come by.'

The mother and son embraced and parted. Liam got into a waiting taxi and Mrs McKearney went back to her house which Malone was waiting to canvass. She was still wearing a towel when she answered the door.

'Hullo, well, if it isn't Mrs McKearney. Sorry if I called at an inopportune time. And a very good-morning to you.'

She knew who he was because she had seen a bleary photograph of him, shown to her by her son, but she had never seen a clear photograph of him as the Malonogram had not yet reached her. His striking appearance confused her. Had his features been plain, her attitude towards her estranged husband's target would have been as cold-blooded as befitted the tradition of her family. 'Good-morning,' she said formally. 'Yes, you have indeed called at an inopportune moment.'

'The departure of a loved one, for whatever the reason, is always distressing,' said Malone, 'and I know how you must feel. Naturally I'm not going to stay more than a minute. Can you offer the Malonist Party your hand? A fat lot you'll get out of the other two parties, whose policies speak for themselves.'

'Will you be bringing your country's invaders home from Ireland?'

'That very serious subject is under consideration, Mrs McKearney. Speaking from my own experience when the Germans occupied my country, uniformed aliens are not a pretty sight on someone's streets,' remarked Malone non-committally.

She misinterpreted his remark to mean that his party intended to withdraw. That, combined with his looks, softened her.

'But your name is Malone. That sounds like an Irish name. The Germans didn't invade Ireland.'

'Yes, Malone is an Irish name and I never said they did.'

Her confusion increased and she thought for a while and continued to rub the herbal cream into her face with the cosmetic iron. This was a typical gesture of hers when she was nervous or agitated.

'And are you a Roman Catholic?' she asked, looking at him sideways.

Malone knew she liked his looks and he wanted her vote. He stepped closer to her, looked her straight in the eye and laughed – the legendary racy Cossack's laugh that melted the hearts of the hardest of women. '*In nomine Patris et Filii et Spiritus Sancti.* Rexy's yer man and the blessing of the Pope is upon you!' he said, making the sign of the cross. With the fourth movement of his hand he slapped her on the behind.

She gaped at him like a teenager at Elvis Presley. After a long silence she said she'd left a tap running in her kitchen and asked Malone to wait while she turned it off. When she returned she told Malone she would give him her vote and shook his hand. As she shook Natalie's hand, she pushed a rolled-up piece of paper into her palm. It was not until she got to the Malonemobile that Natalie opened it. The words were written in capitals with a piece of charcoal.

COME TO MY HOUSE ALONE AT 6.00 TONIGHT WITHOUT FAIL. IT IS A MATTER OF LIFE AND DEATH.

* * *

'Why have you sent for me?'

It was raining heavily and Natalie was wet.

'Come inside,' said Mrs McKearney, who was wearing a bottle green dress and a lime green blazer.

'Whatever business you wish to conduct with me must be conducted on your doorstep. I'm not entering your house and I've left behind a note of your name and address in a sealed enveloped marked "to be opened only in the event of my death or injury to my person". So say what you want to see me about and get it over with.'

Mrs McKearney beckoned Natalie in. The look in the older woman's eyes convinced her that she was neither armed nor dangerous. Her house was clean but untidy. On the walls of the living-room were photographs of IRA patrols dating back to 1939. One of them showed her husband's father, then aged twenty, a good-looking man standing by a barbed wire fence with a bag over his shoulder. There was a framed photograph of her husband taken at the same age, closely resembling his father. An orange, green and white flag covered the wall above the photographs. A life-sized crucifix occupied the facing wall and well-polished Catholic relics adorned the tables.

'Why have you called me here?' Natalie asked.

'Please sit down.'

She sat on the arm of a chair and held her hands together in front of her. Mrs McKearney poured two glasses of whisky. She gave one to Natalie and drank the other, which she refilled and emptied before filling it a third time. Then she began to talk.

'I didn't know what sort of a man your Mr Malone was until today. To us, one Brit in politics is as bad as another and one Brit killed for our cause is no worse than another. But once there's any personal connection' (her voice cracked as if fighting tears) '. . . then our mission is broken.'

'What do you mean, broken?'

'My son has never kept anything from his mother. He's been summoned by his father. My husband's an important figure in the offensive wing of the Movement. He is also a man of considerable wealth. He poses as a Protestant and his income is derived from races won by the famous racehorse, Shamrock Kitty. Apart from the maintenance of his house and the generous allowance he gives me, his income goes to IRA funds and the sponsoring of its operations.'

'What has that got to do with Mr Malone?'

Mrs McKearney poured herself another glass of whisky which she drank. Her brain had become befuddled and her tongue looser than her husband would have wished.

'My husband has already planned Mr Malone's execution because of his pied-piper appeal to the masses and his pro-British stand. My son's as good a hand with a rifle as his father is. He will be present in case anything unforeseen happens and will take over the execution. I know there are others involved because my son has connections in Kilburn, where he's been spending a lot of his spare time.'

The police had already been told about the incident in Kilburn. The hotel Malone would use in Belfast would be surrounded by Special Branch detectives. Natalie was not satisfied this was enough.

'Where does your husband live?' she asked.

The woman produced a map showing some countryside outside Belfast. She drew a cross at a point occupied by a house the size of a castle.

'That's where he lives. There's a respectable Protestant pub in the village of Haagan nearby. He drinks there very day. As he's a perfect mimic, he even imitates the brogue the Protestants use. He's known locally as Raymond Morgan. He attends Protestant services in the local church regularly and will go there for the morning service on Christmas Day just before the execution at 1.15, when Malone will be leaving the hotel to visit the orphanage.'

'Do you think that what your friends do is right?'

'I am committed to the withdrawal of troops and the only way to get anything out of the British is by perpetual violence. I've been a Republican all my life and I would die for the Movement, but nothing, and I repeat nothing – would induce me to condone the killing of a fine man like Malone. He looks so much like my husband did in his youth.'

'You sound as if you were in love with him.'

'I have only met him once but I know a good man when I see one.'

'What do you want me to do? How can I stop your husband committing this act?'

'He has a weakness for beautiful women. His sexual tastes are rather perverse.'

'In what way?'

'I can't be specific. He just likes things to be odd. He doesn't like being indoors for that sort of thing. Sometimes he likes to go outside,' she added vaguely.

Natalie was tired and bored. She expected direct answers. She was intolerant of incoherence, slowness and evasiveness.

'My patience is as limited as my time,' she said coldly. 'You're going to have to do better than that if this thing is to be averted. What's the best way to approach your husband?'

'I'm doing my best to tell you.'

'It's no good doing your best if your best isn't good enough. Try again.'

'He likes beautiful women and anything that is kinky. It makes me feel ill to talk about it and I'm thankful I don't know any details. It was that as well as his temper that made me ask him to leave here, although I still love him to distraction. I don't want him to do wrong and I don't even think I know what is right and what is wrong.'

Mrs McKearney started weeping.

Natalie had never known how to handle people when they cried. 'I'm not hard, but I don't know how to handle other people's tears, Mrs McKearney,' she said in a voice that was harsh and cold but not intended to injure. 'What time will your husband be attending this church on Christmas Day?'

'The service at Haagan village church starts at 11 o'clock. There's only one church in Haagan, a Protestant church. The service ends at midday. That will leave him one hour and fifteen minutes to drive to the Belfast city centre and assemble an Armelite rifle on the roof to the Chaucer Hotel. A bomb will also be timed to go off at the same time. I leave it to you to give the right warnings but I'll have no part in that.'

Natalie remembered *The Day of the Jackal* and feared that whatever security regulations were enforced, nothing would prevent a professional assassin from executing his mission.

'Your husband,' she asked cautiously, 'is he a religious man?'

'No.'

'What I am trying to say is – does he have any scruples about what is done in a church and what isn't?'

'When he was a decent young lad he would have cared, but now he has no conscience about how to behave in the House of God. If he did have any conscience, he would not frequent the house of the wrong god!' Mrs McKearney began to cry again.

'I do wish you'd stop crying, Mrs McKearney,' pleaded

Natalie in a matronly tone, 'it doesn't help anyone. Perhaps you could tell me about your husband's feelings towards women. Does he like them to be aggressive or submissive?'

'In the home submissive, but if encountered to satisfy his carnal lusts he likes them to initiate the entire seduction.'

'I get the picture. I'll go to the church and I'll see that he is delayed. I'll need a photograph of him as he is now, frontways and in profile.'

Mrs McKearney showed Natalie a photograph album, full of pictures of a man between thirty and fifty with a well-proportioned, forceful face and ruggedly attractive features. He did not have the kind of face that a layman would associate with the IRA. Mrs McKearney explained that her husband always carried a Church of England hymn book with the initials R.S.M. (standing for Ruari Sean McKearney and Raymond Sidney Morgan) in gold letters on a dark red background, and that he occupied a pew to himself at the back of the church furthest away from the door.

'All right, I know what to do,' said Natalie at length. 'Don't think it's convenient for me to do this. It isn't. I'd much rather be with my family, but because I am concerned only with my interests and those of my friends, I'll do this job. But I warn you, if you are double-crossing me, there is one sealed document in my bank and one at home saying who you are and who your son is and where he is. The document even brands you as an informer against your own cause. I know you've got most of your life behind you and wouldn't have many years left to rot in jail, but your son won't get off as lightly. Terrorists are not treated well in prisons. I'm sure you wouldn't want your dear eccentric son disfigured or worse than that, buggered, which is what happens to most good-looking young men in prisons.'

After another long fit of weeping, Mrs McKearney forced herself to speak. 'I'm not double-crossing you. I'm so confused. Once I thought I knew right from wrong. Now I don't know. I wonder if my priest would be able to help me.'

'Screw your priest! All I care about is stopping this assassination,' said Natalie and got up to go. She left without saying goodbye to Mrs McKearney and made a long statement at a neighbouring police station. All she had to do now was to delay McKearney's departure from the church.

* * *

Ruari McKearney was in his forties. He was well-built. He had thick greying hair and had obviously been handsome in his youth. He had secretly been an active campaigner for the Irish Republican Movement since the age of twenty. Unlike many of his fellow Republicans, who tended to spend their money as soon as they'd earned it, Ruari McKearney was thrifty. Like his father and grandfather, who had both been active in the struggle for Home Rule, he was an expert in breeding horses and training them. He was personally responsible for the breeding and training of a number of horses to become Grand National winners. His best horse, ironically named Shamrock Kitty, had never lost a race, and the money it won had been used partly to buy a hundred acres of land and a luxurious castle-like country house which McKearney owned, and partly as a regular source of income to subsidize Republican funds. McKearney was known in his local community as Raymond Morgan. He posed as a respectable and genial Protestant. No one working either in his house or on his land would have susspected that over two-thirds of the Republican offensive in Great Britain was supported by his income alone.

His colleagues in the Movement, his wife and his son, were the only people who knew of his heavily influential Republican connections. Apart from them, his image as clean-living, decent Lord of the Manor was inviolate.

Ruari's son, Liam, was a professional jockey as well as a

trained marksman. His job was to ride Shamrock Kitty. Liam knew better than to question his father's orders. He could handle Shamrock Kitty better than any other jockey in Ireland, although he had no share whatever in any money won by the horse. Once the wages of the servants and retainers on the McKearney estate were settled, the money earned by Shamrock Kitty went towards the IRA alone. Liam had been raised as a Catholic and militant Republican and there was an unwritten rule that it was expected of him to do as he was told. He didn't want to be knee-capped, even through orders issued by his own father.

Ruari was a ruthless, inflexible and uncompromising figure in the IRA and one of its most prominent masterminds. So senior a figure was he in the Movement that he was rarely, if ever, seen to take an active part in any of its operations. He was, however, by far the most coveted marksman the IRA had ever had among its ranks. For that reason alone, he carried out the executions of prominent British politicians himself. Not once in his life had he missed his target. Not once had he failed to kill. Not once, with his face covered as it invariably was, by a slit Balaclava, was he ever suspected, let alone detected.

But Ruari McKearney had two major weaknesses, neither of which had as yet impaired his infallibility as a deadly accurate marksman. One of these, the demon to destroy three Irishmen out of every four, was drink. The other, that usually only destroyed two out of every four, was women. Women to him were as harmful as heroin. Although he did not know it at the time, it was a woman who would bring about his ruin.

Liam McKearney had not seen his father for a year. His father was in his study which was encased in a secure, three-foot thick, concrete-walled vault that not even his cleaners had access to. To enter the study, Liam had to push three different numbers, each consisting of four digits, before the solid metal door could open. He found his father sitting behind a plain elm desk, cluttered with rifles and other guns that he had taken from his vast armoury for cleaning. Some of these guns were for shooting birds at his weekly pheasant shoots. Others were for shooting people, and one, an Armelite rifle, its barrel freshly and lovingly cleaned by its owner, had been laid to one side. A person, not a bird, was going to be its target. The person was Rex Malone.

Liam entered his father's study wearing a jockey's outfit, holding his cap in his hand. He was only going to ride Shamrock Kitty once. When the race was over he would be preparing himself for his role in the assassination. His father was dictating a speech he wanted a senior cell commander and ammunitions expert to make at the funeral of a hunger striker. He was speaking into a tape recorder. Liam sensed it would be unwise to interrupt him, and stood timidly, like a novice policeman on duty, prepared to wait all day if necessary.

'Our rules, staunchly adhered to by our beloved martyr just departed, are taken from history. We remember the famine. We remember the Fenians. We remember 1916 and the executions. We remember the Brit murders of the lads that gave their young lives marching beneath the Flag of Green. And I trust that our dear departed will be an example to all of you this sorrowful day, and that it will give you greater strength to free our country.'

Liam cleared his throat, afraid of using more radical methods of attracting his father's attention.

McKearney ignored his son's presence and continued dictating, his voice rising to a thunderous crescendo: 'After centuries of slumber, our nation shall once again strike, please God, at the despoilers who have infringed her liberty and murdered her sons and daughters. Our nation shall strike, and strike hard, and make the evil English tyrants go down on their knees for mercy and forgiveness!'

'Father?'

The ranting of Ruari McKearney continued: 'With the help of God and his blessed mother shall all our comrades and all our holy martyrs in heaven look down upon our tortured, crucified country!'

'I've arrived, father,' said the boy, relieved to have interrupted Ruari before he had started a new sentence.

'Turn round!'

The boy turned, fearing that his father would find something to criticize about his appearance.

'Would you be getting your hair cut, son, dear,' he said.

In comparison with his father's heavy brogue, Liam's Irish accent was not very pronounced, due to the length of time he had lived in England. He replied, 'Jesus Christ wore his hair long, so why shouldn't I?'

Ruari picked up the Armelite rifle by its barrel and swung it violently against the desk like a golfer. 'Jaysus Chroyst may have worn his hair long,' he bellowed, 'but Jaysus Chroyst didn't happen to be roydin' any of my fockin' hosses!'

· PART THREE ·

The Salvation of Miss Natalie Klein

Haagan village church was named after General James Haagan, a Puritan who fought in Ireland on the British side under Oliver Cromwell. It stood at the end of Haagan village street. It was a medium-sized quaint old church attended by parishioners from an area of thirty square miles. Its visitors were well-dressed, middle to upper class Protestants, a few of whom took part in the Orange Free Marches and many of whom admired McKearney, whose mansion had a Union Jack flying from one of its turrets. The pews were full and McKearney, who was regarded by the more snobbish parisioners as a social superior, sat alone at the back.

Natalie entered the church before the service had started. She was dressed conventionally in a khaki-coloured Austrian hunting coat with its collar turned up. On her hair she wore a band attached to a veil which discreetly covered her face and gave her an air of wealth and respectability. The coat was modestly buttoned to the neck. Beneath it she wore the clothing of an Amsterdam prostitute. She sat at the end of a pew facing McKearney whom she recognized from across the aisle, both by his face and his gold-initialled prayer book. He was dressed correctly in a tailored country suit of brown tweed. A middle-aged woman sitting next to her gave her a strange look because she had not knelt down as churchgoers do before a service. Like someone caught in the act of being different from everyone else, she did so hurriedly. She put her hands together copying everyone else and closed her eyes. She remained thus positioned for three minutes, during which time she planned how she would attract McKearney's attention.

Christmas hymns were sung. Prayers that seemed interminable, and which Natalie could not find in the church hymn books, were read. A man from the congregation went up to the front and read a long passage from the New Testament which rambled on until she nearly fell asleep. A clergyman gave a noisy, aggressive, ear-piercing sermon on the subject of thrift and moral decency.

After one of the prayers she raised herself from her knees and lurched violently to the right, forcing herself to fall. Instinctively, McKearney stepped into the aisle to help her up. She looked him lecherously in the eye and thanked him in a pronounced Northern Irish brogue.

'It's my pleasure, my friend,' said McKearney affably.

'Do you mind if I stand beside you? I'm feeling faint.'

McKearney stared at her pretty profile.

'It would be the making of my day,' he said.

The congregation had begun to sing 'Once in Royal David's City'. McKearney joined them and Natalie was struck by his good musical ear and leant against him. She could hear the quickening of his heart and raised her coat to show a thigh covered with a fishnet stocking. Suddenly, for no apparent reason, she was reminded of her visit to the IRA pub in Kilburn and of the man who had asked if the Marquis de Sade had ever done any good for Ireland. It amused her to think that among his many debauches when not behind bars, he devoted himself not to Ireland but to ordering his valet to whip him in his rooms in Marseilles, scratching on the chimney the number of lashes he had received.

An idea flashed through her mind as the long hymn continued. She turned towards McKearney, away from the congregation, and undid her coat. He extended his hand which she took in her own and bit. The gesture excited him and his breathing became heavy. She put her mouth to his ear and sang softly, making up the words as she went along.

'In a southern sun-drenched city
Stood an ancient chimney flue
Where a valet lashed his master
Watching how his member grew.
When the master's eyes went wild,
The valet meekly bowed and smiled.'

'I'll have to be taking you. This is all too strong for me,' said McKearney in her ear. His harsh Northern brogue had suddenly become southern in intonation. She led him towards the door of the church, continuing to sing with the congregation:

'The master ordered: "whip me harder.
This is like a piece of cake."
But when he reached five hundred and sixty
The valet said: "I need a break."
On the chimney he inscripted
The number of strokes that he'd inflicted.'

Some disgusted onlookers stared at McKearney and Natalie leaving. A few of them overheard what she was singing. It was supremely ironical that a man who had maimed and slaughtered not hundreds, but thousands, should follow a woman like a brainwashed sheep.

'I'll be taking you to the outer perimeter a hundred yards from here,' she said nervously, but remembering to use the right brogue.

'Anywhere as long as it's fast.'

She led him to a four-foot high gravestone by the wall of the churchyard.

'Would you be lying on your back, dear?' she said.

The service had started late. It was now 12.30. This left him with only half an hour to get to the city centre and even with no traffic the deadline would not have been easy to keep. As Natalie leant over to kiss him on the mouth, she hit him on the head with a stone, hard enough to knock him out but not hard enough to kill him. No one saw her leave. She drove her self-drive car to the airport and returned to London.

* * *

The Reverend Wentridge-Toomey was a short, pompous, bald-headed man of forty-five. He had been shaking hands with members of his congregation as they left the church. Among them was a farmer who was an old friend of his with an English accent.

'I see that scoundrel, Morgan, picked up a tart again today,' said the minister. 'If he must do that sort of thing he might at least do it in private and not in a Christian church.'

The farmer chuckled.

'We all have our vices. If we didn't we'd have nothing to repent over. Mr Morgan may have a weakness for members of the opposite sex but he's seen as a pillar of the community.'

'I still think his behaviour today was a bit much, but I suppose you're right. At least the blighter has the decency to fly a Union Jack from his residence,' said the Reverend Wentridge-Toomey.

The blighter who had flown a Union Jack from his residence regained consciousness and although he was confused he knew how late it was. He assumed the experience he had had before he lost consciousness was a dream. He opened the suitcase in the boot of his Ford Capri. He checked that the Armelite rifle at the bottom was untouched and ready to load. He covered it with gift-wrapped presents, eased his weight under the steering wheel and headed for the city centre, blindly overtaking and forcing oncoming vehicles to swerve onto the verge. On the outskirts of the city he checked his watch. The time was 1.05. He could still carry out the assassination and went through two red lights. An army patrol car forced him to the side.

'What's your game, my man? You've been through two red lights,' said the militia-man, and asked him for his licence.

McKearney handed over his licence together with other documents and smiled.

'You realize that you've broken the law,' said the man. 'Get out of your car.'

Panic took hold of McKearney. He wondered whether to drive off but decided to act the part of the dumb Irishman.

'To be sure I was trying to make a citizen's arrest of the man who went through in front of me,' he said.

'Oh, you were, were you? Now I'm arresting you. Are you getting out or am I going to have to use force?'

McKearney got out.

'OK, Paddy, stand up against the car with your hands above your head.'

'A little courtesy wouldn't go amiss. I fly the Union Jack I'll have you know. You're not talking to a papist upstart.'

The militia-man and his colleague searched McKearney and removed a Colt .38 from his inside pocket.

'All right, Paddy, let's have the shooter, and we'll check the boot while we're at it.'

'The gun's for self-protection. Those are Christmas gifts

for my family. I'm late for lunch already. It's Christmas Day. Can't you show some charitable spirit?'

'Not a chance, Paddy, we're going through the lot.'

The Armelite rifle was found almost immediately. It was check and mate for Ruari Sean McKearney.

* * *

Liam McKearney had been staying at the Chaucer Hotel for a week, using an American accent and posing as a tourist visiting relatives unable to put him up. When his father had not appeared by 1.10 he realized he had been detained, and assembled his rifle on the roof. Malone was late leaving the hotel because of catering difficulties at the orphanage that had slowed everything down, so he decided to take the Labrador that accompanied him on official visits for a walk.

Liam McKearney focused the rifle sight on Malone's forehead as he stopped in the street to let his dog lift its leg. He had only to pull the trigger and his mission would have been accomplished. Liam had recognized him from the day of his departure from England. He remembered him by the slanting eyes that looked ahead as he waited for his dog. The index finger of Liam's right hand would not respond to instructions from his brain. It remained rigid like that of a nagging wife in rigor.

Bomb-diffusing experts had already halted the timer on the explosive device found in the bathroom Liam used, next door to Malone's. When police and security guards surrounded him and disarmed him, the index finger of his right hand was still rigid. A terrorist squad sergeant kicked him in the stomach and knocked him to the ground, causing blood to flow from his mouth. His captors closed in around him as he lay whimpering, his index finger still ramrod straight.

'I couldn't do it. I couldn't get my finger to bend,' he said, speaking in staccato sentences. 'The man went out unguarded. He's a fine grand lion of a fellow.' Liam started to cry, his tears stimulated by a kick in the kidneys.

Foreign and British press reporters assembled on the scene. The British press, ranging from right to left, were unanimous in variations of the front-page headline:

IRA PLOT TO SHOOT MALONE FAILS and in smaller print 'I couldn't do it. The man's a fine, grand lion of a fellow' blubs gunman.

Thousands of votes that would otherwise have gone to Labour went to Malone on the strength of these headlines alone.

* * *

The Malonist Party had made a lot of gains but nationwide opinion polls still showed it to be equal in popularity to Labour, now entirely in the hands of the hardline Left. It was either thirty-nine to forty-one or vice versa. The balance had only to be tilted fractionally for a landslide to be engineered.

'I have to take a few days off for family reasons and I'm not allowed to say what it's about,' Natalie told Malone.

'Nothing bad, I hope.'

'No. Just very boring. Do you mind?'

'No. Why should I mind?'

'That's very kind of you.'

'No, it isn't. It's kind of you to canvass for me.'

Murphy had hoarded three plastic bags of heroin behind a brick in the wall of his room. Natalie had found them after his death and locked them in a metal case with a combination lock. She had originally meant to save the stuff in case she suffered from a malignant disease in later years. She knew several pubs in South London which were rough and visited by heroin addicts. She disguised herself as a down-and-out and went to a tattered place called the Warwick Arms. She carried the plastic bags in a sackcloth hold-all which she carried over her shoulder.

Four bleary-eyed punks in their early twenties were standing over a gaming machine. One of them was holding an Alsatian dog by the collar. He was desperately trying to raise enough money for an injection. The names of the four young men were Ted, Nick, Bozo and Badger. They were all homosexuals. Badger's nickname was due to the pungent aroma of unwashed clothes and stale sweat that surrounded his person. He wore an imitation leather jacket, torn jeans caked with dirt and cowboy boots with flapping soles. He had fair, greasy hair, a broken nose, an ear-ring in his left ear, and three days' growth of beard. A two-inch scar inflicted by a flick knife covered his right cheek. His eyes appeared black because the pupils covered the irises. His complexion was yellowish and very unhealthy because he was feverish and jaundiced. At first, Natalie feared he might be carrying a virus that could be passed on to her. She was relieved when she found out it was only cold turkey.

Ted was bald. He had shaved his head deliberately to flaunt a tattoo on the crown which said 'Smack is Cool'. He wore an old denim suit and running shoes. His teeth were rotten and his breath was foul.

Nick looked fractionally cleaner than his companions. He wore grey trousers and an open-necked brown shirt. His greasy black hair was styled in a 'fifties look and he had tattoos of two athletic-looking youths locked in an embrace on his left arm.

When Natalie approached them, she sensed they were shy and introverted beneath their outward image of the hunting and the hunted that makes heroin addicts so menacing to look at.

She exaggerated her Welsh accent. 'Are you winning, then?'

'No. It's a screw-up tonight. I can milk this bastard dry most nights and now my dole's fucked,' said Badger, who needed the drug most and who would have made a badger smell like a rose-scented bath.

'The machine's snarled up on us. It's all take and no give,' said Ted. Nick and Bozo, who were also hardened addicts, eyed each other, not as friends, but as wild animals working out how to destroy a weaker animal to stay alive.

Natalie looked at Badger, who was trembling and sneezing. She fidgeted from one foot to the other, trying to put him and his friends at ease by pretending to be a junkie herself.

'You shooting?' she asked Badger.

'I've got cold turkey coming on. Another half-hour and I'm busted.'

'I've got over three pounds of smack. I've kicked. I can load you but you're going to have to work for it.'

'I'll do a redrum for you if you want, but I've got to have a shot first.'

'You'll get your shot when you've earned it. What's a redrum?'

'Backwards for murder.'

'What I'm going to make you do will be easier and on the right side of the law. I've got enough to keep the four of you out of the shit for a month. But don't try anything hot because I'm armed.'

She turned towards them, away from the other customers, and flaunted an illegally purchased Colt .38.

'What's the deal?' asked Badger.

'I've got an estate car outside. Three times a week at about 11.30 at night, I'll take you to people's houses. We'll bring the dog. We won't feed him till after the visits. We'll knock on people's doors.'

'What for?'

'It's not for you to ask what for. You must say a few things when the doors are opened. I'll tell you what to say at the last minute. Then, after you've done that, we leave.'

'Is that it?'

'That's all it is. It's simple. Do you vote, by the way?'

'I ain't votin' for no one.'

She could tell these people were of lower than average intelligence and spoke slowly to them, as if they were foreign.

'I suppose you want to know why I want you to do this,' she said. 'I'll tell you. You won't really understand my motives because they are complex, but I am doing it as a joke, or as a bet I've had with someone which, if I win, will bring me a lot of money. It's no good my explaining what sort of joke it is or why pestering people at this hour is a joke, but for my intents it is, and that's all I can tell you. I'll tell you what to say just before you bang on the doors. That's all you have to do to get a free shot. Will you do it?'

'Where's the stuff?' Badger asked.

'Outside.'

A police constable at the end of his last beat had just taken his seat at the bar. This was PC Bush, who had a temperature of 101° and whose wife had just left him. He wanted to postpone going home for as long as possible and he promised himself he would not be making any more arrests that night.

'Double rum, barman,' he said. 'and a couple of aspirins if you've got 'em. I haven't had flu as bad as this in years.'

Natalie winced and whitened when she saw PC Bush. So did her companions, but for a different reason. The idea of being caught with three pounds of neat heroin on her person was less daunting to her than catching the policeman's germs.

PC Bush suspected the five of them were hot but couldn't face the formalities of another lot of arrests. He didn't really notice as they moved towards the door. He had forgotten about them by the time he staggered home.

The four junkies followed Natalie to a deserted car park. She took out a metal case with its combination lock showing. She pointed the Colt at them with her right hand, unloading one of the three polythene bags of powder with her left.

'Nothing false, palsy, or you lose a kidney.' She was a keen reader of James Hadley Chase and found gangster jargon amusing.

Badger and his three companions were too feeble and slow-witted to kick the Colt from her hand and take her goods.

'Can you prove it's real?' Badger asked.

She cut a small hole in the bag and put a tiny amount of the powder in the palm of Badger's hand which he licked.

'The stuff's fine. Her word goes. We'll do it. Right, everybody?'

Ted, Nick and Bozo agreed.

'It will mean travelling round the country,' Natalie said. 'You'll have to sleep in the back of the car. I will sleep in a hotel with the goods. You'll have shots whenever you want them but you won't be able to go to your homes every night.'

'We don't live nowhere. We crash out under bridges nights,' said Badger.

She took out a map from the glove compartment and worked out how best to cover the rough working-class districts of cities in the marginal constituencies. While she was perusing, Badger developed cold turkey and said he needed a shot. He produced a dirty looking spoon with congealed egg on it and waved it at Natalie, who winced and turned away.

'Have you got what you need – water, lighter, hypodermic?' she asked.

'I've got the works. We share the hypo.'

'That's pretty dangerous and unhygienic, but it's your business. Here's your first ration.' She closed the box and locked the combination. 'It's the smallest ration you can be given; it's just enough to last till we get to where we have to go. Then you'll be given enough for a proper shot. Will you do all that yourselves once I give it to you? I'm not very good with my hands and I've got other things to do besides hanging about heating up spoons.'

'I know how to do it myself, thanks.' Badger prepared his injection and Natalie watched him with the conflicting emotions of morbid curiosity and shock. She had been spared the pain of watching Murphy inject himself and was suddenly overwhelmed with a feeling of sadness when she saw Badger doing what Murphy had done in private.

As the drug flowed to the vortex of his brain he stopped shaking and smiled benevolently at Natalie.

'I never did ask your name.'

'Megan.'

'Megan. That's a funny name.'

'Lloyd George's daughter was called that. It's not so strange.'

'I didn't know Boy George had any daughters.'

'Forget it!' she snapped. 'We've things to do and I'm not hanging around talking crap.'

After half an hour's drive, they came to the main city of a marginal constituency that had finally gone to Labour at the last election after two recounts. Natalie aimed for the rougher areas of the city and chose an unlit residential street, its litter strewn on the pavement and its walls daubed with graffiti. Many of the houses in that street displayed Labour Party stickers in their windows. These were the people whose loyalty had to be broken.

'Here you are, Badger,' Natalie said, when she saw him sweating and shaking again, and she handed him some powder.

She turned on the light in the car so that he could see to heat the egg-caked spoon which he wiped on his dirt-caked jeans. As he rolled up his sleeve to inject into an area of skin that was already heavily infected, she watched him, despising him. It was likely that he had sold heroin at higher prices to finance it and she found that both sickening and amoral.

'It's nice to watch you getting your ass out of your misery,' she commented disdainfully.

'What do I do now?'

She gave him a raw onion without saying anything.

'What do I do with this?'

'You eat it – all of it, and then you breathe straight into the face of the person you're talking to. It's 11.30 now. Go up to that door with the Labour sticker. I want you to hammer violently on it as if the building were on fire, until the door is opened.'

'Is the building on fire?'

'No. You can see it isn't. Don't ask questions. You're here to carry out my orders. The person opening the door will be rude and abusive, partly because of your personal appearance but mainly because of the lateness of the hour. The door will be slammed shut but wedge it open with your foot. Then I want you to lean right into the person's face so that he or she can smell the onions and say:

' "I'm canvassing on behalf of the sodding Labour Party. We're so bloody overworked that there are some places that have to be canvassed late at night and yours is one of them" – be sure to say this very aggressively – "I've come to check you'll be voting for us." '

'I can't remember all that in one go,' protested Badger. 'Besides, they're already voting Labour because of the sticker.'

'The whole point is to pretend you haven't seen the sticker. I'll talk to the person in this house. You stand behind me, and listen to what I say and how I say it, and repeat it at the next house along. I'm going to need the dog.'

'Are you going to hurt the dog?'

'No.'

She took a bar of chocolate from her pocket and waved it in front of the dog. It had not yet had its daily meal and it leapt into the air trying to get it from her hand. She banged

Gestapo-style on the door. There was no answer. She went on banging until footsteps could be heard. She rubbed the chocolate round the door handle and threw the rest through the letter box so that the dog, now in a bad temper because it had been duped, would try and snarl its way into the house.

A middle-aged woman answered. She wore a quilted dressing-gown and hairnet, and could have been Ena Sharples's sister. She opened the door hurriedly, fearing the news that a relative had had an accident.

The sight of the five dishevelled strangers clutching Labour Party leaflets dispelled her fear, transforming it to the manic aggression that often accompanies relief.

'What the bloody hell's up?'

The dog started barking and wrenched at its lead, trying to get within reach of the chocolate that had landed on the woman's staircase. Its teeth were gnashing and its jaws salivating as if it had rabies. The woman was terrified.

Natalie blew the offensive smell of onions into her face and jammed her foot in the doorway to stop the woman slamming the door.

'Was you asleep, missus'?' she asked gruffly in a ham vaudeville cockney accent which lapsed from time to time.

'I bloomin' well was and all. Hubby's got to get up at five to go to the factory. Control your bloody dog!'

'Don't start giving me no flak, sister. I'm just carrying out me orders. I'm here on behalf of the Labour Party. Unlike some slatterns I could mention, we work round the clock and have to do our house calls at this hour whether constituents like it or not. You're lucky we came.' Natalie went closer to the woman and gripped her under the arm until she let out a wail of pain. 'And we need your vote,' she added in a menacing whisper.

'Didn't you see my sticker?'

'Sod that, missus! We haven't time to look for bits of paper.'

'Well, now you're here, I'll tell you: in the past the Labour Party has always taken us to the polling station in a car it supplies. If you send us a car we'll vote for you.'

There was a risk the woman would persuade friends to give her a lift.'

''Fraid them easy times are over, grandma,' Natalie said. 'The Labour Party's got better and more important things to do than dole out sodding chauffeurs for lazy slobs who can't be bothered to turn up.'

'We'll be wanting a car!' said the woman adamantly.

'A car! A car! The Labour Party doesn't owe you a car. You gets to the polls on Shanks's bleedin' pony!'

'I'm not so sure I want to vote Labour after being dragged out of my bed by you and hearing you be so rude.'

'When we win, which we will, we'll have ways of tracing the names of the people who didn't vote for us. They may be picked up in vans at the dead of night, too, and never 'eard of again. We're going to do a lot of good when we get in but we're also going to keep order like Stalin did. We're going to be fair but if anyone isn't loyal to what we stand for, we're going to lock 'em up till they know better, so don't you go putting on no flippin' airs or bleedin' graces neither! A car indeed! What will you expect next, a flippin' 'orse and carriage, and a flippin' load of liveried footmen?'

'I'm reporting you to the police and worse than that, to our local paper. I'm not voting for you after this!'

'When we get in, all Facist newspapers like your local rag are going to be state-owned like in the Soviet Union where at least people are taught to have a bit of respect for Socialism.'

'I wish you'd all piss off. I need my sleep. My husband's been laid up with bronchitis all winter and he's too frail to go to work but goes just to have something to do.'

'Socialists aren't interested in people's trifling medical ailments, only the advancement of decent ideals.'

The woman started to cry, and struggled with Natalie in an

effort to close the door, but Natalie gave her a painful kick in the shin and kept the door ajar.

'Just leave me alone,' begged the woman. 'We're not voting Tory if that's what you're afraid of. After this, I'm going to vote for that other lovely man.'

'What lovely man? Can't you be more bloomin' coherent?'

'His name's Malone and he's getting my vote.'

Natalie slapped the woman across the face. It hurt her more than it hurt her victim and she consoled herself by telling herself that her victim's humiliation would only be temporary and in the interests of a supreme and ultimate justice. She regarded the woman as being good and kind, and had to shout to prevent herself from crying.

'I'll see to it you're sorry if you vote for him! We'll find out if you do, you stupid old bitch!'

'That alone confirms my decision. And your threats don't scare me. They just encourage me to do what bullies like you don't want me to do. I'm going to vote for him if I have to crawl to the polling station and thugs like you aren't going to stop me!'

'Bloody posh bigot! Fascist pig!'

The woman slammed the door in Natalie's face. Natalie saw her tear down the Labour sticker in her window and spit on it. Through her unorthodox methods, she had gained one more supporter for Malone.

Natalie, the junkies, the Alsatian and the onions all moved on to the other houses in the neighbourhood with Labour stickers in their windows. For the next few days she took the boys from one constituency to the next. The same tactics were used and the same results obtained. The first night they knocked off at 4 a.m., and drove into a lay-by, where Natalie gave Badger enough heroin to last the night, and a ration to Ted, Nick and Bozo, who needed a smaller dose. She changed into neat, tidy clothes, took the metal case with her to a four-star hotel and registered under the name of Sally Keanes, quoting her occupation as a pharmaceutical rep when questioned casually by the concierge, who just wanted to make conversation. She was not concerned about the junkies because they would be unlikely to escape from their self-imposed prison in the lay-by.

She was given a comfortable bedroom with a double bed, coloured television and an adjoining bathroom containing a magenta-coloured bath with old-fashioned taps and a matching magenta water closet and bidet. She lay down on the bed and stared at the ceiling. A feeling of gentle melancholy, which startled her because it was out of proportion to her circumstances, descended on her without warning. She longed to tell Malone what she had been doing that night. She wished she could watch him laugh at her description of her recruits and her methods of getting them to do what she wanted. She was proud of the new power she wielded in his honour, and yearned for his words of flattery and praise for the courage that she had not known she possessed. She would have liked to hear the reassuring Cossack's laugh at her imitation of the accents of the strangers she had encountered, and her description of the dialogues between her and the unfortunate people whom she had disturbed and whose nights she had ruined. She wanted to see the flattering look of approval that delighted her so much, and she was tempted to pick up the telephone and tell him what she had been doing and why. The wiser part of her told her not to tell him what she had been doing and she realized that when he asked her where she had been, she would have to lie to him.

'When I want to fight someone I fight them in the market-place fairly and squarely,' he said repeatedly. For a man who had suffered so much in childhood, he was neither capricious or devious. To him Machiavelli was a dirty word. The principles of fairness and honesty were as essential to him as rice to a Chinaman. But Natalie believed that what she was doing was right and yet she knew Malone would think it wrong. She felt depressed because he was honest, because he was uncorrupted and because he could not and would not recognize the need to do wrong, even in the interests of right.

She poured herself three-quarters of a glass of neat whisky. Ten minutes after she drank it the depression lifted, to be replaced by a feeling of sadness. She felt an onslaught of guilt that a man whose family had been gassed by the Nazis should lack vindictiveness so much that he believed battles must be fought fairly, whereas she, who had been raised in comfortable surroundings, should believe the reverse to be true. Combined with the guilt was a feeling of anger that someone who had been through so much should think this way, and yet the anger was mixed with a confused but overwhelming sense of awe, respect and even reverence. As her mind underwent a tortured fight over what was right and what was wrong, she drifted into a drunken sleep and was woken abruptly by the strange sensation of water running into her ear. She thought at first the ceiling had been leaking, but as she came to her senses she realized that what she felt were her tears.

* * *

None of the junkies slept that night. They did not trust Natalie and feared she would not come back on time.

Ted was the first to break the long silence. 'Why do you think she wants us to go to people's houses quarrelling with everyone like this?' he asked.

'I think it must mean that she wants them to vote Labour and she thinks that being rude and making threats is the only way to get people to do what she wants,' said Badger.

'But that can't make much sense,' said Ted. 'Surely if you want someone to do what you want, you try to be nice to them, not nasty.'

'I'd have thought that myself, but maybe she doesn't know

how to be nice to anyone. She's not even all that nice when she talks to us. Perhaps she's hard and cruel.'

'She's neither hard nor cruel. I think she's mad.'

'Hard, cruel or mad, what difference does it make as long as we get free shots?'

Nick, who had not said a word up to now, interrupted them.

'I don't think the way either of you do about her. I think there's something false, something phoney about her. Look at the way she's always changing from one accent to the next. Sometimes it's Welsh, sometimes a sort of educated English, sometimes it's cockney. And I don't think she shouts at these people because she wants them to vote Labour at all. I think it's for another reason, but God knows what. Maybe there isn't any reason at all. Maybe, you're right after all. Perhaps she is mad. She certainly behaves as if she is.'

'Of course there's no other reason why she quarrels,' Badger said. 'I'm certain it's her way of getting people to vote Labour and if it's not, it's because she's mad, as you say. I couldn't give a shit why she asks us to do these things. I need another shot now and I'd kill someone at her request just for that!'

By 6.30 in the morning, Natalie had not returned to the lay-by. Ted, Bozo and Nick were shivering because of withdrawal, which was still quite mild because they were not addicted as seriously as Badger. He lay in the back of the Citroën estate car, viciously scratching himself all over with his dirt-clogged nails. He had ploughed furrows over his face, clawing through the flesh until he reached the bone, and looked as if he had been through an obscure tribal rite.

At exactly 7.30 a.m. Natalie arrived. She was horrified when she saw the state Badger was in, with loose strips of shredded flesh hanging from his face. The feeling of gloom and self-doubt returned to her again, accompanied by the fear that she had taken on more than she could handle. She forced herself to shake off the mood.

'When did withdrawal symptoms start, Badger?'

'6 o'clock this morning.'

'I gave you your last shot at 11.30 last night.'

'If you give it as early as that, I need another at six the next morning.'

'Then in future I'll get to you by six and that goes for the others, who need a smaller dose than you. Here's your ration. Has your dog been fed?'

'No.'

'I thought as much. All you think of is yourselves.' She gave the dog four packets of a gruel-like substance which contained chunks of dried meat and vitamins. A well-cared for domestic pet would only have eaten a quarter the amount, but this dog ate the lot as soon as it was put in front of him.

'When did you last feed this dog?'

'Two days ago.'

'Disgraceful! I'm handing him over to someone who is good to animals when I get back to London.'

'Anything to get rid of him,' said Badger. 'We can't look after him. He was my father's dog but after my father died I took him over.'

'I bet your father had no idea you were a good-for-nothing junkie.'

'I didn't start shooting until after he died. It was the grief that started me on the stuff. Now, although I've got over the grief, I can't kick the habit.'

'I'm sorry about your father. I didn't mean to be callous. When did he die?'

'Six months ago.'

'I'm sorry.'

'Please think no more of it.'

'All right. Have you taken the dog for a walk?'

'No.'

'I'll take him, then. What's his name so that I can call him?'

'Smack.'

She was about to lead Smack away. Badger heated the spoon and made a horrible moaning noise as he waited for the powder to melt.

'I do wish you'd do that in front of the car where I can't see it,' she said, 'it's disgustingly sordid to watch.'

Ted, Nick and Bozo had their injections. By eight o'clock they were ready to travel to another area. The next major city was a hundred miles away. Lunch-time would be a particularly inconvenient time for housewives. Natalie and the junkies worked thoroughly and relentlessly, leaving nothing but hostility in their wake.

Their bad reputation soon gained nationwide publicity. They did not need to canvass every rough street in every marginal, or cover a quarter of that amount of ground, for local papers and even Fleet Street papers to carry such headlines as: 'LABOUR DENIES HIRING HEAVIES' and 'THUGS DON'T WORK FOR US, LIES LABOUR'. The latter of the two headlines covered the front page of the *Daily Mail*.

The opinion polls had changed, but not very dramatically. The Malonists were now a little ahead of Labour but not comfortably enough to ensure a nationwide victory. The Tory Party continued to lag a long way behind the other two and the votes of the people intimidated by Natalie and her recruits rarely went to it. These votes went invariably to the Malonist Party because the harassed voters were more willing to support a civilized pioneer for the underdog than bullies claiming to sympathize with it. Natalie thought it would be worth taking a few people displaying Tory stickers but did not put so much energy into this less important project.

* * *

The southern constituency of Hammerdean was not typical

of the many constituencies they had covered during their three-week-old programme of terror. Hammerdean was a Tory seat where the polls showed the Tories to be marginally more popular than the Malonists, with Labour lagging behind. Even the other southern constituencies, encompassing the stockbroker belt, were, if only fractionally, more Malonist in inclination than Tory.

It was 6 o'clock on a cold crisp morning. Natalie returned from her chosen hotel to the boys, who had spent the night in an unused car park. She seemed in more of a hurry than usual, and threw the sachets of powder at them.

'OK, boys, get on your spoons and load! We've a hundred and fifty miles to cover. We're doing Hammerdean and we're heading for white working-class areas only. I've got to dress in a certain rather peculiar way which means you'll all have to sit in the car till I'm done.'

Samuel Johnson Street was one of several streets that Natalie had to cover in Hammerdean. It was clean and tidy and consisted of newly-painted Victorian houses. These were owned by working-class, thifty, cautious-living whites, many of whom were racially prejudiced, not so much on grounds of nationality, but of colour.

Natalie walked down Samuel Johnson Street wearing a mink coat, a string of imitation pearls and an imitation diamond bracelet, all hired from a theatrical shop. She was surprised to see so many Conservative Party stickers in the windows and regretted that she would have to work harder and faster than she had anticipated.

She banged heavily on the door of the first house, which belonged to Ethel Adler, a tired, frightened, haggard, thirty-five-year-old housewife, battered regularly by her husband who was a history teacher in a grammar school. He thought it wasteful to vote National Front if he could vote for the Tories more effectively, regardless of the decline in their popularity. Mrs Adler was the daughter of an abstemious

Methodist preacher and she had always voted Tory because of her views on immigration. Although she was classified as a starry-eyed reactionary, she was timid and submissive in her private behaviour, believing that a woman's place was by the hearth and that it was her duty to allow her husband to use her body whether she felt in the mood for this or not.

Mrs Adler had five young children, all of whom had flu and rattling coughs. They hung around her, coughing, and gave an impression of Hogarthian squalor.

George Adler had given his wife a vicious beating the night before because his evening meal was burned. In addition she had flu. When she staggered to her front door and opened it to find an ostentatiously dressed woman, over a decade younger than herself, blowing smoke into her face from a cigarette in a 1920's gold-plated cigarette holder, she bent over and had a violent coughing fit from which she took five minutes to recover.

Natalie would have been less frightened had Mrs Adler pointed a gun at her. She had learned to face Badger's repulsive withdrawal symptoms. She had been threatened on several occasions with knives and cudgels and people threatening to slash her face with a razor. Once she had even been pushed down a steep flight of steps, cutting her head open above the hairline. She had been faced with every kind of violence and emerged unshaken and even amused. But this woman was more dangerous in her eyes than anyone she had met on her visits before. This woman had a cough, a fever and germs.

Natalie had not been faced with germs so far during her terror binge. She turned away from Mrs Adler, took a long swig of whisky and told herself she would have to go through with it. In her mind she saw a flashback of the film that had impressed her as a child. She saw Taras Bulba's son galloping over the ravine and the pieces of rock disturbed in his wake, kicked into the ravine by the horse's hooves. She remembered her promise that she would be as brave as he in adversity, for a brave person is not a person who is not afraid to do things others are afraid of. A truly brave person does the thing that frightens him most in the world, a thing that may seem trivial to others.

She was about to turn away, but the galloping horse's hooves thundered through her brain.

'I'm afraid I must come in, madam.'

Mrs Adler beckoned her into a living-room, adorned with wedding photographs and a painting of a cat. In the corner was a small framed newspaper photograph of Enoch Powell. The children, their faces worn with flu, ran around the woman in circles while she told them to go to bed but they ignored her.

Natalie sat down and put her feet up on the table, flaunting a pile of Tory Party leaflets.

'Any chance of rustling up a gin and tonic with ice and lemon?' she asked, mimicking a Sloane Ranger accent.

Mrs Adler started coughing again and wrung her hands.

'We always vote Tory here. I don't keep drink in the house, though. My husband's an alcoholic.'

'No drink? But, my dear, whatever do you do when you receive guests? Surely you don't serve – what's that strange stuff you've got over there – Lucozade?'

Mrs Adler went on wringing her hands. One of her children was sick on the carpet. Mrs Adler began to cry. Natalie desperately tried to fight the hideous fear that obsessed her by thinking of the pieces of rock being kicked into the ravine by the horse's hooves. She forced herself to speak.

'I'm most awfully sorry breezing in on your humble but worthy home like this. At my public school our headmistress taught us to be charitable towards the . . . er . . . less well off. Well, I think this lounge is an awfully good show. Jolly well done!'

Mrs Adler stared at her aghast. The children were hacking again. Natalie continued to blow smoke in the woman's face.

'Oh, aren't I beastly? I had no idea this was Nanny's day off.'

'We've no Nanny.'

'You mean you're *between* Nannies? But how perfectly mizzy for you! A damned tiresome period! I know it only too well, as I have so few servants myself, but at least I've got a nursery-maid, so that helps a bit.'

Mrs Adler wiped the sweat from her brow. Had she been less lonely and sad she would have asked Natalie to leave.

'Some tea?'

'Tea?'

'Would you like some?'

'I don't drink tea. I either take gin and tonic or nothing at all. Now to get to the point. I notice you've been good enough to sport a Tory Party sticker in your window. I'm so glad you've voting for us, which is why I thought I might just drop in on you to express gratitude on the Party's behalf.'

'I had been intending to vote Tory,' said Mrs Adler, 'but now I'm not sure I really want to. You're so patronizing and if all Tories are like you, I don't want them in office.'

'Come now, my good woman, I didn't mean to sound patronizing. It's just that all the Tories I mix with seem grander than you. One would expect a Labour person to live in a place like this, but it's a bit of a slap in the eye if it's a Conservative.'

'That's enough to make anyone vote Labour,' said Mrs Adler after another long coughing fit that Natalie thought would never stop.

'Damned nasty cough, what! Bet you've got something seriously wrong with your chest. I know a cracking good chap in Harley Street who's dashed hot on chests. You may be able to afford him. He only charges fifty guineas for a consultation, which is nothing nowadays, is it?'

'That's about the total of the housekeeping money I get monthly. If the Tories want to win they ought to send out better people than you. I never thought I could possibly be persuaded to vote Labour till I met you.'

'But, my dear woman, you'd be bonkers to go and do that. Besides you do *own* this charming little house, don't you?'

'Yes.'

'Do you realize it's Labour policy to force all owners of private property to surrender it to the State? You'd be able to live here, of course. But instead of paying a mortgage, you'd have an absolutely beastly little man coming round asking for rent – at least that's what one of Daddy's chauffeurs says.'

'There's a third party, called the Malonist Party, too,' said Mrs Adler. 'To me that sounds like the only party that doesn't go to these horrible extremes. Do you know anything about Rex Malone?'

'Not an awful lot, except what the papers say.'

'Do you think he's a nice man?' enquired Mrs Adler cautiously.

'I don't know him. Only his policies, which to people who really matter, sound pretty lax, liberal and do-gooding. I'm sure you know the kind of thing I mean.'

'What are his policies on immigration? My eyes aren't so good these days and I wouldn't be seen dead in glasses. I never get a chance to read the papers.'

Natalie looked at the framed newspaper photograph of Enoch Powell in the corner of the room and blew more smoke in Mrs Adler's face.

'Well, being more English than the English, most papers say he's a bit racist actually, now you come to ask. At least Daddy's butler says that, but there again he's black.'

(The remark about Malone's policies on immigration was untrue, but she knew the woman's persuasion and took advantage of it.)

'I'm thinking of voting for him. My husband never reads

the papers but I listen to the radio a lot when he's at work, and politics is the only thing he listens to me about. I've made up my mind I'm going to vote for Mr Malone.'

'Bully for you! I can't force you not to, although I'd like to. I've got to go now, and do say "toodle-oo" to those poor neglected children for me. Jolly bad luck being caught between Nannies, what!'

'I've never been able to afford a Nanny!'

'I'm sure your dear friend, Mr Malone, will help you out, now you've decided to vote for him after all the trouble I took coming here.'

'Who's that thug banging at my window?'

Natalie turned and saw Badger's sweat-drenched face and mad eyes.

'I need another shot!' he yelled.

Mrs Adler went to the window, coughing and trembling with terror at the hideous spectacle of scarred flesh.

'Don't mind him, my good woman,' said Natalie, 'that's Badger. He's a smack-soak as you can see, but he works dashed hard for the Conservative Party once he's topped up, don't you, Badge?'

'For the *Conservative* Party?' gasped Mrs Adler.

'Why yes, dear, someone's got to. It's mizzy for Badger but his services are indispensable and he's going to drive our supporters to the polls.'

Mrs Adler ushered Natalie outside and tore down her Tory Party sticker. She staggered upstairs and collapsed on her bed, falling into a deep sleep until her husband got her up to cook his evening meal. She told him about her experience that day. Though for the wrong reason, he too agreed to vote for Malone.

When she had recovered from flu Mrs Adler went to London to visit the offices of the *Fleet Street Gazette*. The paper wrote a long article about unreasonable behaviour displayed by canvassers for both the Labour Party and the

Conservative Party and concluded that so far the Malonist Party was the only party whose canvassers behaved decently. When Natalie read the article she felt another wave of guilt about her underhandedness and the manner in which it contrasted with the honesty of Malone, whom she knew she would never be able to tell about her effective, if very unsubtle exploits without losing his friendship.

* * *

LIONEL CRANFIELD DENIES HOMOSEXUAL TENDENCIES

The headline appeared over a short article on one of the inside pages of a Sunday tabloid.

'The leader of the Opposition, Mr Lionel Cranfield, has firmly denied any homosexual tendencies,' read the article. 'When asked to explain his flippant remark to a gathering of supporters of withdrawal from Ulster, "I find the para-military uniforms worn by the IRA at funerals sexually attractive," he furiously denied wording the statement in such a way. "I only meant to say I thought they looked neat and tidy," he told reporters, adding, "I am a happily married man and get no pleasure out of staring at anyone but my wife." '

Cranfield wore horn-rimmed spectacles. He was thin, nondescript and bald. His popularity was more due to the electorate's dissatisfaction with the Tories than to any attractiveness that might have accompanied his colourless, introverted personality.

Politics had always been his principal interest. Privately, he associated the values of the extreme left with the needs of oppressed minority groups, in particular homosexuals. He had married to save his public image. His wife was tolerant of the homosexuality he denied and appeared with him in public. They occupied separate rooms at different ends of a secluded luxury bungalow surrounded by two acres of wasteland and protected by a barbed wire fence. In their respective places, husband and wife received their respective lovers.

Though graced with a brilliant mind that he had trained to associate with thoughts instead of emotions, Cranfield suffered from a serious and incapacitating handicap. He was an intermittent depressive. The attacks were chronic and when they came, which they did several times a week, they would last for as long as three hours at a time. It was during these moods that his promiscuous indulgences got out of control. He would confine them to a gym attached to his bungalow. Once he had consumed enough alochol to drown his gloom, his physical needs became more addictive and his methods of obtaining young men, extravagant and restless. The men were financed by Labour Party funds. Mrs Cranfield tried to persuade her husband to be more moderate in his indulgences. Sometimes weeks would pass by without him returning to his old habits, but as the General Election came closer, his episodes became more frequent and much harder for him to control.

There were no windows in the gym and he was discreet in his binges once within its walls. He usually wore a mask. No visitor to the premises was to know who lived there, because Cranfield's official residence was a spartan flat in Greymills City, the capital of the constituency of Greymills. His binges helped him work. If he had had a 'good' night, he would be cheerful the next morning and free from the attacks of gloom for at least three days.

He was unperturbed by the short article in the tabloid about his statements to reporters. His remark about the uniforms would be taken as a joke, he told himself. Besides, his buck-toothed grinning wife's photograph next to the article bearing the caption 'Opposition Leader's loyal wife', would help to dispel public suspicions. Greymills was a vital Labour stronghold and as safe as a fortress as far as he was concerned. It had had a twenty thousand majority in the last General Election, the strongest Labour seat in the country.

The Greymills Labour Party had a number of respectable, industrious volunteers working for it. But some of the volunteers were Hell's Angels, soccer fans and unemployed youths, who, when not working for Cranfield, indulged in crime to fight the boredom of the dole. They had been primed to be polite when canvassing, but within the Labour Party's headquarters, they shocked other workers by being rowdy and gross. Most of them were heterosexuals and they would bring their women along with them. Cranfield noted those who were not heterosexuals and made a point of being cold and dismissive towards them.

It had been a tedious, uneventful Sunday morning for Cranfield's boys. Eight of them sat at a table in the headquarters, banging down their fists and singing a coarse song called 'Maggie, Maggie, show us your leg'. Suddenly, they were alerted by the appearance of an exquisite-looking boy in his late teens or early twenties, wearing a tight-fitting leather suit. The bomber jacket bearing naval insignia was zipped to the neck. He wore a leather peaked cap with no hair showing underneath it. Joey was among the boys. He was a homosexual and stared at the newcomer with a glazed expression of lust on his face.

'Come on, Joey, you're just a bloody poofter!' said one of the Hell's Angels.

'Lay off Joey, will you?'

The man who said this was known as Cecil Buck. He was Joey's lover and was loyal to him, despite his fear of the tougher boys. The newcomer feared there would be a fight, so he interrupted them by swinging a bicycle chain in the air, chewing gum in the slow rhythmic motion of a lion about to pounce. There was a long silence. Eventually, the boy spoke. The others were struck by his voice rather than the words he uttered.

His voice was abnormally deep and sounded like a caricature. It alternated between being harsh and .gentle. The accent, like its pitch, was carried to an extravagant extreme. It was exaggeratedly Irish and alternated abruptly between a Southern and Northern accent. The boy's voice might have deceived an Englishman but not an Irishman. As he spoke at length, it sounded less theatrical and more genuine.

He had painted the insides of his front molar teeth with Bitter Aloes, forcing his tongue to curl and lodge itself in the back of his mouth to prevent the Irish accent lapsing.

When the Hell's Angels had finished staring at him in bewilderment, they asked him who he was. The boy did not answer and strode to the table with a navvy's lurch and heaved his weight onto it. He examined Joey expectantly, still swinging the bicycle chain above his head.

The Hell's Angels got nervous. They couldn't work out whether the newcomer wanted a fight or whether someone among them owed him money. In their fear they decided to make the maximum amount of noise by banging their fists on the table and continued their song which had been interrupted:

'A rich girl uses cotton wool. A poor girl uses bumph,
But Maggie keeps two vampire bats and feeds them once a month.'

The boy blushed because he thought the song was vulgar. When he pulled himself together he spat out his gum and slapped it on the table.

'Would you be talking about the bitch that orders innocent Irish women and children to be slaughtered on the streets of their own country?' he shouted, pointing at Joey.

'You're right. We want her out.'

'That's just what I'm here for, to come to talk to Mr Cranfield about what he proposes to do to bring the stinking bastards home.'

‘You mean the Army?’

‘You’re onto it! And this is the only party that can do it. Where’s Mr Cranfield’s office?’

‘You go through that door over there,’ directed Joey, ‘then down a long corridor with red doors. It’s the second door on the left and his name’s on the door.’

The boy met his adoring stare and took Joey by surprise as his eyes clouded over with a look of fear and claustrophobia.

‘Thank you kindly for your help,’ said the boy. ‘I’ll be bringing myself back when I’ve had a word with Mr Cranfield.’

Lionel Cranfield had been drinking because he felt tired and gloomy. He had worked all night. The liquor had exhausted him even more but had washed away the gloom. When the mood was not brought on by tiredness alone, it was exacerbated by the conflict between his two images. One of these was the addictively promiscuous homosexual. The other was the respectably married politician and public figure. The additional fear that he might lose the election had increased his feeling of pessimism.

The liquor had heightened his spirits. It was a Sunday. He had no major commitments that day, so he looked forward to a day in bed, ideally with a companion. He felt as if he had been given a pre-med before an anaesthetic and no longer cared what he did.

He replied, ‘Come in’ to the loud knock on the door, which was flung open, banging against a table. He thought at first the intruder was the father of one of the boys he had used. When he saw the delicate-featured figure in leather he had a sudden urge to rush over to the boy, who was standing with one leg on a chair, flaunting the artificial virility simulated with a rolled-up scarf. The boy was chewing gum slowly and purposefully. He walked over to Cranfield, toying with his bicycle chain.

Cranfield felt hot all over.

'May I have the honour of an introduction, sir?'

'Sean Kennedy!' snarled the boy.

'You make that sound like a swear word, Mr Kennedy.'

'It's the name my father bore, God rest his soul,' exclaimed the boy and crossed himself, adding, 'he was shot by the British,' in a voice scarcely above a whisper.

'I'm sorry to hear that. Not all the British are bad. I'd like you to think I was on your side.'

The boy stared at Cranfield, menacingly chewing gum. He pulled out a copy of the *Morning Star*. The paper had an editorial urging the electorate to vote Labour to ensure withdrawal from Northern Ireland.

The boy shook the paper out like a dish cloth and rattled it in Cranfield's face. Then he eased his weight onto Cranfield's desk and leaned on his hands with one leg bent and the other straight.

'You have the hands of a lady,' said Cranfield shyly.

The boy sat bolt upright. The suddenness of the movement startled Cranfield.

'I may have the hands of a woman but I have the heart of an Irishman.'

Cranfield was a little puzzled by the fact that his companion seemed to be struggling to keep a straight face, which was not in harmony with the passion behind his words. He attributed this strange finding to the boy's nerves.

When he had finished reading the editorial, he took his glasses off and looked at the boy. He wiped the sweat from his brow with his sleeve.

'OK, son, dear, so you've read the facts. What are you going to do about Ireland?'

'It's very flattering to be called "son" by a boy less than half my age. I like you for it.'

'You're not answering my question. Only if you take a proper stand will I get my family and friends living in this country to vote for you.'

Cranfield put his glasses back on again and stared at the boy's thighs.

'Naturally we're going to bring the troops home,' he said.

'You don't sound all that convinced. There's nothing I wouldn't do to stop my homeland being ravaged by British torturers and conniving politicians.'

Cranfield bent over to pick something up which he had deliberately thrown on the floor. Withdrawal from Northern Ireland was high on his party's agenda but he decided it would not be in his immediate interests to say this to the boy.

'Did I hear you say there was nothing you wouldn't do for Ireland?' he whispered conspiratorially.

'I'd sink to prostitution for the Cause.'

Cranfield swivelled round on his chair so that the boy would not see the expression of torture on his face. 'Go and lock the door, Mr Kennedy,' he gasped.

The boy did as he was told. He advanced towards Cranfield and ran the index finger of his right hand along the outline of the older man's nose. Cranfield broke out in a cold sweat but managed to prevent himself from throwing himself onto the boy.

'Will you come to my gym?' he said hoarsely.

'I'm not a physical fitness type.'

'My gym has no windows. I'm sure you know what I want you for.'

'I'll have to be warning you. I've got a venereal infection. I got really sore about the British after a rally and to let it all out I went wild down a Belfast public convenience,' said the boy in a despairing tone, but for a reason unbeknown to Cranfield suddenly burst into hysterical giggles.

'You're a very giggly young man, Mr Kennedy, even when you speak of tragic things.'

'Has no one told you that an Irishman always laughs when he wants to cry and vice versa?'

'In that case I shall make a point of not saying anything

funny to you,' said Cranfield, and an awkward silence ensued which was broken by Kennedy.

'I know four boys who will be able to help you in the kind of things you might want to do.'

'Are they as beautiful as you?'

'In this life you must learn not to ask for too much, but they are not infected and they'll be doing the things you might ask.'

'Then bring them to me, in God's name!' shouted Cranfield.

'I'll bring the boys but I'll be telling you one thing, and that is that if on coming to power, you don't do what you promise, I'll have every limb blown from your body.'

'You don't need to make that kind of threat. I keep my promises. Now you bring me the boys.'

'Before I do, might I be asking what precisely you intend to do with them?'

'Not to hurt them. Only to do the kind of things we gays usually do except with a bit of relish.'

'Relish?'

Cranfield blushed profusely. He fought to find words but none came. Eventually he managed to express himself with the stammering repetition of a child in a court of law.

'I . . . don't really know how to put it. Considering your circumstances, you might get the wrong idea.'

Cranfield clawed the blotter on his desk. This was something he always did when he was nervous.

'Would you get to the point? I've not got all day to sit around listening to British politicians who can't even string a sentence together.'

'It's not easy to tell you what I want because you might get the wrong idea and feel insulted. I want this particular thing done because it reminds me of something that is noble.'

'Get on with it or I'll leave this office.'

'It's all basically because I associate it with heroism. All the paraphernalia has a fatal attraction for me. I like the boys to wear *these* clothes.'

'Which clothes?'

Cranfield looked flustered. He awkwardly produced a photograph from his inside pocket. It showed a Provisional IRA funeral. The pallbearers and mourners wore berets, dark glasses and leather jackets. He passed the photograph with shaking hands over to Kennedy, who looked at it for a while and handed it back.

'What you are asking me to do is really rather odd,' he said mildly. 'Besides, who supplies you with this clothing?'

Cranfield beckoned him towards a locked cupboard in the corner of his office. It was an aluminium chest with a combination lock which he opened, spilling its contents on the floor. The chest contained leather jackets, berets, pairs of dark glasses, manacles, chains, whips, strange-looking suction tubes and instruments of torture.

Kennedy did not look as surprised as Cranfield expected.

'Am I to understand that you are going to whip the boys?'

'That's all part of it.'

'I'm not sure I can persuade my boys to do this but I'll try and talk to them.'

Cranfield became inappropriately excited.

'You've got to do your best. I try to get a group of boys together and use all this gear when my spirits get low and I need a lift. I've got six boys working for me on this project alone.'

'Project?'

'Yes. I like to call it that. They don't know who I am because of the mask. I can give you two computerized cards opening the outer and inner gate leading to the bungalow. I'll give you directions to get there and if your boys agree, I'd like them brought along tonight.'

'Fine.'

'Wait a minute. I want to show you something.'

Cranfield stripped and dragged on one of the paramilitary uniforms. He looked at his image in a full-length mirror. 'Do I look ready for it?' he asked intensely and grabbed Kennedy by the arm. Kennedy struggled desperately to keep a straight face.

'I think you're a raving lunatic,' he said, his voice raised in mock anger. 'You're making mockery of what the heroes in these glorious uniforms represent . . .'

He tried to finish his sentence but collapsed in hysterical giggles which intensified when he struggled to control them.

'What's funny?'

The boy pulled himself together.

'I'd never expect an Englishman, however liberal, to understand that Irish history had been so tragic from the beginning that if an Irishman can't occasionally look upon it as a black comedy, he'd never have the guts to fight back against the British. Every Irishman and woman would be slitting their throats if they didn't know how to laugh sometimes about how sick it all is. So if you want to know why I broke down just now, that's the reason. It's my way of showing grief at seeing the honour of Erin mocked and her sons and daughters butchered.'

'I'm sorry I offended you. I didn't mean to. In using these uniforms for this purpose I don't mean to mock or degrade the dignity of the fine men like yourself who fought and still fight for Ireland. Perhaps I do these strange things because it excites me to associate something perverse with what is fine and noble.'

He might have been a sympathizer with all political movements committed to British withdrawal, but his private activities had nothing to do with his political beliefs, despite what he had told the boy. He had often asked himself why he had this fatal attraction for men in IRA uniforms. In his immediate consciousness there was nothing directly political about his obsession. It may have been the dark glasses, combined with the macabre, carnival-style elegance in not just one person but a mass of identically clad people, that set his blood on fire. Indeed, he saw a rare and perverse, indefinable beauty in something associated with evil in England. This was combined with the slow, reverent beat of 'The Wearing of the Green', the rousing marching song played at a Dead March pace. The song was associated with IRA funerals. When he played it over loudspeakers in his gym it provided the greatest erotic cocktail he could ever hope to experience.

Kennedy appeared satisfied with his explanation. 'All right,' he said, 'I'll go along with you, but I still think there is something sinister and ludicrous about the way you entertain yourself. I don't know why you can't have a fockin' game of darts when you get blue like everyone else. I'll only help you in return for what you promise to do when you gain office.'

'Do you think I will get elected?' Cranfield asked, as if confiding in the boy.

'Of that I have absolutely no doubt. I know you *will* gain office and if I didn't I wouldn't bother to waste my time agreeing to do all these things for you.'

* * *

When Kennedy turned up at the bungalow in the grey Citroën with Ted, Nick, Bozo and Badger, Cranfield's first reaction was one of shock. As he looked at them more closely, he felt the barrier between the extreme ugliness and physical degradation in Kennedy's boys, and the contrasting beauty of Kennedy himself, inexplicably thin. He regarded supreme hideousness to be as rousing as beauty.

'We're all going to do a different kind of job now, boys,' Kennedy had said. 'If you don't go along with it, I'll have to withdraw your junk rations, so you'll have to do what I say and what our new friend says, however odd it might be. Our friend's name is John Bowden. He is going to whip you. It won't hurt you at all. As you're all itching and scratching most of the time between getting cranked up, you'll find it will relieve the itching. You'll have to put on funny-looking clothes, and do general sexual duties. I know you all know what I mean by that – the things you had to do to pay for your shots before I found you first.'

The boys said they couldn't care what happened to them as long as they could have their injections.

'Good,' said Kennedy. 'Mr Bowden wants to heat up your gear for you and give you the injections himself. He thinks the way you're doing it with just one needle and no disinfectant is unhygienic and you'll end up with hepatitis, thrombosis, gangrene, Aids and God knows what else. I've got a set of clean disposable syringes. Before you get together and do whatever he asks you to do, he has very kindly agreed to fix you all. He was a doctor before he retired and he knows how to do these things better than I do.'

Badger remarked, 'It's funny but that man looks like Lionel Cranfield, the Labour Leader, except he's bald.' (Cranfield always wore a wig in public.)

'It's also funny, but I happen to look like Paul Newman.'

Cranfield had been persuaded, if reluctantly, to give the boys their injections, because Kennedy had told him their hands shook too much to find the right arteries. He said he was much too squeamish to give the boys their injections himself.

Kennedy had taught himself to use a video camera. Once he had found a hole in the wall of the gym, he inserted the camera lens that could zoom and pan according to its user's whims, and supported it by a pile of books on top of a table. The hole in the wall was nowhere near the door Cranfield would leave by, which gave the boy plenty of time to move his apparatus. There was no one else in the bungalow, as Mrs Cranfield was busy campaigning on her husband's behalf.

There were ten young men in the gym besides Cranfield, who was not dressed in an IRA uniform but as a woman. This time, he had not bothered to wear a mask. He wore neither wig nor make-up and when the camera zoomed on him his features were unmistakable. The ten young men wore IRA uniforms. An empty seven-foot box representing a coffin lay on the floor. The video camera got a close-up shot of Cranfield heating the white powder in four clean spoons, disinfecting the skin with a cotton wool swab and injecting each of the boys, who queued up like Dickensian workhouse waifs pining for their gruel. Once the boys were loaded, they assembled in two regimented lines on Cranfield's instructions, preparing to go through the sinister and bizarre ritual, which was accompanied by the slow but rousing marching dirge sung by the Dubliners, a group specializing in Irish songs. The song was 'The Wearing of the Green'. Through the walls, an occasional whipcrack could be heard but the cry of pain from its consenting victim was partially drowned by the lachrymose stirring refrain:

'I met with Napper Tandy and he took me by the hand.
He said: "How's poor old Ireland? How does our country stand?"
'Tis the most distressful country that I have ever seen;
They be hanging men and women for the wearing of the Green.'

Kennedy was not a boy to be easily shocked, but on this occasion he was absolutely aghast. He was knowledgeable about sexual perversion but he had never witnessed something on such a sickening and vile scale as this. The things he saw that night were more extreme than those he had seen in any pornographic film or book.

He fainted. In about two minutes he came round. Perhaps it was the continuation of the song that had woken him.

Between the acts of depraved bestial degradation, the two

regimented lines marched backwards and forwards past the camera, followed by the transvestite who cracked the whip in rhythm to the song:

'Have you heard it, Paddy dear, the news that's going round?
The shamrock is forbidden by law to grow on Irish ground.
St Patrick's Day's forbidden and his colours can't be seen,
For the English have forbidden by law the wearing of the Green.'

Then the even more sinister perversions, each more harrowing than the one before, started. The camera had not fallen from its perch when Kennedy fainted. He had overcome his initial shock and watched the carnal carnival with morbid curiosity. He had filmed all he felt he needed to film.

Badger, Ted, Nick and Bozo staggered out and got into the Citroën. Kennedy left no address and told Cranfield he would be bringing his boys back the following night.

'It was all a bit rough,' Badger said mildly, after his injection. 'What is shamrock anyway? Is it an opiate weed like hash?'

Kennedy laughed. 'No, of course not, you idiot. It's a sort of wild weed. It's like clover.'

'Then why is it forbidden to grow on Irish ground?'

'It's an old saying. It's a symbol of being Irish. In the days when that song was written, if you were Irish, you weren't allowed to wear it in your buttonhole.'

'It was a good song, though. Can you sing it?'

'I can indeed but I'm trying to drive a car now.'

'You won't make us go back to that perve tomorrow, will you?'

'No. As of tomorrow, you'll all be free. There's what I've got left of your heroin. It's now up to you to distribute it among yourselves. After that there'll be none left and you'll have to manage on your own. Besides, no form of prostitution is as nasty as what you had to do tonight.'

'You're right. So are you just dumping us?'

'Yes. I'm giving you £20 each, and I'm leaving you at Greymills Station. You've all been very good, but now the time has come for us to part.'

'That's fine by us,' said Badger, as the Citroën approached Greymills Station. 'But tell me one thing – why are you so odd?'

'Because sometimes they make 'em odd, Badger dear – so long!'

* * *

Kennedy made two copies of the video he had recorded. He deposited one in the safe of the National Westminster Bank in Camberwell Green and kept the other two with him. As he watched the film in the privacy of his bedroom in a five-star hotel in Barfax East, he was surprised he was no longer horrified by what he saw. Repulsion and shock were replaced by a macabre curiosity and that in turn was replaced by something akin to attraction for the clothing worn by the men, the attraction grossly enhanced by the background song. But Kennedy had a capacity for self-discipline and he forced himself, if with a great effort, to suppress his erotic fascination for something with such sinister associations. Besides, he had been on his own for long enough. He longed for the company of friends and the fact that it was 2 a.m. did not deter him from dialling the number of a house where he knew he would be welcome.

* * *

Malone had been addressing nightshift factory workers all night. Hortense and Miss Bechtold were alone in the house when she was woken by the telephone.

'Yes, who's that?' came the shrill, anxious voice, the accent more markedly French than usual.

'It's me. I'm sorry if I woke you.'

'Natalie, where on earth have you been? You never went to see your family at all because Rex rang your father who said he hadn't seen you. Whatever have you been doing all these weeks? We've all been worried about you.'

'I'm sorry. I should have told you. I've been ill – very ill and staying with some friends.'

'And are you now fully recovered?' Hortense's tone suggested she was not convinced she was being told the truth.

'Yes. I'm better. But it's been a bit heavy. It's something to do with a man.'

'Ah, now I understand you! You should have said that first. Is it bad?'

'May I come and stay in your house for the weekend? I can come tonight. And I want to see you again.'

Hortense was used to Natalie's abrupt methods of propositioning herself and instead of considering it rude, she considered it rather charming.

'You know very well you will always be welcome and I won't ask you a lot of difficult questions, because I know how nasty this sort of thing is. If ever you want to confide in me or tell me about this man, I'll always be there to listen. You *do* know that, don't you?'

There was no answer from the other end of the line, only the sound of loud breathing, the onset of tears.

'Are you still there?'

'Yes.'

'I will leave the key in the corner by the door. I won't be up to see you, though. Everyone will be in bed.'

'You *are* kind! What bedroom will you be putting me in? I don't want to wander round waking people up.'

'The bed is made in Arianne's room. She's with her aunt. And don't take one of your 4 a.m. baths. It gets on Miss Bechtold's nerves and she's often complained in the past. It's not that I mind. And you can stay as long as you like. I'd like you to think of it as your home. You know that, don't you?'

'Again you're very kind, but I only want to stay the weekend. And there's something else I want you to understand.'

'Yes?'

'I think much more highly of you than you will ever know.'

A pause ensued. Hortense thought she was genuine but was puzzled by her intensity. Natalie broke the silence with her usual terseness. 'I'm coming now. I won't wake you when I come. Bye!'

She left her two bigger-than-average suitcases in the hall. One contained her clothing and cosmetics. The other, her pills.

Malone returned to the house at 6 a.m. When he saw the two matching navy blue suitcases with the silver initials N.K. staring ostentatiously at him, he reacted with a mixture of pleasant surprise, indeed relief, that the owner of the two suitcases had come to no harm, and anger that he had been let down and lied to.

Hortense had a long talk with Natalie the next day. She lied repeatedly to Hortense and her task was made more difficult by having to speak French.

Malone found the two women in the kitchen.

'You *are* mean, Ma,' he said. 'You never told me Natalie was coming to stay and you didn't give me a chance to look forward to it.'

Natalie was touched by the remark and hugged Malone. It was the first time she had really felt proud of her exploits. Tears would have come easily to her at that moment had they been summoned, but she felt glowing and triumphant. She remembered her conversation with Hortense when they had first met. 'We must all find Napoleon within ourselves,' Hortense had said, at a time when she needed strength. She had sought him and had almost found him.

Malone interrupted her pleasant thoughts. 'You know

you've caused a lot of trouble, missy. You told me you were going home. When I heard nothing from you, I had to ring up Selwyn. He said you hadn't been home at all. Next time you disappear, you should have enough consideration to tell someone at least what you're doing, because for all we knew you could have had an accident.'

'You're right. I ought to have kept in touch with you. I'm sorry.'

'So am I' he replied tersely. The dry remark amused her. When she laughed out loud, he softened. He took her hair and wound it round his wrist.

'Next time, I shall have to hold onto this to stop you getting into mischief.'

She looked at him sideways, her eyes happy. She felt no envy for Hortense, only admiration for her determination to consummate his personal glory. Both she and Hortense were trying to do good. Natalie had chosen wickedness in the interests of ultimate goodness. Hortense had chosen purity and honesty as she knew no other path. She thought fleetingly of the two sisters in *Justine*. She saw much of Justine in both Hortense and Malone. In their own ways they reminded her of the completely virtuous sister who did no wrong in the face of adversity. Natalie herself identified, though not to such an exaggeratedly unsubtle extent, with Justine's sister, Juliette, who committed one crime after another for personal vanity and advancement.

Miss Bechtold entered the room quietly.

'The night editor of the *Malonist Voice* on the line for you urgently.'

'Thank you. Put him through and put the telephone on the table, please.'

Miss Bechtold did as she was told, tidied a pile of papers away from the table and left the room.

'Yes, Stanley?' (That was the *Malonist Voice* night editor's first name.)

'It's about our Anti-Heroin Campaign that's to be started in Monday's edition.' (The night editor's voice was loud and clear, so Natalie could hear every word he said.)

'What about it, Stanley? You said this was an urgent call.'

'You approved the Monday front page headline: BABY ADDICTED TO HEROIN.'

'Yes. Naturally, I did. We went through the lay-out together and we're going to have a picture of the baby alongside it. What's the problem?'

'One of the team has just got a significant scoop from Greymills. It's pretty sordid. We feel it would be more suitable for the front page than the baby story.'

'Greymills? That's Cranfield's constituency, not that it will alter the vote much. Let's have the story and keep it brief, for Christ's sake.'

'An unemployed tramp aged eighteen knifed three other tramps in a water closet near Greymills Station. He then gave himself a massive overdose of heroin, enough to supply his needs for a week. The man's syringe was embedded in the neck. The police are convinced he killed the three others to get the drug off them.'

'Bugger what he killed the others for! Have you got a picture of the man with the syringe?'

'Yes. It's as close up as Manning' (a bright, ambitious photographer on the *Malonist Voice*) 'could get.'

'Good. Shove the picture on the right-hand side of the front page.'

'All right. I've thought of a series of headlines but I feel I ought to consult you, in case you can think of something better. What about "Evil Cancer Worsens"?'

'No, Stanley. That sounds too much like a late night film. What about "Hang the Bastard Who Gave It To Him".'

'Should we put an exclamation mark after that, sir?'

'What the hell for? This is the *Malonist Voice*, not the bloody *Soviet Weekly*.'

The night editor laughed. 'If we use so many words, there won't be much room left for your own photograph, sir,' he retorted.

'You'll have to work it out, Stanley. I'm not your Nanny.'

'Very good, sir.'

'I take it you've got the names of the syringe man and the men he killed.'

'The syringe man's name was Eric Samuels but he was known as "Badger". The others were Edward Mason, Nicholas Ward and Bill Oliver, known as Bozo. There's just one more thing, but we haven't got enough facts to make a story out of it yet. A clean-shaven boy with an Irish accent was seen speaking to all four of them while entering the station.'

'So what? He was probably asking for directions or something. I don't see what that's got to do with it.'

'Perhaps the boy with the Irish accent sold it to them. I think it's worth sending someone up there to look into it.'

'Screw the boy with the Irish accent!' said Malone, adding in a quieter voice away from the telephone, 'for God's sake, Natalie, that was one of Hortense's favourite jugs you've just knocked over and smashed. You're a bloody nuisance.'

'The boy really is worth following up,' persisted the night editor, although it was not his job to tell his proprietor where to send reporters. His job was to organize the lay-out of each page.

'The boy is not worth following up, Stanley. He's not relevant to the story unless for any reason he comes back into the limelight,' replied Malone.

'I still think there could be more to it than that, sir.'

There was a pause, because the night editor was nervous of Malone. Then he added, 'I'd better just let you know this.'

Malone sighed heavily into the mouthpiece. 'What, Stanley?'

'An eye-witness thinks the boy's first name is Sean.'

Malone sighed more heavily into the mouthpiece to show

his frustration and leant over the table supporting his forehead with the receiver, his eyebrows raised in the exasperated expression he always wore when addressing an idiot.

'I think you'll find that quite a lot of Irishmen are called Sean,' he said quietly.

'But Mr Malone . . .'

'Goodbye, Stanley!'

* * *

Hortense was going through a list of canvassing sheets when Natalie entered her study.

'Hullo. Have you come to give me a hand?'

'I'm in some unpleasant emotional trouble. I'd like to stay here with you these last ten days to help you, but my mind is so disturbed that I'd be a hindrance. I need a week to think something over. I've a hard decision to make and when I've made it, I'll come back.'

'Is it because of that young man you were talking about?'

'Yes.'

'Is it unrequited love?'

'It's very much worse. It's unrequiting love.'

'Anything you can tell me? It will make you feel better.'

'I'd like to tell you but it's so bad I can't.'

'I understand. You know where to come when you've sorted it out.'

'I don't know what to say except how unworthy I feel of your friendship.'

'Think nothing of it!' Hortense went back to her sheets. As she leafed through them she sang a song of Edith Piaf's called 'Padam, padam'. She liked to sing this song when she was happy. When Malone had visited her rooms in Paris before their engagement, she sang it when unwrapping flowers he sent her. He would watch her without her knowledge. In spite of his toughness the song would bring tears to his eyes.

Padam, padam, became quieter as Natalie walked from the house.

* * *

Elliott was busy, too, when she descended on him at the shop, but he wasn't singing. Two of his workers had left the office without permission. He was kneeling, doing a demeaning carpentry job. He swore as his hammer hit one of his finger-nails.

'Stop that. I need to talk to you.'

'You've been away for weeks on end and left me on my own. Then you turn up and bark. All I ever get from you is one long, thunderous flood of orders.'

'When I was away I was fighting to stop us being nationalized. You'll never find out what it's been necessary for me to do to help us both, to help us all!'

'All right. Now you're here, perhaps you'd like to help me.'

'I've had a lot of trouble while I've been away. I need help and I don't know where to go. I can't even tell you. I need a rest, even if it's only for a few days.'

'All right. Where do you want to go?'

'I want to go to Marseilles.'

'You mean – now?'

'Yes.'

Marseilles was Natalie's favourite city. Its seediness delighted her as well as its bouillabaisse restaurants surrounding its harbour, its backstreets worn by time and crime, its foul-mouthed whores, its gutters swimming with old syringes, litter, the sordid dregs of the dregs, the wafts of garlic, the permanent sound of an accordion and the street fights occurring near the harbour and in the backstreets. The fights attracted her because she liked to place bets on the combatants and shout encouragement like a common street woman at the combatant she'd placed her bet on.

She liked to watch the Legionnaires picking up the toughest women in the roughest bars. She liked seeing streetfighters being arrested and dragged screaming into vans, their faces covered in blood and the sirens wailing. She liked the white holsters the police carried their guns in, contrasting with the colour of the blood of their captives. She loved the perpetual sound of car horns and most of all she loved to swim across the harbour when drunk and watch the reflection of the city's lights on the water.

On her visits to this city, she was completely happy, as if injected with an opiate, and because Elliott wanted her to be happy, he also agreed to accompany her there, although he did not like the place himself. When she was happy, he too was happy and in a perverse way he had grown to have pleasant associations with this city.

'All right,' he said, 'we'll have the shop manned. We leave for Marseilles tomorrow.'

* * *

Notre Dame de la Garde is an imposing, fortress-like church at the top of a steep hill overlooking the city of Marseilles. To get to it, one travels up a long mountainous road. From the church itself, there is a magnificent view of the tiled, pink-tinted buildings against the outline of a bright blue sea.

'*Voici la Mère*' states a gold mosaic with a blue Virgin Mary in the centre, confronting one on arriving at the church, as if demanding that one enter.

The crypt, which is reached by a slow, inefficient lift, has a gold mosaic ceiling and is on the third floor. The confessionals are in the crypt. They are carved intricately out of oak. A misleading notice saying, '*Un prête est en permanence à votre disposition*' stands nearby.

Natalie feared she would become mentally ill if she did not tell someone about the heinous nature of her crimes. She had tried to make an appointment to see a French psychiatrist (less daunting to her than an English one) but flew into a rage at the British Consulate because of the slow-wittedness of the staff, and abandoned the idea of getting in touch with any doctor. There was only one alternative: she did not want spiritual guidance, all she wanted was an ear and the opportunity to hear the words on the air floating into the consciousness of another person. She got drunk, hired a taxi to take her to Notre Dame de la Garde and decided she would take on a man of the cloth.

A bus carrying a group of quiet, provincial English tourists, many of them either middle-aged, retired or locked in humdrum professions, was unloading as Natalie entered the building. Her instinct when seeing the confessional was to open it, expecting to find a telephone inside. There was no face, no hand, no voice, nothing but a grid and no knowledge of the kind of person sitting behind it. The more nervous she became, the noisier and clumsier became her behaviour.

'God knows what makes a Catholic tick!' she said, intentionally to herself but in a voice that echoed round the crypt. She ignored the tourists who turned round to stare at her. If she couldn't release the words describing what she had done, she made up her mind she would have to kill herself.

The grid of the confessional was hewn out of oak leaves. She put her mouth to the grid. Her words started to fall on the air like poisoned bile that had to be released from the body if its owner were to survive. They came in French, which was somehow less painful than English. It took her fifteen minutes to say what she'd done. Her listener had not expressed shock.

'Well, what's your opinion?' She addressed the anonymous character the other side of the grid. She didn't see why she should call him '*vous*' if she couldn't see his face.

'Have you no tongue?'

Silence.

'Answer me!'

She rattled on the door, afraid to open it and find no one behind it. The rattling noise was like that of an unfastened shutter in a violent wind.

She turned round, about to go and saw a crowd of astonished English tourists. Her natural exhibitionist streak came into its own.

'Where the hell's the man?'

They stared at her aghast, which is what the more destructive side of her wanted. They knew she was mad.

'No wonder the Vatican's going bust! It's a scandal that these booths should be unmanned. If the Catholic Church wants the show to go on, it should see that these men worked in shifts. A Borgia pope would soon have got everybody cracking.'

The people hissed at her to stop shouting, but she ignored them, continuing with more zealousness than before and banged her fist on one of the chairs in time to her words about how the Vatican should run its affairs.

'Excuse me, my name is Timothy Nicholson. You're in trouble, I see.' The man identifying himself wore a thick untrimmed beard and off-white, ill-fitting linen shorts, showing lily-white legs bitten to pieces by mosquitoes. His hideously inelegant appearance disgusted her.

'Can't you see the joint's a shambles?'

'I'd like to know you better. I'm a sociology teacher. I'm from Lincolnshire . . .'

'I couldn't care less whether you're from Lincolnshire. The Vatican is run by a bunch of half-witted cowboys.'

'It's no good blaming me. I'm C of E. What are you?'

'I'm Malonist. What the hell do you want of me anyway?'

'Well, I'm into ethnic groups and funny people who don't fit in. Are you free tonight?'

'I'm sure that's very interesting. I'm not free tonight. I'm going back to London.'

As she went away, she felt exorcized, partly because of the funniness of the incident and partly because she had heard her words on the air. She was not afraid to return to London any more.

* * *

The Malonist Party headquarters was crowded the night before Polling Day. The walls were draped with the party's yellow and white flag. When Malone entered, his supporters broke spontaneously into the Malonist Anthem, which had rather banal words and which was sung to the tune of 'Cockles and Mussels':

'We know it's a pity that life ain't too pretty,
But the man who can save us is Rexy Malone.
For the poor it's salvation and the rich admiration.
He caters for all sorts, does Rexy Malone.'

Malone raised his right hand appreciatively. The anthem was followed by a standing ovation while he scrambled up onto the platform, deliberately refusing to use the steps. He went to the table where his wife and children were sitting. His agent pushed a microphone into his hand. The chanting of his name died down.

'Before I talk to you tonight, let me say first that I don't need this.' He handed the microphone back to the agent. 'I would like to introduce you all to my wife and family, because without them I would never be where I am now.'

'Come, come, you are far too modest!' exclaimed someone near the front of the hall.

'No, not modest, just truthful.'

Then he introduced his children to the audience, explaining how old each child was and what each was doing in life.

'Now we come to Sarah. Although my wife and I persuaded her that work was hard to find in her choice of profession, Sarah had always wanted to go on the stage. I'm sure you will all remember a song called "Don't Put your Daughter on the Stage, Mrs Worthington". We tried to persuade Sarah to do something more stable, but she has been very successful. In fact, I don't think there's a single person here who hasn't heard of Sarah Malone. As you all know, she has been playing the part of Miss Brodie at the Aldwych.'

'Congratulations, Sarah,' said another supporter.

'It looks as if you've got your Cabinet lined up with you already, Rex!' This was Gladys Bingo, who was sitting in the front row. She was going to say something else but broke into a hacking smoker's cough, which for some reason prompted the audience to sing the Malonist Anthem again. This was followed by the chanting which irritated Malone, who banged the table for silence.

'Ever since I became associated with this constituency as the Malonist candidate, I have done my best to help individual constituents with their problems – to the point where people of all parties have unanimously agreed that as candidate, and with your help, your future Prime Minister, I have been able to get things done that needed doing,' continued Malone. 'If elected, I pledge myself to help, not just a privileged few but everybody, and I repeat everybody – the skivvy, the navvy, the mucker, the raker, the butcher, the baker, the candlestick-maker – all those who need guidance, those whose will to live is boosted by a kindly word, a friendly hand on the shoulder, the sick who are turned away from NHS hospitals and doctors' surgeries because richer patients occupy time and beds free of charge when they can well afford to go private, the unemployed victims of a Tory government who turn to crime in their idleness, the elderly who are so often neglected and alone, and believe me, I know what real loneliness is.'

Applause ensued. He waited for the applause to die down,

hoping that his audience would not slow things down by singing the Malonist Anthem again. They didn't.

'We *will* fight privilege!' he said, banging the table with his fist, 'and we *will* fight complacency! We intend to get this country back to where it belongs.'

To his dismay the audience broke into the National Anthem, which dragged on slowly as he repeatedly banged the table for silence.

'I don't see that this is an occasion to get carried away,' he remonstrated. 'Most of us will fight discrimination against women, which still exists and is an important subject to speak about tonight. When I first bought the *Malonist Voice,* I was shocked by the lack of female workers. "Why aren't there more women working here?" I asked. "Because there are lots of bundles for them to lift," one of the regional managers replied. "And when did *you* last lift a bundle?" I asked. 'Not for some weeks," was his glib reply. Far too many women have been kept out of jobs on the notion that they can't lift bundles.'

An ovation followed, comprised of shrill female voices. Cameras clicked. A TV camera circled him. He went on speaking when the noise had died down. 'When will society stop treating a woman on her own in a public place as a freak?' When only silence awaited him, he continued. 'An important AA survey has shown that many women travelling on their own are treated with deference and ignored in the hope that they will go away. Even in the days of female equality, hotels are among the last of the male bastions. Women are often ignored at reception desks, given the worst tables and made to feel as if they were looking for trade in bars. If I'm elected, the AA shall name the worse offenders and knock the stars off their value. That will teach the hoteliers a few manners!'

Both men and women applauded. He waited through another rendering of the Malonist Anthem.

'I've always been a campaigner for the rights of underdogs exploited at work, but there must be a time when bullying picket line violence must stop. Imprisonment of strikers who set fire to blacklegs' houses is not fascist law, as the *Morning Star* is always telling us. It is not Tory law either. It is English law and it is law because it is just.'

A solitary male voice in the back row muttered angrily, but was silenced by the stares of loyal Malonists. Malone continued: 'To return, if exhaustively, to women's rights: if I'm elected, a secretary's wage will be equal to that of an executive. Secretaries' wages are low because of the belief that they are frivolous and anxious to find men who will support them. A secretary *will* be able to afford to buy luxury goods. She will be able to afford to get her hair done without having to borrow money. She'll be able to get it done on her own wage.'

'There's no one who could afford that now,' Gladys Bingo called out.

'Things will be very different when I'm elected,' added Malone, noncommittally. Then he covered a number of other controversial issues, unleashing a cocktail of Leftist and Rightist values which baffled and mesmerized his audience.

Afterwards, he left through a side door with his family. He had been working the previous night and had had a long day. 'I'm all in, Mr Tonky,' he said to his driver. 'If I hear that bloody song again, I'm going to throw up.' When he got home, it took Tonky at least five minutes to wake him and tell him where he was.

* * *

The Malonist Party won the General Election on a landslide. The obscene film about Cranfield's private hobbies, shown to his own supporters in the crowded Labour Party headquarters at Greymills on the eve of the polls, and the news of the film's existence, spread through the country with Concorde-like rapidity, and had a startling effect on nationwide votes.

Natalie Klein's unorthodox canvassing activities also played a major part in the landslide. The Malonist victory was equally, if not more so, due to Malone's charisma and personality. Even if she had not committed these acts, he would have won anyway, if with a less comfortable majority.

Malone was with his wife and family in the Barfax Town Hall when the result was announced. The Malonist supporters broke spontaneously into the Malonist Anthem, followed by 'Hark, the Conquering Hero Comes.'

The Greymills Labour Party headquarters had also been crowded on the eve of polls. Kennedy had to get to Greymills in time to divert Cranfield from the eve-of-poll address to his constituents. He had paid a Greymills video hirer to bring a recorder to the headquarters to play the film on a cinema-sized screen. He had rung up Cranfield at his bungalow to tell him he would be there to drive him to his headquarters in the absence of his own driver, who was ill.

'Where have you been all this time?' asked Cranfield in a startled voice. 'And what became of those boys?'

'They all walked out on me. They thought your requirements were too heavy. Also I've had flu and haven't been able to get to a phone box. I've had no one to look after me.'

Cranfield accepted the explanation.

'I'll expect you at the bungalow at six o'clock. My wife's using her own transport and she'll probably be late anyway.'

Kennedy said he'd be there at six. The train to Greymills left from Euston and he used the London Underground to get there. A chalked notice on a blackboard apologized for any inconvenience caused by a woman throwing herself under a train. Suddenly, he realized he had forgotten to record Greta Garbo's *Anna Karenina*, which was being screened that night. It was a film he had been waiting for months to record. His negligence made him bad-tempered. He paced up and down the platform, swearing and elbowing aside crowds of waiting travellers to make a path for him. He saw a uniformed man whom he decided he would use as a scapegoat for his double-edged frustration.

'Why does it take so long to drag a dead body off the tracks and get the trains going again?' he barked.

The man was startled. First he looked at the ground. Then he looked at Kennedy, but there was something in his face that made him feel uncomfortable about looking him in the eye.

'It's no good asking me. I don't know nothing about railways, do I?'

Kennedy pinned the man against the wall. His head banged against a poster advertising the film *A Clockwork Orange*. 'If you don't know anything about railways, what the hell are you doing wearing a railwayman's uniform?' shouted Kennedy.

'I'm not wearing a railwayman's uniform. I'm wearing a flippin' busman's uniform!'

* * *

'Come in, my lovely Sean Kennedy!' exclaimed Cranfield when the young man arrived, only just in time, at his bungalow. 'We've still got a few minutes before I'm due at headquarters. Some tea?'

'Yes. Four lumps of sugar.'

'Four? That's a lot.'

'I can't taste it unless it's sweet. That handsome picture over there in the corner – would that be your father?'

'Yes,' replied Cranfield, walking towards the photograph, a little nervous of the young man.

'What a fine face he has!'

'Yes, he had a fine face.' Cranfield eased the picture off its hook to examine it more closely as a wave of nostalgia came over him. Kennedy used the opportunity to put something in his tea. It was enough to knock him out for a few hours but not enough to kill him. Cranfield sat down again and drank the rest of the tea. 'Funny taste, this tea,' he remarked.

'To be sure it's fockin' disgusting! The tea-bags must be years old but until you mentioned it I was too polite to pass remarks. Haven't you got any proper tea?'

'No,' said Cranfield and his head suddenly fell forward.

'Are you all right?'

'It's nothing. Just exhaustion. I'm suddenly so tired I don't think I can even stand.'

When Cranfield fell to the floor, Kennedy dragged him by his legs to his bedroom and locked the door. It was nearly time for the eye-of-poll address. Supporters were filling the hall which was draped with red cloth. When Cranfield showed no signs of appearing, Kennedy mounted the platform and walked towards the screen that had been erected next to a video recorder. He banged the table for silence.

'Comrades! Ladies! Gentlemen! And decent working people! First, I expect you're wondering why our dear Mr Cranfield isn't here yet. He's been held up. The Soviet Ambassador and he are having a brief talk about arms reduction and the scrapping of Cruise missiles.'

Lukewarm applause ensued.

'Next, I expect you'll be wondering who I am. Sean Kennedy's my name, I'm Comrade Cranfield's new secretary and I'm here to entertain you till he arrives.'

'I like that leather!' said a fifteen-year-old-girl with peroxide curls. 'You're Irish, aren't you?'

'Aye, daughter.'

People in the audience clapped and chanted 'Brits out.' Kennedy raised both arms in a gesture of goodwill until the clapping and chanting died down, then continued: 'First, I'm a great believer in personalization. A politician, particularly if he's a good democratic man like Mr Cranfield, shouldn't be shown to the world as a wooden, two-dimensional character giving orders from behind a desk. He should be seen as an ordinary human being, a man with hobbies, a family man, but above all he should be seen as one of us, one who had dedicated his life to fighting injustice, a man, who, unlike all the other conniving British politicians, wants to free Ireland from the neo-Nazi jackboot.'

He was interrupted. A group of middle-aged women, drunk on cider, started singing,

> *'Oh, come to my heart, Sean Kennedy.*
> *There is room in my heart for thee.'*

'I appreciate your support, but to return to what I was saying. I'd like you all to see Mr Cranfield, not as your future Prime Minister, but as a people's man, a man of the litter-strewn streets, a man playing darts in your local, a man at the disco, at the fish and chip shop. I could go on but won't. Here in my hand is a videotape. It's a home movie showing our dear leader at home surrounded by his friends and relaxing with his hobbies. The film is a fine and moving one, and while we're waiting for him, we'll watch it. In it we will see him as the noble, home-loving human being that he is. He's even given the film a name. It's called *The Wearing of the Green.*'

'Show it!'

Kennedy took the video from its cover ponderously and slowly.

'Show us the film!'

'To be sure a little patience wouldn't go amiss, now.' He put the tape in the machine waiting for the sound of 'The Wearing of the Green' which preceded the visual side of the film.

It began with a close-up of Cranfield dressed as a woman, preparing the heroin injections for the four junkies. The camera had shown a close-up of his face to which he was holding the spoon of powder in concentration. On withdrawal, it showed him injecting the drug into the junkies' veins. The majestic, dirge-like song continued and the sexual perversions, which were becoming increasingly more vile and revolting, were shown. A woman in the front row with her nine-year-old son, gasped in horror and covered her son's eyes.

'Wanna see it! Take your hands away!' whimpered the boy, who was a tired, over-excited, whiny little fellow, yearning, like all children, for forbidden knowledge.

His mother let out another startled cry, louder than before, and dragged her son from the hall, boxing his ears every time he turned to look at the screen.

Kennedy had disappeared through a side door. He changed into different clothes and returned to London, bitterly regretting that he would never witness the audience's reaction to the film. The leather trousers, jacket, cap, wedged shoes and bandage to flatten the chest were rolled into a bundle and thrown off a bridge into a river. 'Goodbye, Sean Kennedy!' said a complacent voice. 'We have very important business elsewhere now.'

As the film unrolled, 'The Wearing of the Green' was drowned by the pandemonium that had broken out in the Labour Party hall. 'Shame! Pervert! Traitor! Filthy smack pedlar!' These were the mildest words of abuse that these people, once loyal to Cranfield, were now screaming about him. One woman, a hardened Glaswegian, raised on her mother's immoral earnings in the slum ghettoes of the out-of-work, fainted as the material shown on the screen became more repulsive than even the vividest imagination could envisage. Hissing was replaced by booing. Booing escalated to rioting. Newspaper reporters trying to photograph the scene in the crowded hall were knocked and jostled and prevented from taking pictures. As the screaming and shouting died down, Cranfield's former supporters gradually left the hall in droves. Occasionally they chanted, 'We won't be alone with Rex Malone.' The film was still running when the hall was empty.

The news of Cranfield's sexual perversions and involvement with drugs dominated the national press on Polling Day. As yet, no one knew who Sean Kennedy was, but not many socialists in Greymills voted Labour that day. Those who did vote, in a last-minute change of mind, voted for Malone.

* * *

The Malones had been in Number 10 Downing Street for three days. It was 10 p.m. Hortense had gone to bed. Malone was with Natalie in his study watching *News at Ten*. A news bulletin from Rome announced that a Mafia attempt had been made to assassinate the Italian Head of State.

'And now on the home front,' said the reader, 'it is suspected that there has been some foul play on the part of one or more people involved in the election campaign of former Opposition Leader, Mr Lionel Cranfield. Mr Cranfield, who resigned immediately after the election, was featured in a pornographic film, believed to be a forgery. The film, which was referred to as *The Wearing of the Green*, shows perverse sexual activites of men wearing provisional IRA uniforms and was shown to Mr Cranfield's constituents and supporters on the eve of polls. It is suspected that one man, rather than several, might be responsible. The culprit's political beliefs are not yet known, but police believe he is either mentally deranged or a member of a splinter Irish rebel organization, wishing Cranfield to be defeated, despite his expression of support for withdrawal from Ulster. The man is still at large. He is armed and dangerous. He is being sought in connection with drugging Mr Cranfield's tea with a barbiturate dose strong enough to kill him, to prevent him from making his eve-of-poll address. Mr Cranfield is responding well to treatment after an emergency stomach pump operation and his condition is said to be satisfactory.'

'Satisfactory to whom?' said Malone, baffled by the story but in a playful mood.

The announcer continued: 'The man is thought to be approximately eighteen years of age.' (Natalie raised her eyebrows approvingly.) 'He is five foot seven inches in height. He wears black leather and a leather peaked cap. He has delicate, effiminate features and speaks with a heavy Irish accent, thought to be Northern, and is known as Sean Kennedy. There is one particularly strange characteristic about this man and one that is easily noticed; he is said to take abnormally large quantities of sugar in his tea.'

'He sounds like a man after your own heart, Natalie,' Malone said jokingly. She laughed uneasily, and lit another cigarette with the one she had finished.

The announcer continued: 'If you see a young man taking abnormal quantities of sugar in a bar or café you are not to approach him, but to inform the police immediately.'

Natalie laughed nervously.

'Watch it. I could turn you in.' He wound her hair round his wrist and then let it go.

A police artist's impression of Sean Kennedy filled the screen. It bore a close resemblance to Natalie but the face was less oval than hers. Malone was becoming bored with Sean Kennedy.

'Lastly, he has been seen on numerous occasions driving a grey Citroën Safari estate car registration number FBL 705K.'

Malone switched the set off by remote control. 'But that's the car I gave you to drive,' he said, and looked very surprised. 'I don't understand. Do you know this man, Sean Kennedy?'

'Yes, as well as one can know anybody, I suppose,' she replied and smiled complacently.

'What kind of company are you keeping, Natalie, for

Christ's sake? What the hell do you think you're doing with your life? Consorting with dubious Irishmen showing pornographic films with intent to pervert the course of justice? I don't understand how you could waste your time being so irresponsible. Don't you see that now this man has been seen driving a car registered in my name, it will look as if I hired him to dope Cranfield and show his constituents a film – which incidentally is really quite horrible – I've seen it. Do you know where Sean Kennedy is?'

'Yes.'

'Where the hell is he, then?'

'He is in this house.'

'In this house? In this house? Don't be so bloody stupid! How can he be here?'

She did not answer but looked shiftily at him.

'Go and find him, wherever he is and bring him here!'

She walked over to where Malone was sitting.

'Didn't you hear what I said?'

'Yes, I heard what you said. You asked me to bring Sean Kennedy here. This is he.'

It would be an understatement to say Malone looked astonished. He gaped at Natalie, who broke the silence by mimicking Sean Kennedy's voice: 'And if you don't believe me, here's my fockin' photograph b'Jaysus!' and she handed him a photograph of herself taken the day she had first approached Cranfield.

'Why the hell did you *do* it?'

'Because, through my own unhappy experiences, right only comes of doing wrong.'

'And who are you to judge how right is obtained by your own experiences, that are few? Do you think my past experiences have been happy? I saw my family herded into a truck and dragged to the gas chambers. I've been through the Nazis and through the war. All you've ever had to suffer is the memory of some idiot calling you a coward for some reason I don't understand, and the wrongdoings of a couple of bent psychiatrists. I'm a better judge of how right is brought about than you. I've lived almost twice as long, and believe me, right is *not* brought about by wrong.'

'I have to interrupt you. The Marquis de Sade wrote about two sisters, Justine and Juliette. Justine did nothing but right and suffered in return. Juliette did wrong and was rewarded for it. It's her I identify with, not her sister.'

'I'm not interested in these sisters!' rasped Malone. He took off his jacket and loosened his tie. Even as Prime Minister he had not given up this habit, and it made Natalie feel very lecherous.

'You may not be interested in them, but their respective philosophies are important and show how the writer must have seen a very sad world.'

Malone paced up and down the room with an unlit cigar in his mouth. He bit the end off and spat it out. 'I don't want to hear another word about de bloody Sade!'

There was a long silence.

Natalie looked at the floor. Then her eyes followed Malone as he paced up and down.

'I had to do it! I had to!' she said, wringing her hands. 'I wanted you to win. I did it for you and for Hortense because I love you both.'

'Don't think I'm not grateful to you for your loyalty. But you should have asked me before you did all these things. And on top of it, that film. What connection did you have with that film?'

'I didn't even know what was in it when I put it on. I was told it was about Cranfield beating up his wife, which I thought would be good propaganda value. I didn't have time to look at it.'

'Who gave you the film?'

'A commie.'

'A commie? A commie? What's his name, Natalie?'

'He wouldn't have given me his name even if I'd asked. I met him in a pub.'

'Why do you think a communist would want anyone other than Cranfield as Prime Minister?'

'Because the commie was obviously to the Left of Cranfield. The enemy on the other side is not as bad as the enemy in your own ranks. At least, that's what Khrushchev said. He said if he were a citizen of this country he'd vote Conservative, didn't he?'

'You still don't know who the "commie" is?'

'I've no idea.'

'I don't think you understand how very serious this is. You haven't seen the film. I have. In a minute I'm going to show it to you.'

'Oh, no, please don't. I hate anything that's nasty.'

'It's time you grew up, Natalie. Cranfield's abnormal fetish about IRA uniforms is nationwide knowledge.'

'Why does he do that sort of thing?'

'That's a silly question. I've no idea. What I do know is that he is ill and that he has been seen to handle heroin.'

'Heroin?'

'Heroin. He has been seen to give it to men hired to wear IRA uniforms. There are eight men in this film, four of whom are now dead. The names of the dead correspond with the people mentioned last month in the *Malonist Voice*. One of them killed himself, as you know. These people put these uniforms on when they needed heroin,' he added, if in a somewhat confused manner.

'We are talking at cross-purposes. I'm rather innocent, I know, but surely if a man were suffering with withdrawal symptoms of heroin, his first reaction would not be to put on an IRA uniform. It would be to go out and buy the stuff.' She suddenly got the giggles.

'You haven't listened to a word I've said. It is thought that either Cranfield supplied these boys with heroin in return for their services or that his appearance was a forgery, perpetrated by someone who wanted another party to win.'

'I can't keep up with any of this. I don't know anything about any uniforms or any heroin. All I know is that a commie gave me the film and told me if I wanted to get rid of Cranfield, I was to show it to his constituents.'

'How did you get talking to him?'

'I can't remember. I was drunk, for Christ's sake!'

'I had no idea you were capable of such crass stupidity.'

Malone regarded her with the familiar, suspicious fox-like stare, his head raised. She stared at the carpet that had not been changed and which had been heavily dented by Mrs Thatcher's high heels. Neither Malone nor Natalie spoke for five minutes.

He said: 'I'm showing the film to you whether you like it or not. If you've seen any of these people or recognize any faces, you're to let me know.'

'No, please! I don't want to look.'

'Because you don't want to see it again. Is that why?'

She thought she was going to faint. She didn't. He inserted the film. She let her eyes cross but did not close them. 'Of course I've never seen it! It's horrible. I'm going to be sick.'

He ignored her amateur dramatics. He asked, 'Do you recognize any of these faces?'

'No. Only Cranfield. But it's probably a forgery.'

'I don't believe you. Was it you who drugged Cranfield's tea?'

'I give you my word. I would do some bad things but I would never do a horrible thing like that. It must have been the commie.'

'It must be very convenient for you to make references to the "commie" whenever you are accounting for deeds which you condone but which you find unpleasant. It was foolish of you not to have had a look at the film, and also to have accepted it from a stranger.'

'Yes, it was indeed foolish.'

Another silence followed. Natalie looked for a long time at Malone and Malone looked for a long time at Natalie. He was so revolted by what she had done that his first impulse was to report her. To him, foul play constituted the lowest order of human depravity. Her dog-like affection for him, his wife and family confused him and prevented him from being directed by his instincts. The soppier side of his otherwise tough nature caused him to feel a numb sense of forgiveness, even an urge to reform her fallen character. He felt angry with himself for not being ruthless and not turning her in. He couldn't make up his mind whether the active pursuit of ethics had right of way over compassion towards a thuggish but fundamentally vulnerable girl the same age as his children. He let himself weaken.

'I can still be your friend, can I not?' she said.

'You know very well you will always be my friend and I yours. Your heart was in the right place if your hands were not.'

* * *

'John!' When Natalie had gone upstairs, Malone was still pacing up and down, shouting for his eldest son. The young man didn't hear his father call above the sound of running bath water. Malone called again.

'Yes, Father?'

'Come down at once.'

'I'm in the bath, Father.'

'Then get the hell out and come down this instant.'

'Yes, Father.'

'Did you know what Natalie was doing?' rasped Malone, as John shuffled into the room in a bath towel dressing gown.

'Yes. She told me on the eve of polls. What are you so concerned about? You wanted to win, didn't you?'

'I'm disgusted to hear a child of mine talk like that. I raised you to be decent and honest and on occasions you deceived me or anyone, I beat you. I beat all of you and I taught you not to condone thuggish, unjust acts.'

'By the time she told me it was too late to stop her.'

'You should have noticed all along.'

'Didn't she help you win?'

'Win! Win! After what's happened, I don't see myself as having won – not fairly – and the only way to win is the fair way. By the code of ethics that raised me I ought to resign.'

'You're taking this too far. OK, because of her misdeeds you won on a landslide. You would have won anyway.'

John stared at his father, trying to read his mind. Besides, the country needs you. If you resigned, think of the lives that would be ruined, the millions of people who would be disappointed. And what alternative is there to you? The Tories, under whom working conditions are like those in the workhouse days . . . the Stalinist Left, that until his resignation had been under the rule of a sexual maniac.'

Malone pondered for a while and didn't comment either on the validity or the flaws of his son's argument.

'Get out now, John,' he said, 'I need to be alone.'

* * *

Natalie stayed with the Malones for another two weeks. Weekends were not spent at Chequers but at Malone Hall. After the arrests of Humphrey Buttercrow and Dr Morganton-Bradshaw and the closure of the Bodmin Moor and Jersey clinics, several of the Bodmin inmates had been reported missing. Helicopters scanned the moor, hovering with telescopic equipment over the shafts. A body, thought to be that of an inmate killed on Buttercrow's orders, was found down one of the more shallow moorland shafts, and dental records confirmed it to be that of Dolores Murphy, whose landlady had originally reported her missing, suspecting her of deliberate rent evasion.

Natalie was with the Malones in the middle of dinner. Malone had forgiven her for her 'stupidity' and gross dishonesty. She was sitting on his right-hand side, joking flirtatiously with him, happy because she knew she was the centre of his attention. Every time she spoke, he would delight her by responding with the seductive Cossack's laugh that had made him so popular. It stimulated her to tell more anecdotes, many of them comic and outrageous, some of them coarse.

'Excuse me, Mr Malone,' interrupted Miss Bechtold, as she entered the room. 'We have Chief Superintendent Joseph Blair from Scotland Yard to see you.'

Natalie hated being interrupted and continued to eat in silence.

'What does he want?' asked Malone.

'He wants to know if Natalie Klein is staying in the house and if so he wants a word with her. He is in the living-room.'

Natalie rose to go.

'There's no hurry. You can go when you've finished your chicken.'

She looked across the table at Hortense, who smiled as if it were a matter of no consequence.

'I'd better go, now,' she said.

Malone waved his right hand in the air and shrugged his shoulders, a well-known gesture of his if someone refused to take his advice.

'Have it *your* way, then,' he said and picked up a bone to chew while Hortense admonished him.

* * *

Chief Superintendent Blair was sitting uncomfortably in an Empire chair by an occasional table with chessmen on it.

'Are you Natalie Klein?' he asked.

'Yes. What do you want?'

'Do you recognize this woman's face?' asked the Chief Superintendent. It was a photograph of Dolores Murphy looking more like a criminal than a victim of savage murder.

She looked at the picture. Then she looked at the board. In a subconscious effort to be bold she moved one of the white knights out. The white knight shook in her hand. She banged it aggressively onto a square and its carved ivory sword broke under the pressure. She put her hands in her pockets.

'No, not off-hand. I don't think I've ever seen her before but I don't have a very good memory for faces.'

The Chief Superintendent put his face close enough to hers to be able to kiss her. His eyes seemed to bore into her own as if trying to drive them back into their sockets.

'I think you do recognize her, Natalie. After all, you were in love with her brother once, weren't you?'

'If you are referring to Seamus Murphy who died fourteen months ago in a road accident, I can assure you I never met his sister. He was ashamed of introducing his girlfriends to his family. He may have had a picture of her by his bed, but I never look at women's photographs by men's beds. I'd be too frightened of recognizing a rival.'

She hoped her remark would amuse her interrogator. It didn't. She picked up the second white knight and moved it out.

The hostile glint in his eye had become friendly. 'Would you like a game?' she said, taking advantage of the situation. 'I'm prepared to play without my queen if it will put you at your ease.'

'I would advise you not to waste your time and mine by being frivolous. Dolores Murphy visited you several times after her brother's death. The man you live with, Mr Charles Elliott, finally reported her to us because she was becoming a nuisance.'

'I never saw her personally. It's true our firm dealt with the disposal of the late Mr Murphy's remains, but Mr Elliott deals with that side of it. He has contact with the customers. I don't. I have a somewhat unfortunate manner when I'm ill at ease, so I keep away from them. All I do is the admin. work.'

'Why do you think Mr Elliott complained that Miss Murphy was harassing and upsetting you personally?'

'It's his way of saying she was harassing him but he was trying to sound like a gentleman, because he is a gentleman.'

'What was she harassing him about, Natalie?'

'She was harassing him because first she wanted Mr Murphy buried. She was dreadfully drunk and aggressive, by the way, or at least that's what Mr Elliott said, and then once Mr Murphy had been buried, she changed her mind, demanding that his body be exhumed and then cremated. On top of that she refused to pay any charges. If you were an undertaker, I bet you'd call that harassment!'

'There's no need to shout. I am not deaf. Are you saying you never met her?'

'No, I never did. Mr Elliott said she'd been pestering him several times a week with abusive phone calls. You know what Irish people are like, but eventually she stopped upsetting Mr Elliott. I think she stopped because he threatened to take her to court if she continued to be a nuisance to him. Upsetting the other customers, too, he said. If I'd met her, I'd have sent her packing.'

'You did meet her. And you did send her packing. But you killed her first before you packed her.'

'You must be raving mad! I've never seen the woman.'

'I think you had better come along with us. There are one or two things that need to be cleared up.'

Malone came into the room with Hortense. 'What the hell's going on?' he said. 'And why are you touching my chessmen? What have you done to my white knight? Where's its sword, sir?'

'We're very sorry about this, Prime Minister. We regret that we will have to take the young lady along with us. There are one or two questions that need to be put to her.'

'What about, for Christ's sake?'

'We are detaining her on a suspected murder charge.'

'I hope you know what you're talking about.'

'We know our job, Prime Minister. We voted for you. We hope you know yours.'

Natalie asked, 'Will you allow me to say "goodbye" properly to Mr and Mrs Malone?'

'As long as you don't take all night.'

She kissed Hortense on both cheeks. Hortense said she would leave the front door key in its usual place for her and ignored the Chief Superintendent's cynical stare. She went to say 'goodbye' to Malone and hugged him. He picked up the heavy painted porcelain bust of Napoleon. 'I want you to take this with you,' he said. 'You've always said how much you liked it.'

'But I can't take this away.'

'You may keep it until you come back. Hortense and I want you to be reminded that, though you may be a fool and a wrongdoer, a coward you are not.'

'All right, Prime Minister. You will have to excuse us now. Come on, young lady. There's no way you can get out of coming so you won't be handcuffed. That will mean you can hug that blithering china job – pardon me, Prime Minister – for the rest of your life if you want.'

* * *

Natalie Klein was found guilty of the murder of Dolores Murphy, as well as other offences, some major, some only minor. She was charged with first-degree murder, tax evasion, theft, attempted poisoning to pervert the course of justice, unlawful impersonation for the same purpose, making and showing a film designed to deprave and corrupt with underlying dishonest motivation, trafficking in hard drugs, among other much more trivial offences. She was found guilty on all counts and sentenced to life imprisonment. She publicly disassociated Malone from her illegal methods of electioneering and he was proved innocent on a jury's unanimous verdict, which only added to his popularity.

* * *

Jeremy Klator completed his slow, uncomfortable journey in the London Underground tow-cart. The wagons moved in fits and starts and aggravated his rheumatism. His fellow travellers delighted in spitting at the convicts, two of whom manned each wagon. Klator found these people immature. He thought it was all right for adolescents to abuse the convicts just for the sake of it, but he considered adults indulging in this sport to be childish and vulgar. After two hours, he got out at Harley Zone One and went straight to the hospital which was linked to the Underground tow-cart station by a tunnel. He waited in the reception area of the makeshift cancer clinic.

'Mr Klator! Do come in, sir,' said the chief consultant, Dr Lipman. The tone of his voice was not compatible with an impending announcement of bad news, so Klator waded boldly into the subject that tortured him.

'Is my son still very bad?' he asked, putting his hand on the consultant's shoulder.

'No, sir. We have splendid news. See these?'

Lipman produced four different scans and held each one against an illuminated screen.

'What does all that mean?' asked Klator.

Lipman shook his head and smiled, respecting not only his stoicism but also his rank of Keeper Elect of the Malonist Vault.

'The cancer has gone,' he said. 'If it had not been for the money Mr Malone put into cancer research, we might never have managed it.'

There was a pause and then both doctor and layman embraced.

* * *

Highgate Cemetery was not as wet and windy as it had been when Klator left it. There was a light breeze, and a pale watery sun was just visible through the dense clouds. Klator's son, Miguel, had not yet got to know his father. He was only five. He looked forward to the visits of the friendly, sympathetic visitor who came regularly to his bedside. He did not know that the man was his father, but he had always wanted to run away from the hospital with him. He had never been out of doors and stared at the bleak but refreshingly different surroundings with a smile of delight so consistent that it might have been moulded onto his face by a plastic surgeon.

Klator led him by the hand into the inner chamber of the Vault and lifted him to his shoulders so that he could see Malone's effigy. Miguel wandered silently round the vault, fascinated by all the statues. Klator raked the leaves outside while his son explored. Raking was something he liked to do himself without the help of the Vaultmen. As he worked he whistled a strange tune. He thought the tune was that of a song called 'Greensleeves' but was not certain. His whistling was in such perfect pitch that the notes might have been plucked by a lute or a lyre.

* * *

'Once to Every Man and Nation' was still being played in the women's prison on the isolated isle known as Northern Zone Eight. The younger warder had been staring in curiosity through the door of old Miss Klein's cell. She turned to the other warder.

'She can't see me but she seems to be beckoning me. She keeps laughing aloud.'

'That's because she doesn't know she's here. She's reliving her childhood. She's perfectly happy.'

'She's still beckoning. I think she wants someone. She has such a mischievous look on her face.'

'Go on in, and see what she wants, dear.'

'Yes, 00 82 95 616?' said the young warder crisply.

The prisoner had a wild, mad expression on her face. She had been hearing the galloping horse again. Like alcohol, the auditory hallucination made her feel elated and victorious.

'What do you want, Klein?' asked the warder.

The old woman laughed wickedly.

'An ice-cream, please, miss.'

'That is not available. Any other requests?'

'Yes. I have a message.' She looked around shiftily, as if about to play a practical joke. She gave a strange laugh and pointed at the warder.

'There's a good-looking boy in the cinema who'll fuck you for a shilling.'

The young warder smiled charitably. She had once been a nurse and senile dementia was as charming to her as the sound of children's voices.

Old Miss Klein held the bust of Napoleon with an effort. It had become heavier as she became frailer. She saw herself standing in front of her parents reciting the lines she had been made to learn because she had tried to prove she was not a coward. She heard Hortense's voice saying '*You are not a coward.*' She heard the horse galloping towards the ravine.

> *'They that had struck so well*
> *Rode through the jaws of death.'*

Her parents were waiting for her to remember the next line.

One of her brothers appeared in the cell. He prompted her as he had before. '*Half a league back again*,' and walked backwards, disappearing through the wall. She saw herself throwing a brick at a red car and cackled maniacally at the sight of the dented panel on the driver's side. The horse's hooves were becoming deafeningly louder but much slower, as if something that had to end one day, had ended. She thought she was going towards the ravine but she was not afraid. Malone was standing on the other side. He seemed to be saying: '*Tibya izvyenili*.'* She extended her arms in greeting. Both warders rushed into the cell.

'Klein 00 82 95 616 say "yes" if you can hear me,' requested the older warder, who felt her pulse and found nothing. She pulled the veil from the old woman's face.

Her serene open eyes were deceptively alive, as was the smile of joy that had frozen on her face. It was as if the young soul imprisoned in the frail, decaying frame had found as much personal glory as the man whose porcelain bust lay smashed on the floor.

The senior warder looked pleased when she saw the old woman had died. She took two gold coins, both with an engraving of Malone's face on them and spun them in the air in a gesture of triumph. She slapped them onto the old woman's eyes. In the aftermath of a nuclear holocaust it was natural to cling to ancient traditions, even if it was less natural to show reverence towards someone who had just died.

'This is my lucky day,' said the senior warder. 'I've got to make my way to Fleet Strip One.'

'I remember you saying something about that. You're going to sell the information Murphy's sister had about the old woman, aren't you?'

'That's right. I've got the filthy evidence on tape, ha! ha!'

* Russian for 'You are forgiven.'

'Well, what did Murphy's sister know?'

'You'll have to read it in the *News of the World*,' said the older warder. 'Do you realize that their sales are going to be boosted so much by this story that they will be issuing their readers with free radiation-proof black rubber mackintoshes?'

The innocent young woman looked confused and bewildered.

'I never really understand you when you talk about things like that.'

'Don't worry. A paper like that will give you a bloody revolting ride for your money!' replied the other.